THE
STONE OF DARKNESS

Published by Mundania Press
Also by Resa Nelson

The Dragonslayer's Sword
The Iron Maiden

Our Lady of the Absolute

THE

STONE OF DARKNESS

RESA NELSON

The Stone of Darkness Copyright © 2012 by Resa Nelson

A Mundania Press Production
Mundania Press LLC
6457 Glenway Avenue, #109
Cincinnati, Ohio 45211-5222

To order additional copies of this book, contact:
books@mundania.com
www.mundania.com

Cover Art © 2012 by Ana Winson
Edited by Erena Kelley

Trade Paperback ISBN: 978-1-60659-333-2
eBook ISBN: 978-1-60659-332-5

First Edition • May 2012

Production by Mundania Press LLC
Printed in the United States of America

3 2126 00128 641 3

10   9   8   7   6   5   4   3   2   1

Acknowledgments

As always, thanks to all the great folks at Mundania Press for all their help.

Also, as always, many thanks to fellow writers Carla Johnson and Tom Sweeney for helping me strengthen and sharpen this novel.

CHAPTER ONE

Astrid hated lying in wait for the monster-lizard commonly known as a dragon. Keeping still for hours took a hard toll on her body, leaving it stiff and achy.

Slowly and mindfully, she placed one hand on the tree limb on which she sat, lifting her body just enough to shift and find a more comfortable position. She winced as the rough bark scraped against her legs. Resisting the temptation to snort in disgust, she realized there was no comfortable position remaining. Not after spending all morning perched ten feet up in a sturdy oak like some type of predatory bird.

At least the view is beautiful.

Her tree stood alone on a ridge overlooking the exquisite rolling countryside of the Southlands. She watched farmers in the valley below as they walked the fields and flicked handfuls of seeds to sow the early spring crops. The mild air warmed her skin. The heavy scent of basil drifted on the wind and made her nose twitch.

Don't let your attention wander, Astrid reminded herself. *Just because you haven't seen the dragon yet doesn't mean it's not here. It could spring out of nowhere, rise on its hind legs, slam its belly against the trunk of this tree, and knock you to the ground.* She wrapped her fingers around the branches to steady herself.

Midway through her second year as a dragonslayer, Astrid had followed the winter route from her home in the Northlands and spent the past few months here in the Southlands, mostly in DiStephan's birthplace, the small city of Bellesguarde where everyone had known or heard of him. It struck Astrid as a friendly and open community that welcomed every traveler. Simple stone houses jammed against each other, creating narrow city streets made of cobblestones. Women wore wide flowing skirts as colorful as the wildflowers that graced the hillsides. They tied simple kerchiefs on their heads to keep the playful wind from blowing their hair across their eyes. Their husbands wore leather breeches tied at the knees, colorful woolen hose on their calves, and simple but roomy white blouses. The people of Bellesguarde rose as gently as the sun and took their time enjoying each day, working only as much as needed and then spending their time in relaxed conversation and what seemed to Astrid by their thick waists, constant dining.

The sharp sound of a breaking twig snapped her attention back to the grounds on the other side of the tree.

The ridge on which the oak tree grew was the natural boundary of the grounds owned by the wealthiest man in Bellesguarde, Master Antoni. His stone manor stood in the distance. Although rising three stories, its narrow width made it seem smaller than its true size. A slim tower stretched six stories high on the left side and was adorned with an enormous iron flower on top, making the manor look like a gigantic toad shooting its tongue skyward to catch a blossom floating on the breeze. An expanse of green stretched before Astrid, a grassy lawn cropped short by the family's herd of sheep. But as she turned to look, Astrid saw a small goat grazing below.

Oh, no, he sent the wrong animal as bait!

Despite her sudden impulse to jump out of the tree, scoop the precious goat up in her arms, and bolt toward Master Antoni's manor, Astrid paused and drew upon her many months of experience. She'd learned to look before leaping.

The lawn lay wide and open beneath her, but two new rows of simple wooden fences formed a narrowing passageway from the distant grounds of the manor to this grassy lawn. When the goat entered this area, its neck pressed against a string that triggered a gate positioned to swing shut behind the goat, locking it into an area surrounded by fencing on one side and the edge of the ridge on which Astrid's tree perched on the other.

At first glance, Astrid believed it was impossible for a lizard to be lying in wait anywhere nearby. When she'd carefully investigated the lawn and its perimeter at sunrise, she'd spotted none of the trenches lizards typically dug out of the ground. She knew the telltale signs: freshly turned earth, unusual piles of leaves or sticks, sharp claw marks in the ground.

She listened as she turned her head. All she heard was the occasional bleating of the young goat and the tearing sounds as it yanked bunches of grass blades for its breakfast. A cool breeze grazed her face, carrying the scents of freshly baked bread from the manor, basil and thyme from its herb garden, and the juice of chewed grass. As she scanned the lawn below, the smaller trees and bushes lining the edge of the ridge swayed gently in the breeze. Nothing seemed out of place. It looked safe enough to take the young goat back to the manor and politely admonish Master Antoni's sons for their mistake. Astrid dropped from the tree limb, bending her knees deeply to absorb the shock as her feet hit the ground.

A lizard vaulted over the bushes lining the edge of the ridge. Its silvery blue scales shimmered as they reflected the sunlight. Measuring the length of two horses, the lizard hit the ground running, its short legs bowed and squarely bent. Its yellow tongue flicked like fire above the spittle hanging from its slackened jaw.

By the time Astrid withdrew her sword Starlight from its sheath, the goat screamed as the lizard turned its head sideways and clamped down on the smaller animal's front legs, filling the air with the sound of crunching bones.

Astrid sprang forward, only to realize her mistake. Dozens of arrows shot by Master Antoni's sons arced in the sky above from behind a pile of old branches near the castle, darkening the sky like a sudden rainstorm. She could have kicked herself for forgetting the plan. She'd promised to keep cover during the first shower of arrows only to forget when it counted.

Quickly, she darted to take cover behind her tree. She cried out as an arrow pierced through the edge of her trousers and into a fallen log, pinning her. Moments later, blood blossomed through the green fabric covering her calf. Her emotions ran so high that she never felt the arrowhead graze her skin.

A familiar low-throated rumble made her look up. The lizard straddled the young goat, its massively thick and squat legs bowed. Spittle hung in threads from its slack jaw. It raised its head and saw Astrid for the first time.

As Astrid struggled to pull free from the arrow, the lizard stepped over the slaughtered goat and toward her with a cold, calculating look in its eyes.

CHAPTER TWO

Astrid reacted more from instinct than experience. In one swift move, she grabbed the feathered tail of the arrow with one hand and used the other to swing Starlight in a short stroke to cut the wooden shaft in half. Letting the remaining shaft stuck to the fallen log slide through the hole the arrow had made in her pants leg, she pulled free.

She turned in time to see the lizard's snout inches from her face. It slammed a front paw into her chest, knocking the air out of her lungs. She crashed to the ground. Gasping for breath, Astrid tightened her grip on Starlight, but the lizard knocked it out of her hands.

The lizard's spittle dropped on the side of her face. Its snout grazed her nose as it sniffed her skin, seeming to taunt her. Astrid stretched her arm toward her weapon, wincing at the animal's sour odor. Starlight was just beyond her reach.

Astrid balled her hand into a fist, took a roundhouse swing, and punched the lizard in the eye.

The animal started, raising its head slightly and shaking it in disbelief. Straddling Astrid, it now left enough space for her to sit up quickly and punch it in the eye with her other fist.

Even more surprised, the lizard took a small step back, giving Astrid enough room to dive underneath its front leg and retrieve Starlight.

As Astrid rolled over and scrambled to her feet, the lizard spun, its eyelids shut. It snapped at the air surrounding her. Dagger-like teeth scraped against her wounded leg. Sharp pain seized her. Astrid cried out. She bounded away from its mouth and seized the moment: the lizard hesitated, its body low to the ground and its legs bent like stair steps.

Astrid sprang onto one of the lizard's bent legs and onto its back. The lizard twisted its body in response, but Astrid had already driven Starlight in between the scales covering the back of its neck. The beast writhed, throwing Astrid onto the ground. Crawling away from the dying lizard, she watched it closely until she saw its body go limp.

Only then did Astrid feel the sharp pain throb in her calf. She raised her ripped and bloody trouser leg to examine the damage done by the arrow and look for signs that the lizard had bitten her.

Still bleeding, the grazing wound made by the arrowhead looked minor. The bleeding was minimal and likely to stop as soon as it could be treated properly.

She found rips in her trousers made by lizard teeth, but she found not even a scratch on her skin. She'd escaped being bitten.

But as Astrid leaned over her leg, the spittle that had landed on her face dripped onto her bleeding wound. Crying out in horror, she used her shirtsleeve to wipe the spittle off the wound, accidentally spreading the spittle across her broken skin.

No, no, no! Astrid frantically wiped the blood and spittle away from the wound.

But it was too late. She'd already seen the lizard's spittle mix with her blood, which meant it had probably already entered her body. Everyone knew it wasn't the lizard's bite that killed; it was the poisons contained in its spittle, poisons no one could survive.

Astrid knew she would be dead by tomorrow.

Chapter Three

"Miss Astrid!" a chorus of voices cried out in the distance.

Like a herd of heavy-footed sheep, a group of eleven young men thundered down the path between the manor house and the ridge where Astrid lay on her back next to the lizard she'd just slain. Even if they hadn't been shouting, she would have known they were coming by the way the ground trembled beneath her bones.

She gazed at the sky, taking in its sharp blue tone and the absence of clouds. With every breath she noticed the scent of basil still in the air, although not as noticeable as it had been earlier today. As a breeze kicked up, it bent her tree's branches and moved their shadow just long enough for the sun to warm her skin.

I'll miss this. I'll miss all of it.

Peter, the master's oldest boy, dropped to his knees by her side and held her hands. Worry creased his face and the light in his eyes diminished like a flickering candle about to go out. But when Astrid turned to gaze at him, his concern lifted like fog. "She's alive!" he shouted.

His brothers and friends gathered around the lizard's carcass, poking it from a distance with sticks. At Master Antoni's insistence they spoke Northlander in Astrid's presence, giving them the opportunity to stay fluent while respecting her struggle with foreign languages. "Of course she's alive," his middle brother Joseph replied. "She's a dragonslayer."

Popping up to his feet, Peter grinned and extended a helping hand to Astrid. His grin faded when she looked away and shook her head. He faced the others and the tone of his voice deepened into authority. "Leave that thing alone and come here. Something's wrong with Mistress Astrid."

Reluctantly, Joseph took a final poke at the dead lizard and led his brothers and friends to gather around Astrid. Joseph removed a skin of water strapped across one shoulder and offered it to her. "Have a drink."

Peter took the skin from his brother's hand and glared at him. Kneeling next to Astrid again, Peter lifted her shoulders and wedged himself behind them to help her sit up. He then raised the skin and squeezed a stream of fresh well water into her mouth.

It felt good to rest against Peter's chest and let him prop her up. Astrid relished the clean taste of the water, grateful for every gulp. Why hadn't she noticed the simple pleasures the world offered until now?

"Here's the problem." The youngest brother John pointed at the wound on her calf. "She's injured."

With a sudden burst of energy, Astrid slapped John's hand away before he could touch her leg. "Keep away from it! There's dragon spit on it!"

Everyone except Peter jumped back from Astrid, horror shining in their eyes. She felt Peter shudder, and the waves of his fear reverberated through her.

Peter's voice trembled. "It's our fault. This was our idea, and you got hurt because of us. We're no better than murderers."

"Nonsense! When I fought the lizard, its spittle dropped on my face. It wasn't until after I killed the thing that I examined the place where—" Astrid stopped, not wanting to tell the boys she'd been grazed by one of their arrows. "When I looked at my wound, the spittle fell from my face onto the wound. It's my own stupid fault. If there's a murderer here, it's me. I managed to murder myself."

"Maybe you'll be all right," Peter said hopefully. "If the dragon didn't bite you—" He paused and frowned. "Then how did you get hurt?"

John twisted his head, peering closely at Astrid's leg. "Look! It's from an arrow."

Astrid said, "It's not your fault, it's mine. I forgot the plan. I came out of the tree too soon. If I had remembered what we agreed upon, this wouldn't have happened."

"And everything would be fine," Peter said softly. He brushed tears from his eyes before they could fall.

"Peter?" John's voice quivered and his own eyes filled with tears at the sight of his oldest brother struggling to keep his composure.

"Go back to the house, all of you," Peter said. "Find Father.

Tell him what happened. Tell him Mistress Astrid needs a quiet place and whatever else we can provide."

His brothers and friends dawdled. They cast fearful looks among themselves. Astrid understood. A dragonslayer's death would ripple through towns and countryside like a rock thrown into the center of a pond. It could take months to secure the services of a new drag-onslayer. Until then, those towns risked attacks by lizards and many people were likely to die.

A girl screamed.

Before she lost consciousness, Astrid saw the master's youngest daughter standing in the path, wide-eyed with horror as she stared at the bloody remains of her pet goat, torn apart by the lizard.

Chapter Four

When Astrid awoke, she discovered herself lying in a large bed covered in soft furs. It felt like floating on a cloud despite the pungent scent of bear and wolverine. Soft sunlight outlined the edges of tapestries that had been placed across the windows facing her, making the room so dim that it took several minutes for her eyes to adjust. She didn't remember being in this room before, and she suspected it belonged to the private family chambers inside the manor.

Someone snored nearby.

Squinting as she propped herself up on her elbows, Astrid made out a figure slumped in a chair next to the bed.

"Hello?" Astrid said.

The figure jerked upright as if waking from a dream, saying, "Let loose the arrows!"

"Peter," Astrid said, smiling, happy to know he was by her side.

He sat in the dark for several moments, frozen in place. Tentatively, he said, "Mistress Astrid?"

"How long have I been here?" she said, realizing how stiff her body felt as she sat up in bed.

"Mistress Astrid!" His dark, shadowy figure hovered above her for a moment, and then he rushed toward the pale light outlining the tapestries. He took one side of one tapestry, pulled it open, and tied it in place, allowing a sharp stream of light to spill on to the floor and brighten the room.

Peter paled for a moment. "Are you a ghost?"

Everything rushed back at her. She'd managed to infect the wound made when an arrowhead grazed her leg with lizard spittle. Most people died from a lizard's bite within a day or two. Sometimes it took as long as three. Why did Peter look so afraid? "How long have I been here?" she asked again.

"A week," Peter said. "I stayed by your side and kept feeling your hand. It's been warm every day, and I watched you breathe and thrash in your sleep."

Had she died? Was she now a ghost like DiStephan?

Cautiously, Astrid raised her hands to her face. Her skin felt warm to the touch. "Have you taken night's bane?"

Peter shook his head.

"That's the only way you can see ghosts. To chew night's bane."

Peter shook his head again. "That's mostly true. There are some who have the gift of ghost sight without night's bane."

"Ghost sight?"

Peter nodded. "They say you never know you have it until you see your first ghost. I must have ghost sight, and you are my first ghost." His voice trembled. "I never meant for you to get hurt, Mistress Astrid. I was headstrong and foolish in demanding the attack of arrows."

"Peter, it wasn't your fault. I agreed to it."

Ignoring her words, he took a cautious step forward, as if he expected her to turn into a wisp of smoke any moment now. "You warned us. You said the dragon's scales protected it and the arrows would bounce off. We shouldn't have let you become part of it." Peter choked as tears spilled down his face. "It's my fault you're dead!"

Astrid wiggled her toes and flexed her knees and elbows. Everything worked, and her body still felt stiff and sore, probably from having spent a week in bed. "I'm not so sure I'm a ghost. Come here and touch my hand."

Still crying, Peter wiped his tears away. "Everyone's always talking about how they wished they had ghost sight, but I don't want it! Please don't haunt me, Mistress Astrid!"

"All right. I promise I won't haunt you." Astrid paused, wondering how to put Peter at ease. "But let's make sure I'm truly dead first. Just give my hand a quick touch. If we discover I'm a ghost, I'll vanish and leave you alone forever."

Peter sniffled but gathered his courage. He walked toward the bed and poked one finger at the back of her hand.

Astrid sighed in relief.

Peter's eyes widened and he grabbed her hands. "You're real," he whispered. "You're warm." He placed one hand on either side of her neck, looking into her eyes. "I can feel the life in you. How can that be? Why aren't you dead?"

Astrid smiled. "I don't know."

Back peddling, Peter stuttered, "Not that I want you dead. I want you alive! We all do. What I mean to say is I don't understand how this is happening."

"It shouldn't be." Astrid hesitated, wondering if she should take Peter into her confidence. Why not? Hadn't he stayed by her side all week? Hadn't he watched over her? Hadn't he shown remorse even though he'd done nothing wrong?

The black stone that had emerged from her foot last year weighed heavy in her pouch, and that weight felt too great to carry alone.

"I need to ask you a question," Astrid whispered, looking at the doorway to make sure no one else was near. "Can I trust you?"

Peter let go of her neck, suddenly acting shy and awkward. But he gathered himself up with pride shining in his eyes and said, "Yes. I have always been good at keeping secrets."

Astrid reached to her waist only to panic when she discovered neither her belt nor the small bag she kept tied to it was there.

Peter reached to the floor and lifted her belt and bag. "I took it off so you could breathe easier."

She relaxed as he handed them to her. Opening the small bag, she felt among its simple contents until she recognized the cool touch of stone.

I shouldn't do this. I've been keeping it secret since it came out of my foot. Who knows what kind of power it has?

But what if the stone had something to do with the reason the lizard's bite hadn't killed her?

Astrid took the stone out of the bag and showed it to Peter. The gem was the size of a fingernail. In the light cast from the window, it sparkled black with a hint of indigo.

Peter stared, his face drawn with puzzlement. "I've seen nothing like this before. What kind of gem is it?"

"I don't know. I've shown it to every alchemist I've met from the Far Northlands to here in the Southlands. No one can tell me what it is or what it's for. But it's the only thing I can think of that would explain why I'm alive."

Someone nearby cleared his throat.

Astrid looked up to see the dark silhouette of a man in the bedroom doorway.

"If no alchemist has explained it to you," he said, "then they're either liars or frauds."

CHAPTER FIVE

He entered the room and stepped into the light. Astrid sighed in relief. She recognized Peter's father, Master Antoni, the wealthiest man in Bellesguarde. Ten years Astrid's senior, he carried himself tall and straight, even though he stood only slightly taller than Astrid. Master Antoni kept his graying hair cropped close to his head and yet sported a dark beard. The servants gossiped that surely he must dye it with henna, but Astrid chose to believe the color natural and untainted. He gazed first at her and then at the stone in her hand.

"Peter," he said quietly, "stand guard at the door."

Without hesitation, Peter snapped to attention. "Yes, Father."

Watching Peter take his position, Master Antoni said, "You seem well, Mistress Astrid."

"Yes," she said with a smile. "We've already determined I'm not a ghost."

"Ah, yes," Master Antoni said. He patted her hand as if to validate what she'd told him. "Peter is well aware that ghost sight runs in our blood. Few have it, but one never knows until it's too late."

"Do you recognize this?" Astrid held the stone in her open palm.

Master Antoni gazed long and hard at it before answering. Even then, he kept his voice low and glanced up from time to time to make sure Peter still guarded the door. "Only from legend, which says such a stone is created whenever a Scalding has experienced a personal time so trying as to sink into the darkness of despair and sorrow."

Master Antoni glanced briefly at Astrid, but his gaze pierced her like a needle.

Margreet. The stone emerged after what happened to Margreet. I felt despair, and that created this black stone.

"Legend tells of bloodstones, which are created from love," Master Antoni said, "and it is love that gives them the innate ability to provide protection, although I've heard some alchemists use questionable means to release that ability. The stone of darkness is quite different." He shifted his gaze from the stone to Astrid. "Even when a new one is created, it holds old powers."

"Old powers?"

Master Antoni's gaze moved to the small pin in the shape of a tree fastened to Astrid's shirt. "Powers known by those familiar with the old gods and the old ways." Looking into Astrid's eyes, he said, "But I would never take you for a Keeper of Limru."

Astrid blinked back tears. A year later, and everything still stung as hard as if it had happened yesterday. "I knew a Keeper of Limru."

"I understood they all died several years ago."

"There was one left."

"One who became a friend? One who is no longer with us?"

Astrid nodded. Even now, she couldn't bear to talk about it.

"And the pin of the Keeper of Limru was a gift? You wear it to remember your friend?"

Again, Astrid nodded. She remembered how Master Antoni had cautioned her about the pin when she'd first arrived. Located in a remote part of the Southlands, Bellesguarde had been conquered by Krystr soldiers months before Astrid's arrival. But the Krystr soldiers had displayed their arrogance by leaving no more than a handful of clerks behind when they left in search of more places to invade. Master Antoni had wasted no time in bribing the clerks and making it clear their lives would come to a quick end if they disrespected Bellesguarde or any of its people. Astrid could be safe wearing the pin on Master Antoni's property, but he'd cautioned her to take greater care once she delved deeper into the Southlands.

"And you found the stone after your Limru Keeper left this world." Master Antoni's words resonated as a statement, not a question. "It could be that all these things led to the stone finding its way to you. And you may be right in believing the stone saved your life."

"What do you know about it?"

Master Antoni shrugged. "Not much beyond a few old legends I learned from an alchemist in my family. Any alchemist worth his salt can tell you everything you need to know."

Astrid held the gem in front of her, and the light cast on the floor seemed to light a glow deep within the stone for a moment. Or maybe it was just a trick of the eyes. "I've talked to every alchemist I've met during the past year. Some believe it's a hardened lump of coal. Others call it a blackstone. They all claim it's worthless."

"Did any ask to keep it?"

"One or two, out of curiosity."

Master Antoni snorted. "They knew more than they were willing to share. Should your path cross theirs again, run the other way."

Astrid sighed. "If it's dangerous to ask an alchemist about the stone, then what am I to do?"

"For now, keep it hidden and don't let anyone know you have it. I can give you directions to a town where you'll find a pair of dependable alchemists." Master Antoni laughed. "And if you should run across any other alchemist you've already met, tell him the stone is in the hands of a friend who has sent you on a mission to learn its value and use. If any alchemist wants to see the stone for himself, send him to us and we'll take care of him!"

Astrid laughed too, but a sudden dread overcame her as she wondered what kind of power she held in her hand.

CHAPTER SIX

A few days later when Master Antoni's physician deemed Astrid well enough to travel on her own, his family held a dinner in her honor in their great dining hall. The tapestries that had covered the windows in her sick room returned to hang in their normal places on the stone walls of the dining hall, surrounded by larger tapestries, all of which illustrated scenes from legends or family history.

Astrid preferred taking her meals earlier than the family meals, so she'd always eaten in the kitchen and chatted with the cooks. For the first time, Astrid walked into the dining hall and felt struck by its size, so large that she suspected loud conversation would echo inside. The chill of the stone floor seeped through the thin soles of her leather shoes, making her shiver despite the warmth radiating from the blazing flames in the nearby fireplace.

A long wooden table dominated the center of the room, and benches stood next to its walls, presumably for gatherings of dozens or maybe even hundreds of people. Peter, who still refused to leave her side, nudged her gently and smiled. "We've family everywhere. You never know when they'll come to visit."

The servants scurried past, hurriedly setting out fresh daggers for eating as Master Antoni, his wife, and their other children drifted into the room. A few of the children chased each other, screeching as they zipped from one corner of the room to another. Master Antoni quietly surveyed the scene while his wife scolded the servants out of habit.

Astrid stood in front of one enormous tapestry whose colors had faded. Men battled with short swords in the foreground, and they all bore a resemblance to Master Antoni. Peter joined her side, pointing out the details of the tapestry. "About 100 years ago, this land belonged to thieves who sailed from the Far East and drove people out of their homes and farms." The men who looked like Master Antoni fought paler-skinned men who reminded Astrid of her dragon ally, Taddeo, when he chose to take human shape.

Astrid pointed to the right side of the tapestry. A handful of fanciful creatures snarled behind Peter's ancestors. About the size of horses, they looked like colorful snakes with long legs and wings. "Are those supposed to be lizards?"

"Dragons," Peter said, correcting her. He paused, studying the images. "The dragon you killed is the first one I've seen up close. These tapestry dragons look smaller and more delicate. And then there's the wings, which real dragons don't have. I wonder why they look so odd." He shrugged and then answered his own question. "I suppose they'd never seen dragons up close. All they probably knew was what they heard from gossip."

Taking notice of something new, Astrid caught her breath before she realized she'd lost it. She pointed at the tapestry. "That man. Who is he?"

Peter grinned. "Only the best dragonslayer we've ever known!" He froze for a moment, and his smile faded. He stumbled over his words. "With exception to you, Mistress Astrid! What I mean is he was the first dragonslayer from the Southlands and the best we've ever produced."

Astrid gazed at the familiar image. Her heart fluttered. "He looks familiar."

Peter stared at Astrid for a moment, his gaze soft with compassion. "He was DiStephan's father. Did you ever meet him?"

Astrid smiled. "Many years ago. When I was a child."

Peter pointed to the center and then to the left side of the tapestry. "You can see all of the Upper Lands here…the Midlands and your Northlands."

The regions spread out like a map showing landmarks identifying each region. Astrid stared at a depiction of Tower Island, a small island with a golden spire off the coast of the Northlands. She felt glad the dragons had regained their territory of Tower Island, surprised at how much she missed them. A wave of sadness overwhelmed her for a moment. She wondered if she'd ever see any of them again.

"It's nothing to feel fearsome about," Peter whispered. "When DiStephan came here each winter, he told us about you. We know you're of the Scaldings. And your father was a dragonslayer, but he died long ago. Which is why DiStephan's family took up the dragonslaying trade. Everyone thinks you're returning your family name to its former glory."

Startled, Astrid turned to look at him. "Glory?"

"Of course. Back in the day of—"

"Peter!" Master Antoni called out. "Stop bending the dragon-slayer's ear and seat yourself at the dinner table!"

"Yes, Sir!" Peter called out before dashing toward the table and taking his place seated among his siblings.

Delicious aromas of cooked beef and vegetables filled the room as the servants streamed in with pots in hand.

Astrid smiled. She took her place of honor next to Master Antoni and his wife, who for once suppressed her daily look of disapproval. As Master Antoni talked of the new crops and current sailing conditions, Astrid wondered what Peter could have meant about her restoring the name of Scalding. Had the boy merely been sparing her feelings? Or could there be some part of the Scalding history she hadn't yet learned?

CHAPTER SEVEN

The dragon Taddeo stood atop the highest point on Tower Island, the tower itself, waiting for the sun to rise. The frigid spring wind tugged at the cloak he kept wrapped around his body. Fine sea mist stung his face, and he tasted its salt on his lips. The wind moaned as it whipped around the tower beneath him, reminding him of the help he could call upon should he need it. The massive iron structure he'd helped Astrid forge last year showed signs of rust, and it creaked in the wind's embrace. Taddeo watched a thin band of gold spread across the horizon, glad to see the day begin.

"Taddeo?"

He turned at the sound of Wendill's voice. Like Taddeo, Wendill took the shape of a man, because it was easier to navigate the tower in that form. Decades ago, after the Scaldings had wrenched Tower Island into their grasp they had transformed everything to suit their needs. They'd built new steps over what had once been a spiraling ramp inside the tower. They'd encircled the island with iron to keep dragons out. And they'd filled in and barricaded the lower passageway the dragons had created and used to travel to Tower Island from their own realm.

Taddeo smiled. He'd always liked Wendill, but he liked him even more since Wendill had helped Taddeo's only surviving relative Norah heal from the horrors wreaked upon her by the Scaldings. "Good morning."

The other dragon crossed the expanse of the stone floor, and the wind whipped his loose hair across his face. "I believe I understand the root of the problem."

Taddeo nodded, waiting for him to continue.

"It will make more sense to show you than try to explain." Wendill motioned Taddeo to follow. He opened the door to the stairway and vanished inside the tower.

Taddeo paused at the top of the winding stairs to give his vision time to adjust from the early light of day to the darkness inside the tower. Moments later, he easily made out Wendill's figure and followed him.

Wendill stopped on a landing where a second set of stairs rose toward a large globe attached to the inside tower wall like a goiter on an old man's neck. "Here," Wendill said. "It happened somewhere around here."

"What?"

Wendill's eyes softened with sadness. "Murder."

"Ah," Taddeo said, remembering. "Yes. The Scaldings killed a girl. I took her shape to set Norah free. But the murdered girl's spirit was released. I saw it happen. It would be impossible for her to haunt this place."

"I see no haunting." Wendill knelt and placed his hands upon the stone step beneath his feet. His hands shifted and melted into the step, his skin taking on the stone's color. "But I sense a residue. It was the act and the unexpected nature of her death that seeped into the stone like poison. I feel its path, running down the entire stairway and into the bedrock of the island itself."

Taddeo frowned. "Has the entire island been poisoned?"

For several long moments Wendill remained frozen in place, looking like a statue carved out of stone. Slowly, his skin regained the color of flesh, and he withdrew his hands from the stone. At first they looked like square blocks of skin, but his wrists, hands, and fingers soon regained their normal appearance. "Our passage is blocked by this poison. Even if we are able to walk through the passage and leave this place, we are likely to take the poison with us. We risk damaging our own realm with the poison from this one."

Taddeo recoiled. His legs wobbled as he sank to sit on a step. "How can this be resolved?"

Wendill sat next to him. "Clearly, we cannot take the poison and spread it elsewhere."

"Does that mean none of us should return home?"

"Not until we cleanse it." Wendill sighed and rubbed his hands through his hair. "I believe there is a way to clear the poison, but I need time to investigate the exact steps required. What I do know is that for the final phase of the cleansing we need the presence of either the one who committed the murder or the one who set the murdered girl's spirit free."

"The one who called for the murder is the Scalding Drageen. The one who actually committed it was most likely his alchemist." Taddeo paused, squinting as he drew upon his memory. "They are the ones Astrid defeated."

"Oh," Wendill said. "That day when I was set free from Dragon's Head?"

Taddeo nodded, remembering how he and Norah had taken their water form and watched the battle from the sea surrounding the rocky outcrop that had held Wendill captive since the beginning of the dragons' involvement with the Scalding family. "Drageen and his alchemist are the ones who took your place. They are the ones now imprisoned in the rock."

"Oh," Wendill said again, disappointed this time. "Then they will not be able to help us. What about the one who set free the murdered girl?"

"Astrid," Taddeo said softly, realizing for the first time that he missed her. "She is in the Southlands now, traveling the winter route of the dragonslayer."

Placing his elbows on his knees, Wendill rested his face in the open palms of his hands. When he spoke, they muffled his voice. "Then it will be months before she comes back to the Northlands. And how will we contact her if we're trapped on this island?"

Taddeo closed his eyes, remembering his time alone on top of Tower Island, a ritual he performed at the beginning of every day. "I believe there is a way."

Wendill looked up, letting his hands fall to his lap. "How?"

"You've been free of Dragon's Head for less than two years, and already you forget who and what we are." Taddeo smiled. "We will call upon the wind."

Wendill nodded. "Of course. But that can wait. First we must focus on the task of cleansing, and for that we must call on something else."

CHAPTER EIGHT

Following Master Antoni's directions, Astrid left Bellesguarde and traveled on foot for the next several days, sticking to the main road that divided the crops and rolling hills of this region of the Southlands. Astrid's nose twitched from an acrid scent. Up ahead, she noticed a small cottage facing the road and steady curls of smoke rising from an opening in the center of its roof. A short stone wall surrounded the cottage, and a large garden expanded behind it. From the description Master Antoni had given, she suspected the cottage belonged to the alchemists he recommended. But it would take several minutes to get there.

Although the breeze was often cool, the sun baked into her skin, reminding her winter had ended and it would soon be time to follow lizards as they migrated back toward the Northlands. She'd seen few lizards on the winter route and remembered how DiStephan had talked about them thinning out to a point where they seemed likely to disappear altogether.

"Do you think there will be any lizards to follow next winter?" Astrid said to the empty air as she walked alone.

Dirt swirled from the road, rising to form the wispy figure of DiStephan's ghost, which shrugged.

Astrid took a deep breath to steady her nerves. At Master Antoni's manor she'd found no way to speak with DiStephan because she'd rarely been alone when outdoors, where DiStephan manipulated any natural element available—such as dirt—to take form and make his presence known. As much as she'd enjoyed her stay with Master Antoni's family, she'd missed DiStephan.

"Were you there when the arrow pinned my leg and the lizard attacked?" she said.

The wispy figure turned to look at her and nodded.

"Did you see its spittle fall onto the wound on my leg? That was as dangerous as if the lizard bit me, wasn't it?"

Again, the figure nodded.

Astrid dug into the leather pouch hanging from her belt and withdrew the dark stone she kept hidden inside. "Is this what kept me alive? Is it why I'm not dead?"

DiStephan's ghost shook its head emphatically. *No.* Its wispy hand pointed at Astrid.

She pushed the stone back into the pouch. "I don't understand. If the stone didn't save my life, what did?"

DiStephan's ghost pointed at her again, even more emphatically.

Stumped, Astrid struggled to understand him. "Something else I carry with me?"

The ghost hesitated as if unsure how to respond.

"Is it the bloodstones? I haven't used any of them, but is having them enough even if they're not here with me?"

Again, the ghost hesitated.

She decided to try a different line of questioning. "Did anything like this ever happen to you?"

The dirt forming DiStephan's ghostly shape collapsed on to the road, leaving the air next to her empty again.

Out of habit, Astrid pulled Starlight from the sheath hanging at her side as she spun, looking for a lizard or any other sudden danger. She froze at the sight of two slender women walking toward her from the cottage. Each wore her hair down to her waist. One's hair was as white as milk and the other's was raven black. Both had brown, weathered skin, creased with lines that develop over the course of a lifetime. They wore bright green dresses down to their ankles, black cloaks, and a rainbow of flowers in their hair. Their blue eyes sparkled brightly as they walked in rhythmical step, side by side. In unison, they smiled and said, "Hello, Astrid."

Swallowing hard, Astrid didn't dare put Starlight away yet. Now that they stood closer, they seemed to be surrounded by a whirlwind of aromas, dusty and old, fresh and crisp, exotic and familiar. "Who are you?"

"I am Glee," the raven-haired woman said, "and this is my sister Fee. We are the alchemists you seek." She not only responded in Northlander but did so with a Northlander accent.

Astrid kept a tight grip on Starlight's hilt. "How do you know who I am? And what I seek?"

Fee giggled, the sound of her laughter musical and lighter than air. The sisters beamed as if they kept a wonderful secret.

"We know everything," Glee said, struggling to keep a straight face. Failing, Glee joined Fee in laughter, leaning on her sister for support.

Unconvinced, Astrid aimed the point of her sword at Glee's face.

"Mightiful joy!" Fee said, staring at Starlight and pointing at its blade. "Look at the dragons dancing on its blade!"

Glee gripped Fee's shoulder, squealing with delight. The sisters rushed toward the blade so quickly that Astrid tilted it upward to prevent anyone getting impaled on it.

The women squinted, coming so close to the sword that their noses almost touched the blade. Fee's pointing finger hovered dangerously close to the polished iron. "See how the little blue dragons shimmer and sway?"

Astrid held Starlight steady with both hands. She'd freshly sharpened its edges this morning, and if she or the women made a sudden move, she could slice their faces accidentally. "Take a step back, please."

Oblivious, Glee said, "And see the history here." She looked up briefly, gazing at Astrid quizzically. "I wouldn't have ventured you're a Scalding just by the look of you." Glee nudged her sister's finger out of the way with her own. "Look at the story the twisting and smiting tells! Can you see the path of love and betrayal and the strange turnings of fate?"

Fee gasped, covering her mouth with her hands. She looked at Astrid. Tears brimmed in her eyes. "So much for one so young."

Glee shook her head, unmoved. "The girl is a Scalding. You know the portents as well as I."

"Oh." Fee blinked her tears away. Her eyes cleared as if she remembered something obvious. "Of course." She smiled apologetically at Astrid and returned her attention to Starlight.

"Portents?" Astrid said. "What portents?"

"Nothing, Dear," Glee said absently. She pointed up the length of the blade toward its forte, the widest and strongest area. "This can't be right. Fee? What do you make of this?"

"What?" Astrid said, glancing at the blade and seeing nothing out of sorts. She wondered if the sisters imagined what they claimed to see, because most people found it difficult to make out the pattern welded into the sword unless they breathed on the polished iron, preferably on a chilly morning.

Fee studied the forte, frowning at first. "I take no issue with what it foretells."

"Foretells?" Astrid said. "How can a sword foretell anything?"

"But look closer," Glee said. "Near the hilt."

Fee paused, studying the patterns in the iron. "This is a complex and complicated matter."

"But the cost," Glee insisted. "Consider the direction in which the results could lead."

Squinting again, Fee reached forward to touch Starlight. Before she made contact, Astrid took a quick step back and raised the sword to position it vertically in front of her chest.

"Please don't touch with bare hands," Astrid said. "It damages the iron."

The sun disappeared behind a cloud, and the sudden shade made Astrid blink as her eyes adjusted to the darkened light now surrounding them. For a moment, Fee and Glee seemed to transform as if they were shapeshifting. The wind billowed up under their cloaks, rising up like wings. Their fingernails looked like talons and their hands like claws. Although Astrid realized it must have been a trick of the light, their eyes seemed to glow golden.

It had to be a trick of the eyes. No one in the Southlands ate lizard meat or drank lizard blood. It was considered unhealthy and unclean. And, of course, anyone who didn't consume lizard meat or blood didn't have the power to shift shape.

When Astrid's vision adjusted, Fee and Glee looked as harmless and jovial as before.

"No harm intended, Dear," Glee said. "We make a bad habit of investigating any source that comes our way. But that isn't why you're here."

"You want to know about the stone that broke out of the sole of your foot," Fee said. Pointing at Starlight, she said, "The blade tells of it."

Suspicion gnawed at Astrid. She'd forged Starlight with her own hands many years ago, and if it contained portents she couldn't imagine how such a thing could have happened.

"She speaks of confirmation," Glee said, winking. "We first learned of you when Master Antoni sent message by way of pigeon.

Come inside where we'll be certain no prying eyes can see us and we'll take a look at your stone and tell you what we can about it."

Astrid reminded herself what Master Antoni had said about alchemists in general, speculating that some had already tried to weasel the stone away from her because they knew or suspected its value. But true to his word, Master Antoni had provided directions to this town and to these women. He'd vouched for these alchemists.

If he trusts them, so will I.

She returned Starlight to its sheath.

Bubbling with laughter once more, Fee and Glee hooked their arms through Astrid's, flanking her as they marched toward the cottage.

CHAPTER NINE

Unlike other Southland homes, Fee and Glee's cottage reminded Astrid of the Northlands. The one-room home had a blazing fire in its center hearth, and its woody smoke curled up through the hole in the thatched roof. After walking in the door, she noticed the wide floorboards and the hollow sound they made beneath her feet. She suspected a cellar lay beneath, although she saw no door to one.

Astrid paused to allow her vision to shift from the bright light of day to the fire-lit room, its edges dark and dim. Although most of the smoke escaped, the heat did not. Astrid smiled because the heat reminded her of her smithery and the joy she felt when she forged blooms of iron into swords and other weapons. Although light perspiration beaded her forehead, the warmth made her feel at home.

"We'll need the stone to examine it," Fee said as she stepped forward to stir the fire with an iron poker.

As Astrid's vision adjusted, more of the room came into focus. A few small wooden benches surrounded the fire. Iron pots, pans, and fireplace tools hung on one wall. Shelves crowded with bottles of powders and potions lined the other walls.

Tools of the alchemist's trade. Astrid scanned the hundreds of bottles. Some were made of clear glass and others were colored green or dark blue or amber. The bottles ranged from the size of a thumbnail to the height of a toddler. On closer inspection, Astrid noticed some contained liquids, while others held balls of sticks, roots, or leaves. The contents of one particular bottle gleamed in the firelight as if it held liquid sunshine.

A large cauldron hung over the fire, and she heard something boiling inside. "Are you hungry?" Glee asked.

Before Astrid could answer, Glee scooped up a wooden bowl from a shelf and used a dipper to fill it with steaming liquid from the cauldron. Handing the bowl to Astrid, Glee said, "Soup of the sing root. Always good for whatever may ail you."

"And equally good for what doesn't!" Fee added. The sisters giggled in unison.

Without hesitation, Astrid raised the bowl to her lips and drank. The spicy-hot taste of the sing root soothed her soul, a reminder of her friend Lenore back home in Guell, who was the best sing root hunter Astrid had ever known. The pungent aroma reminded her of the smells of the sea mixed with tangy forest plants. After a few gulps to calm a hunger she hadn't noticed until this moment, she let a mouthful of the soup rest on her tongue, savoring its other spices and herbs. Although creamier and more complex in flavor, the soup reminded her of the root stew she'd learned to make as a healing meal for dragonslayers. Moments later, she drained the bowl, surprised at how quickly the meal filled her belly and calmed her spirits.

"The world always looks like a happier place on a full stomach," Glee said while she gazed at a row of bottles, seemingly searching for something.

Fee plopped down on a bench and stuck out the palm of her hand. "Let's take a looky-see, shall we?"

With hot sing root soup in her belly, Astrid felt as light and dreamy as if she'd just taken an afternoon nap in a warm bed with a snowstorm raging outside. Not that it snowed in the Southlands. But she remembered such days during the Northland winters. Glee was right: the world *was* a happier place now. And Astrid could think of no reason why she shouldn't trust the alchemist sisters with her strangely dark stone.

Astrid reached into the leather pouch, recognized the cold touch of the stone, and picked it up, handing it over to Fee.

The alchemist let loose a wistful sigh when the stone touched the palm of her hand.

"Did it hurt you?" Glee said, her face creased with concern.

"Not at all," Fee said, her voice airy and light. "It has the mightiful feel of sunlight breaking through a dark storm." She hesitated and reconsidered as she turned the stone over. "Or perhaps it's the darkening feel of a terrible storm blackening out the sun." She closed her eyes and shrugged. "Or perhaps it's both." With a deep sigh, Fee opened her eyes, spat on the stone, and rubbed it onto the lower half of her dress.

Astrid noticed that when Fee lifted the hem of her bright green dress, it revealed a cream colored underdress. How odd that a South-lander would wear the double dresses fashionable among Northlander women. Then again, trade was common between nations, and women often adopted foreign fashions, even if only for a few months or so.

Glee's fingernails tapped against the bottles she examined, the sound of it vaguely musical, as she continued her search. Finally, she cried out, "Got you!"

Glee pulled a clear bottle of black-red powder from its shelf. Holding its cork firmly in place, she shook the bottle hard while Fee placed the stone in the center of her lap and held the lower half of her dress taut, as if holding a tray over her knees.

"For your own protection," Glee said to Astrid, "repeat nothing of what you see or hear today." Removing the bottle's cork, Glee poured a small heap of powder into her own hand, and then handed the bottle and cork to Astrid. "Put the cork back in for me, please."

Doing as she was told, Astrid watched closely as Glee sprinkled the powder over the tautly held section of Fee's dress, the part she'd rubbed with the stone after spitting upon it. After Glee brushed the last bit of powder from her hands onto the dress, Fee gently rocked the taut fabric back and forth to distribute the powder evenly.

At the same time, Glee walked behind her sister, standing between her and the fire. Glee raised her arms over her head and pushed the heat from the flames toward the powdered dress. As she spoke, her voice deepened and lost any trace of amusement. "Promises broken and promises kept. Betwixt our worlds we beg you leapt. Moonstones, bloodstones, sunstones spark. Reveal the meaning of the dark."

For a moment, nothing happened. Then the black-red powder exploded, and thin golden lines, flaming as bright as the fire, rose on Fee's dress. The lines rose vertically, now standing on the fabric as they twisted together like the iron billets used to make dragonslayer swords. The lines kept twisting together until they formed the tiny image of a woman holding a sword, her hair flying free in the wind.

A lump formed so quickly in her throat that Astrid could barely breathe. She recognized the image immediately. It was what she had forged on top of Tower Island as a warning to anyone tempted to invade the Northlands. It was a message announcing to the rest of the world that Northlander women were free and strong and fierce.

Suddenly, the tiny image rose from Fee's dress and shattered into golden ashes that circled them all before drifting up with the smoke through the center hole in the roof.

Exhausted, Glee collapsed to the floor. Fee rested her elbows on her knees, doubling over and lowering her face into her hands.

Astrid sank to one knee, grateful neither sister saw her trembling hands. Realizing she still held onto the potion bottle, Astrid decided to place it back on the shelf before she accidentally dropped it. But when she looked at it, Astrid froze. The bottle's label displayed a drawing she recognized. A symbol she'd seen drawn on maps warning of dangerous territories that should not be entered.

Reading the symbol out loud, Astrid said, "Here be dragons."

CHAPTER TEN

Astrid faced the alchemist sisters and held up the bottle containing black-red powder. "What is this?"

Still breathing hard from the exertion of raising information from the dark stone, Glee hauled herself up on the bench beside Fee, draping a comforting arm around her sister, who still sat doubled over with her face in her hands. Glancing down, Glee said, "Nothing you need concern yourself with."

Astrid's heart raced. Other than the brief conversations she'd had during the past months with alchemists who could tell her nothing about the stone, her only real experience with practitioners of this trade had been with the Scalding family alchemist, who'd been so closely secreted away by Astrid's brother Drageen that she'd never known the woman's name. That alchemist had destroyed Astrid's happy life and murdered hundreds of people, all for the sake of bloodstones.

Once more, she withdrew Starlight from its sheath with her free hand. "I know the symbol on this bottle. It says, 'Here be dragons.' Now tell me what's inside the bottle."

Fee's body shook as if she were sobbing, but she made no sound.

Glee finally looked up, her eyes dark and brooding. "It's the blood of dragons, dried up and pestled. But not dragons like the ones you keep company with. It's the blood of the kind of dragons you slay."

Astrid froze. No one other than DiStephan's ghost knew of her relationship with Taddeo and Norah and the other dragons she'd met. How could Glee possibly know?

As if reading the surprise in her eyes, Glee sighed. "It's in the sword as well as the stone. None of this is happenstance."

"Hush!" Fee mumbled through her hands.

Glee blinked quickly and then took a deep breath. "What harm is there in telling her about her own family?"

Suspicion raced through Astrid like a wave of oncoming sickness. "How did you know I'm a Scalding as soon as you saw me? What can you tell from looking at my sword? And what are the portents you mentioned?"

Fee gathered herself and sat up, her face flushed and puffy as if she'd been crying, although no tears stained her face. "How much do you already know about yourself?"

Astrid spoke slowly and steadily. "I'm the one with the sword. You will be answering my questions, not—"

Fee flicked her fingernails at the sword, and its tip suddenly plummeted to the ground.

It's trickery. Astrid tightened her grip on the hilt. But no matter how much muscle she put into it, she couldn't lift Starlight's tip off the ground. She put the bottle on the cottage floor, then placed both hands on the grip and tried again with no luck.

Fee leaned forward and snatched the bottle back into her possession. When she spoke, her voice was cold and hard. "We have no time to waste on fools."

The sisters' skin paled to a steel color, and their eyes diminished to something small and birdlike. Their nails grew into claws.

Don't, Astrid told herself. *You never have the right to let your opinion of them change the way they look, even if they can't see how you've made them look.* She closed her eyes and concentrated on drawing her feelings about the alchemists deep inside so that they could look like themselves again.

But when Astrid opened her eyes, the sisters looked even more menacing as their cloaks rose and shaped themselves into wings.

Glee's voice turned guttural. "Show some sense, dragonslayer."

Of course. Why didn't I realize this sooner?

Smiling, Astrid remembered DiStephan on the day they'd first met and how he'd disarmed the child seller by feigning incompetence. Instead of trying to raise the sword, she stepped forward to stand Starlight on its point as she draped one arm around its crossguard like placing an arm around a friend's shoulders. "You're shapeshifters." She nodded at the bottle in Fee's hands. "And that's how you do it. You use dried lizard blood instead of eating its meat or drinking its blood." Astrid paused, watching the expressions on their faces change from menacing to surprise. "Funny how the Southlanders frown on that. Unless you're a dragonslayer, of course."

The hovering cloaks fell, and the sisters returned to their normal appearance and demeanor. There was a touch of apprehension in their laughter, even though it still sounded musical and light.

Astrid felt the force keeping Starlight grounded dissipate, but she kept her arm draped across its crossguard. "What are you trying to hide?"

Sighing in resignation, Glee said, "Not hide. It's not about hiding."

Fee added, "Remember we are alchemists. We have a duty to the practice and each other and all other alchemists."

"What duty?" Astrid said.

The sisters exchanged nervous glances. Fee answered. "To respect the workings of destiny."

Astrid didn't necessarily believe in destiny, but she could see the sisters did. "Whose destiny?"

"Anyone's, even our own," Glee said. "But in this particular case, yours."

"Our work attracts knowledge, and it swirls around us all the time, but especially when we practice alchemy," Fee said. "Its power is mightiful, and its edges shine brightly, showing us what we must not reveal to others."

Astrid curled one hand loosely around the grip and placed her other hand on top of the pommel. With a quick flick, she spun Starlight on its point, flashes of light dancing around the room as the firelight bounced off the spinning blade. "If that means you can't tell me about my future, does it mean you can tell me about my past?"

In unison, the sisters took their gaze off the twirling sword and looked at Astrid with relief. "Of course," Glee said. "We can tell you all about your family, especially your grandfather, Benzel Scalding, although he was more commonly known as Benzel of the Wolf because he first became known as a wolf slayer and peddled their skins."

"First known?" Astrid said, letting Starlight slow down until it stood still. "Was he later known for something else?"

Fee and Glee exchanged concerned glances before Fee piped up. "Of course! Your grandfather was the first dragonslayer!"

Chapter Eleven

Fee, Glee, and Astrid sat on the wooden benches eating sing root soup and bread. The fire burned more quietly, and its light inside the cottage was softer and gentler. The spices from the soup intertwined with the smoke, which somehow made Astrid feel at home.

"Did you know him? My grandfather?" Astrid blew on her second helping of soup, and its steam wafted around her face.

"No," Glee said, cradling her own bowl in her hands. "He died long before we were born. "He was very, very old when your father was born."

"It's a mightiful shame," Fee said between sips. "The stories about your grandfather prove he was a great and noble warrior. If he'd lived long enough to raise your father and teach him how to be a man, none of this Scalding nonsense would have happened." She paused, drinking several gulps of soup from the side of her bowl. Fee gazed in the distance. "And the world we live in would be different. Quite different."

Astrid frowned. "Different in what way?"

Fee kept looking into the distance as if she could see the things she spoke about. "We'd be at peace with the dragons, for one thing."

"Speculation, pure and simple," Glee argued. "No guarantee anything of the like would have happened."

"Your family might have come to reign over all of the Northlands. In a case such as that, the Midlands and Southlands would be humbled into keeping the peace. It might have even suppressed the threat posed by the Krystr people."

"Nonsense." Glee shook her head. "No one could have accomplished such a thing, not even Benzel of the Wolf. And the fact of the matter is that Benzel's son was easy prey for the Scaldings. What's done is done, and there's no changing it."

"Prey for the Scaldings?" Astrid said. "But we *are* Scaldings."

"Not quite," Fee said.
Glee cleared her throat and sang:

Benzel the mighty warrior
Set Tower Island free.
The Scaldings gave it to him
As his slaughter fee.

Many years he lived alone
Happy as a dove.
But when a woman crossed his path
He recognized true love.

She gave to him his only child
As she passed away.
Benzel cared and loved his son
Until his dying day.

A small child on an island
Cannot live alone.
Thus the Scaldings took him in
And reclaimed their home.

The boy sang songs of dragons,
Which no one did believe.
They say the boy did not go mad;
It's simply how he grieved.

They gave the boy their Scalding name
And treated him like kin.
He played with other Scalding boys
Until they grew to men.

Now you know the story
Of island and tower.
Children sing of danger
Where the dragons glower.

"Some say it's nothing but a children's rhyme," Glee said, giving a half-hearted shrug. "Who's to know for certain?"

Astrid pondered the words. Hope rose like dawn in her chest. "Does that mean I'm not a Scalding?"

Fee shook her head. "Sorry, Dear. Pay no mind to Glee. Neither your grandfather nor father was a Scalding. But your father married one, so you're half dragonslayer and half Scalding."

The light broke apart and faded inside Astrid. But a new question occurred to her. "And my brother? Drageen?"

"Your half-brother," Fee said, "is half Scalding and half commoner. He has no dragonslayer blood in him. That is why he is incapable of producing bloodstones, much less a dark one like the one you gave to us."

Glee jabbed her sister's ribs with an elbow. "Keep your mightful mouth shut! That's mostly but what people hear and say. Who's to know how much truth is in it?"

Swallowing her surprise along with a mouthful of soup, Astrid said, "I suspected as much. I don't remember much of my parents, and I suspect no one ever told Drageen. I think he believes he's my true brother."

Fee put her empty bowl on the ground, then took the stone from where it had remained resting in her lap and handed it back to Astrid. "You'll be wanting to know what we think of this."

"No!" Glee said, staring into the remaining soup in her bowl. Looking up sharply at Fee, she said, "Fetch the snowdrop seeds!"

Paling, Fee jumped to her feet and ran toward the shelves, searching the bottles with shaking hands. Finally, she found a small jar of small yellow seeds and raced back to Glee, who held her bowl at arm's length. Fee unstoppered the bottle, took a large pinch of yellow seeds, and sprinkled them into Glee's soup.

An immediate stench filled the air, and thunder rumbled inside the cottage despite the bright light of day that poured in from the open doorway.

"There's no time! They're too close!" Glee said.

Turning toward Astrid, Fee shouted, "It's the Krystrs! Run!"

Startled, Astrid looked around the cottage, seeing nothing out of sorts. "But—"

Fee and Glee dissipated into dark smoky outlines of themselves, ethereal and otherworldly. The cellar air sucked them through the floorboards and into the hidden space below, leaving Astrid alone in the room.

Chapter Twelve

Shaking her head in disbelief, Astrid stared at the empty room where Fee and Glee had stood just moments ago. Dropping to her knees, Astrid ran her fingertips along the edges of the floorboards through which the sisters had evaporated. Sooty residue stuck to her skin, smelling of wood and smoke and earthy spices.

Astrid had been a shapeshifter all of her adult life, but everyone she knew altered their own appearance slightly. In her blacksmithing days she'd made herself a bit taller and increased the size of her muscles to make it easier to smite iron. Back in the village of Guell, the jeweler Beamon narrowed and elongated his fingers. The day she'd met DiStephan, his father had changed the color of his skin in order to blend in with the trunk of a tree. For that matter, Astrid had changed the color of her skin and hair as soon as she'd learned how to do so.

But never in her life had she witnessed any shapeshifters who could turn themselves into smoke! Could it be possible? Or had Astrid imagined it?

Astrid squinted as she looked through the gap in the floorboards, following a soft beam of light into the darkness below. For a moment, she thought she saw something move. "Hello?"

A faint voice drifted up, and it might have belonged to one of the sisters, although Astrid couldn't tell which one. "Run!" the voice whispered, drifting like milkweed on a summer breeze. "Don't let the Krystrs catch you."

The air inside the cottage shimmered cold for a moment, and Astrid shivered, realizing she hadn't heeded the alchemists' first warning. "You left me alone!" Astrid cried out, touching Starlight's pommel to make sure she had the sword safely in its sheath as a matter of habit. With her other hand, she squeezed the pouch hanging from her belt until she felt the sharp edges of the stone, making sure she had it, too. To be on the safe side, she pulled the leather gloves tucked beneath her belt and slipped them on.

Clouds of dust rolled through the open doorway, darkening the cottage. Astrid blinked as her eyes adjusted to the darkness. Outside, a multitude of hoof beats thundered to a halt.

No, no, no. Astrid searched the cottage for another way out as the boots of dozens of horsemen thumped to the ground outside. Seeing no other doors, she gazed up at the hole in the center of the roof, through which the smoke from the hearth fire escaped. With the fire blazing directly underneath, she saw no way to get to it without burning herself alive. And even if she somehow pulled herself up through the hole so high above, would the thatch roof support her weight? Or would she come tumbling through it, possibly into the flames?

As the first man ran through the doorway, Astrid made her decision by withdrawing Starlight and pointing its tip at him. The heavyset man wore a dark beard typical of most Southlander men. His eyes widened at the sight of the dragonslayer's sword, nearly twice as long as the short sword in his own hands. As more men trampled into the cottage, the first one yelled, stepped to the side, and delivered a sideswiping blow at Astrid's leg.

Two years ago, she might have panicked and either frozen in place or thrashed ineffective blows in defense.

But a year ago she'd trained with one of the best sword masters in the Southlands, Vinchi. And with Margreet as her training partner, Astrid had learned how to fight men instead of lizards. In the time it took for her to inhale, everything she'd learned came rushing back like instinct running through her veins.

Fighting a lizard required only a sharp blade. Although dangerous, lizards were limited in how they fought and could be killed by simple, direct means. Fighting men required resourcefulness and trickery.

Fighting men required using every part of the sword in many different ways.

Lunging onto her back foot, Astrid delivered a downward blow that would have split the man's head open had he not ducked and stepped back at the same time.

When a second man charged, Astrid grabbed Starlight's blade with her gloved hands. Swinging the sword like a club, she smacked him in the head with its pommel, and he dropped to the ground, unconscious from the heft of the blow.

Another man criss-crossed his sword through the air while he stepped toward her. Blocking his blow, Astrid quickly stepped past him, locking her leg behind his to buckle his knees and using Starlight as a lever to throw him onto his back. Placing one foot on his chest, she put Starlight's point against his neck. She knew only a little bit of the Southlander language and struggled for a moment to find the right words. Staring into the man's frightened eyes, she said, "Get on horses and I let you live."

Someone chuckled.

"Like everyone else, he is expendable," a man said in Northlander.

Astrid glanced up briefly to see the heavyset man with the dark beard speak before returning her attention to the man lying under her foot. What she'd also noticed was a roomful of men surrounding her with dozens more waiting outside.

"But what will you accomplish by killing him? We are many, and you are alone. If you kill him, we will act as one and kill you."

"I am dragonslayer," Astrid said, sticking to the little she knew of the Southlander language to make sure all the men understood her. "Kill me, and I kill you."

The men's laughter startled her, and Astrid looked up in surprise. Perhaps her Southlander needed more work.

"Foolish girl," the man with the beard said as he laughed. "You may fancy yourself a dragonslayer, but everyone knows there is no such thing as a dragon."

Even more startled, Astrid's mouth opened in astonishment.

The bearded man stepped, and she spun, swinging her blade up toward his face. But he ducked and stepped in toward her to wrap one hand around her wrists, squeezing them as he wrenched Starlight away from her.

Chapter Thirteen

Astrid soon found herself with gloves stripped off and her hands bound together in front of her body with leather ties. The first man who had burst into Fee and Glee's cottage had picked Starlight up from the floor and strapped the naked blade to his back. He then picked Astrid up and flung her face down across the back of his honey-brown horse, whose hair felt coarse and smelled of musk and hay.

Dozens of horses grazed outside the cottage while the men scoured and ransacked it. With her head hanging upside down and the blood rushing to her brain, Astrid felt askew. At first she'd planned to simply slide off the horse and onto her feet with the intent of running away. But a much longer leather tie connected her hands to her feet, running beneath the horse's belly. If she tried to slide off, she'd simply end up hanging underneath the horse where one kick could kill her instantly. She considered shifting her shape the way she'd done before to escape such binds. But changing shape required time and great concentration, especially to return her hands to normal after making them small enough to slip out of the ties. And until her hands had their normal shape and strength, she'd be unable to use any kind of weapon. That kind of foolish decision could cost her life.

So while the men rummaged the cottage, Astrid quietly worked at the knots in the leather ties with her fingers. Unable to see what she was doing, Astrid closed her eyes and tried to visualize everything she felt. Each tie had a smooth dark side of finished leather and three softer unfinished sides. She found it easier to gain purchase by squeezing her fingernails into the edges of the finished leather and tugging slowly on it.

There! One length of tie freed itself from a knot and she pulled it loose. Re-examining the knot, Astrid felt it tied in at least three other places. But if she kept working at it, she might be able to free herself and run away. She searched quickly for another smooth side of leather and dug her fingernails into its edges, wiggling it back and forth as it began to loosen.

The air filled with the sound of breaking glass.

The bottles of potions. The men are breaking the alchemists' bottles.

A few moments later, gray smoke mixed with sparks of crimson and azure and ocher shot through the hole in the cottage roof like a geyser. Astrid first noticed the pungent mix of acrid and sickly-sweet scents. She turned her head in time to see the smoke rise and spread like wings above the cottage, although from her vantage point the cottage was upside down and the smoke seemed to pour beneath. For a moment, she thought she saw the figures of two women in the smoke, growing wings and taking flight toward the woods.

The men stumbled out of the cottage, taking slow and staggering steps toward the startled horses while coughing and wheezing.

They must have thrown the bottles of potions in the hearth fire, Astrid realized. *Even I know better than to do something as dangerous as that!*

As long as the men were recovering from the explosion caused by the contents of the bottles thrown into the fire, Astrid knew she had another minute or two to work at loosening the ties. And once they were on the road, she might be able to continue. Assuming she freed all the knots, she could then hold the tie in her hands until an opportunity to escape presented itself.

And if DiStephan's ghost still accompanied her, he would likely create an opportunity for her.

The horses trotted down the road, kicking up dust in Astrid's face. She wheezed and coughed onto the horse's side, pressing her nose against its hair and using it as a filter. Her torso bounced up and down on the horse's back, knocking the wind out of her lungs with every step. She took comfort in the jostling of the empty sheath still attached to her belt. Just as she'd hoped, she managed to keep her hands draped in a way that disguised her working the knots of the leather ties loose. She worked slowly and patiently until the tie connecting her still-bound hands to her ankles came loose and then held it tightly. Now all she needed was the opportunity to slide off the horse and run free.

Within minutes, Astrid smelled the opportunity as they approached it.

Most people never noticed it: the tangy and briny scent of a lizard lying hidden in wait for its prey.

CHAPTER FOURTEEN

Still draped across the horse's back, Astrid took a deep breath. *Get ready to run*, she told herself. Although her wrists were still tied together, she'd freed them from her ankles and now kept her eyes open for a good opportunity to escape while pretending to be helpless.

Careful not to draw attention to herself, Astrid turned her head slowly, resting her cheek against the horse's flank. The animal's body blocked most of her vision, and its gait made her seasick. But she made out a solid line of horses ahead, riding two or three abreast when the width of the road allowed. And the road itself was flanked by old fields of cornstalks, long ago stripped of ears and left to rot in the sun. She'd heard rumors that such abandoned crops marked the path of the Krystr army, who killed farmers, stole the food they'd grown, and left the land in shambles. Fee and Glee had warned the Krystrs were attacking. These men must be part of that army.

Astrid's heart raced and she wavered in a moment of panic. She'd only seen a couple of Krystr clerks last year at a distance. Something about the memory of them made her feel uneasy and unsafe. If the men who had attacked the alchemists' cottage and bound Astrid like an animal were part of the Krystr army, they probably planned to kill her.

Unlike Northlander men, they wore pants and shirts of dull colors and light weight for the balmy weather here in the Southlands. Their faces were brown from the sun, and they wore their dark hair cropped above their shoulders. Most of them stood shorter than the average Northlander man, barely taller than Astrid.

A soft breeze carried the sharp tang of lizard scent, stronger now. The beast must be lying in wait somewhere nearby.

One of the horses ahead suddenly reared, throwing its rider and screaming.

Now! Astrid told herself, letting go of the tie and sliding off her own horse as it skittered and bucked. When Astrid's feet hit the ground, she found herself surrounded by dozens of terrified horses, wide-eyed and looking for a place to run. Clouds of dirt rose from the road, and men shouted as they tried to control their animals. Her horse bucked again, and it threw off the man who had taken her captive. When he landed face-first on the dirt road, Astrid grabbed Starlight's hilt with her bound hands and pulled it free from the straps across his back. She then darted between the panicked horses and sped into the field of dead cornstalks.

Astrid forced her way through the narrow rows with the flat of Starlight's blade resting on one shoulder, slowing down as soon as she felt the unevenness of the ground beneath her feet, caused by plowing, growing corn, and rainstorms. She slowed her pace to a slow jog to avoid tumbling or twisting an ankle.

A thunder of dry rustle filled the air behind her, and hoof beats echoed hollowly, making the ground tremble beneath her feet.

Astrid cut through a few rows away from the approaching horse. Glancing up, she saw the stalks towering above her head wave as she pushed them aside, giving away her location. Turning and shifting to hold Starlight against her chest, Astrid moved sideways, still careful of the uneven ground. This way, she could slip through the field unnoticed.

In the distance, a horse screamed and others whinnied in fear, trampling the ground as if trying to find a way to escape the mayhem.

Dust filled Astrid's mouth, and she fought back the urge to cough while she kept moving sideways. Behind her, cornstalks waved like a stormy ocean and the shouts of men grew closer. They'd be upon her in moments.

The stone, Astrid realized. *No one searched my pouch yet. They don't know I have the stone!*

Astrid dropped to one knee, letting Starlight fall to the ground. Her bound wrists made it difficult but not impossible to open the drawstring pouch and dig out the dark stone. She shoved it inside one shoe and in between her toes. Taking a fleeting glance at her sword, she saw a hand emerge from the cornstalks and steal Starlight away. Astrid rose to her feet and bolted in the opposite direction, knowing that pursuing Starlight could cost her life.

Astrid kept zigging and zagging through the field until three mounted men surrounded her, their horses whinnying and snorting in the dusty and dead field. Instead, she stood her ground gracefully even though the men looked down on her with disgust etched on their faces. They climbed down from their horses and circled Astrid as if she were a dangerously wild animal.

Astrid wished she knew how to shift shape in the blink of an eye into smoke like Fee and Glee, if they hadn't been burned into cinders instead. She'd also learned how to choose her fights, and she'd already done her best to escape. As the men circled her cautiously, Astrid held her bound hands out as an act of surrender, the disappointment of failing to take advantage of the chance to escape dropping in her chest like a stone in a well gone dry.

Chapter Fifteen

Once they dragged Astrid out of the cornfield and back to the road where chaos had erupted, the man who spoke Northlander realized her sword was missing.

"Where have you gone and hidden it?" he demanded, shoving her so hard she fell to her knees. Dust rose into her mouth and nose, the dry taste of it making her want to sneeze. Surrounded by men, she immediately noticed their boots. Their stains and creases made them look well worn. The men smelled as if they'd spent the day walking through a barnyard.

"I didn't," Astrid said, wincing at the force with which her knees had slammed on the unforgiving ground. "Someone took it. One of you." As she looked up, she noticed a few dead stalks of corn rustle gently far behind the men. Hesitating for a moment, she wondered if it might be nothing more than the wind. Possibly. But why were only a few stalks moving out of an entire field?

And why were those few stalks in the same area as where she'd dropped Starlight?

He spoke to the others, who argued among themselves, each showing his sword to the others to prove he hadn't stolen Astrid's sword. After much debate, they mounted their horses.

Once again, Astrid found herself flung over the back of his horse and tied in place. By dusk the group of men and their horses arrived at an enormous encampment in a shallow valley of simple tents, all dyed blue. The men hauled Astrid off the horse and led her into the camp. She couldn't help but think the tents looked like water and the people bustling among the tents were like fish and eels and freshwater crabs. Small fires burned in front of every tent on the encampment's perimeter, forming a barrier of fire to keep out night predators. As the men led Astrid through the maze of blue tents, she noticed other small fires here and there, lighting their way. Finally, they came upon a large tent, its poled top rising high above the others and decorated with fluttering ribbons. The tent glowed from within, lighting up the encampment like a monstrous glow worm.

Astrid's knees nearly buckled as she realized her hunger at the sudden smell of rich and potent spices blended with roasted meat and root vegetables. For a moment, she could have sworn she tasted cream in the breeze. The tinkling sound of tiny symbols and heavy drumbeats pierced the night air escaping from the interior of the large ribboned tent. She winced at the sharp bite of an insect, slapping it away from her jaw with her bound hands.

A hand reached out of the large tent and pulled a flap back, allowing entrance. One of the men shepherding her shoved Astrid inside.

A large brass cauldron stood directly beneath the tented peak that towered high above. Swirling designs decorated the cauldron, in which untamed and unpredictable flames roared. Thick mats made up of many layers of colorful fabrics formed a circle around the fire, but only one man draped himself across them, bedecked in robes thickly striped in maroon and amethyst. Although dark-haired and youthful, his head verged on the brink of balding. With a sharp nose and narrow-set small eyes, he reminded Astrid of a hawk, ever watchful and ready to pounce on its next meal. At the moment, he sat with his back to the brass cauldron of fire, giving his full attention to a handful of dancing women. Servants lined the walls of the tent, standing quietly in the shadows, ready to jump at a moment's notice.

Astrid noticed a large pale cow hide hanging on the wall behind the hawk-like man. Recognizing the shape of the Northlands, she realized with a start that a map had been drawn on the hide. Until now, she'd only seen maps of the Northlands and the many islands to the west. But this map showed the Northlands as a small part of a much larger world than Astrid had ever imagined. While most of the landmasses remained pale, some had been colored a dark rusty red. All of what she supposed were the Southlands had been painted as well as the lower half of what looked to be the Midlands.

Astrid stared at the map in amazement. A continent as large as the Northlands and Midlands combined lay below the Southlands, separated by a narrow sea. She'd heard tell of the Far Southlands and had always assumed it was the lowermost region of the Southlands. But could the Far Southlands be another place altogether?

The greatest continent of all dominated the right side of the map, and Astrid guessed it to be the Far East, its southernmost shores dotted with islands. Yet another large continent covered the left side of the map, and a large ocean stood between it and the Northlands. Although the red portions of the map were small, arrows from it pointed to the Upper Midlands, the Northlands, the Far Southlands, the Far East, and the Far West.

A weary but bright-eyed soldier cut his thumb with his dagger as he approached the map. He smeared his blood on a section of the Midlands.

It's blood, Astrid realized as a cold wave of fear washed through her veins. *They mark the territory they conquer with their own blood. And the conquering path is headed toward the Northlands.*

As the soldier sucked the remaining blood from his thumb, he turned and stared when the music grew louder and the dancing began.

Although Astrid didn't think of herself as a good dancer, she'd developed the habit of letting townspeople drag her into dances of celebration before a community meal, usually one held in her honor on the heels of a slain lizard. She'd come to relish the bellyaching laughter that came with plodding her way through the steps, intricate or not, danced at any particular village. Often she'd remember the right steps in the wrong town and giggled as everyone needled her for bringing another village's dance into the mix. She was used to dance steps that felt like skipping or hopping or galloping.

She recognized the women were dancing because they kept time to the music. But it was a type of dance Astrid had never seen before.

Dressed from neck to toes in bright blue garments that looked like a second skin, the women writhed like upright snakes. Their bellies and chests and hips undulated in a way Astrid never imagined was possible. But the women didn't laugh or giggle or show any joy at all. As they shook and squirmed, their faces were as blank as if they were sleeping.

But it was a sleep made of nightmares, not of peace.

Watching closer, Astrid felt herself go cold at the sight of the clench of each woman's jaw and the down-turned corners of her mouth.

The hawk-like man raised one hand, letting his fingers and palm undulate like the women's bodies as he motioned the nearest dancer to approach. A tall, slim woman with hay-colored hair tied up in a knot danced slowly toward him, seeming to taunt him with the dance. But she continued toward him, acting mesmerized by his beckoning hand. Finally, she slid onto his lap and into his hands.

At that moment, a cold dread washed through Astrid like an unexpected ice storm.

As the hawk-like man touched the dancer in his arms, Astrid realized that none of the dancers wore clothes. Instead, their skin had somehow been colored.

Shapeshifters? Astrid wondered, averting her gaze.

Not likely. If men like these came looking to harm alchemists, how much stomach would they have for shapeshifting?

"Mandulane," a guard called out in Southlander. When he spoke, the one word Astrid recognized was "dragonslayer."

Everyone inside the tent laughed except for the dancers and the hawk-like man, who replied without looking up from the body of the dancer in his arms.

The guard who had announced Astrid's presence smacked himself in the head and muttered. Clearly angry with himself, he dug his fingers around the tie binding Astrid's hands and dragged her to the opposite corner of the tent, careful to cut a wide path around the still-undulating dancers.

Deep in the corner sat an old man with glazed eyes who stared into the seemingly vast space swimming before him. The old man clung to a hollow reed stuck between the edges of a small cauldron and its slightly ajar lid. Oblivious, he wrapped his lips around the reed and sucked loudly, closing his eyes. A thin white vapor escaped his mouth as he leaned back and sighed in relief.

The guard threw Astrid roughly to the ground and barked an order at the seated man.

Several moments later, the old man opened his eyes and squinted at Astrid. Nodding, he reached behind him and drew out a large wooden bowl filled with a gooey blue substance. Reaching blindly for the bowl's rim, he wrapped his fingers around one of many needles stuck into it and smiled as he worked it free.

Chapter Sixteen

Astrid stared at the needle in the old man's hand. Glancing back over her shoulder, she stared at the dancing blue women again.

Of course. They'd all been tattooed from neck to ankle.

Terrified, the small bit of knowledge of the Southlander's language evaporated from Astrid's mind. "No!" she shouted. She jumped to her feet in horror.

The old man giggled in delight, staring at her as he grinned and fingered the blunt end of the needle. "Ah," he said in Astrid's language. "We have a Northern girl in the mix."

The guard's rough hand slammed on her shoulder, forcing her back on the ground.

The old man used a wooden spoon to stir up the thick blue dye. "Never mind that nitwit," he said, still speaking in Astrid's language as he cast a narrow glance at the guard hovering above her. "Except, of course, to do what he says. Otherwise, he'll beat you until you're covered with bruises." He paused for a wink. "Trust me. The pierce of the needle is easier to take than a beating."

Still panicked, especially with Starlight stolen in a far-off cornfield, Astrid trembled and focused on gathering her wits. A sudden thought occurred to her. "I'm already pierced."

The old man raised an eyebrow as he quickly scanned her body. But the only skin showing was on her face, neck, and hands. Her clothing covered the rest. "Give us a peek," he said.

Astrid loosened her shirt and pulled it down to her collarbones, exposing her throat.

The tattooer's other eyebrow raised as he leaned close to peer at her throat. After a few moments, he leaned back and took another drag from the smoke trapped inside his cauldron, sucking hard and long on the hollow reed between the lid and rim. The look in his eyes gained more distance. "No mortal hand pierced your skin," he whispered. "What happened to you?"

Astrid rearranged her shirt to once again cover the image of the dragon scales forming a dragonslayer's blade running down her sternum from her throat to her belly. "Dragon," she said. "Chewed me up and spit me out."

The old man looked confused. "But what I saw is no accident. It's deliberate. It's a pattern. No dragon does that."

Astrid resisted the urge to smile. "That's right. The dragon left me covered in scars. The scars themselves chose to come together."

He rested one hand on the outside of the wooden bowl and rocked it as if rocking a cradle. Fear deepened in his eyes. Barely able to meet her gaze, the tattooer whispered, "Scalding."

Startled, Astrid wondered how he'd made the connection. Had this happened to other Scaldings in the past, relatives she knew nothing about? Astrid allowed herself a small smile, hoping it would scare him even more. *For once, let my family name help me.*

The guard kicked the dirt floor and spoke harsh Southlander words.

The tattooer protested in Southlander, holding up his trembling palms.

The guard snorted.

With her hands still bound together, Astrid opened them like a clamshell to grab the edge of the bowl of blue dye. In one swift move, she spun as she rose to her feet and threw the contents of the bowl into the guard's face.

He screamed, clawing at his dye-covered eyes as he sank to the ground in agony.

Pushing the tattooer aside, Astrid tipped over his cauldron, and white vapor filled the air, forming a misty curtain between her and the rest of the tent.

The old man cried out, reaching in vain for his ruined and escaping smoke.

For a moment, Astrid felt sorry for him, already imagining his unfortunate fate if these men allowed him to live. But he was the one who had chosen to be with them. There was a price to every choice, and the tattooer's decision to work with these men was a price he had to pay, not Astrid.

She dove under the edge of the tent behind the tattooer, escaping into a dark space between the grand tent and the one next to it. While noisy commotion erupted inside the large tent, she crept through the dark space and into another, winding her way through the unlit spaces forming a maze within the complex. Before long, she heard the shouts of men looking for her.

Astrid rushed through a dark alley to a place where light spilled before her. Hanging back in the shadows, she watched the crowded walkway in front of her, lined with tents. She had nowhere else to go. She'd come to the end of her options, and she'd be found in a matter of minutes.

Women screamed. A sudden blaze behind a tent lining the passageway climbed high in the dark. The top and sides of that tent burst into flames. It had caught on fire.

Everyone in sight ran to the tent, grabbing the edges that hadn't yet caught flame and pulling them to the ground while others threw blanket after blanket on top of the burning fabric. While all eyes were on the fire, Astrid slipped out of the shadows and walked calmly behind their backs until she reached another dark alley.

As she ran in the shadows between the tents, more screams rose behind her. *Maybe other tents are catching fire, too. How did I get so lucky?*

But when she reached the edge of the encampment and prepared to run away from it, hands emerged out of the dark, grabbing Astrid's arms. A hand clamped solidly over her mouth before she could cry out.

A woman's voice whispered, "Worry not. We come to help."

Chapter Seventeen

Astrid froze and thought, *Is this a trap?*

But the hand clamped over her mouth was as soft and firm as the woman's accented voice whispering in her ear.

"We learn when it is good to fight and we learn when it is good to run," the woman's voice said quietly. "This time is good to run. Do you agree?"

Speaking against the palm still covering her mouth, Astrid said, "Yes." The scent of burning linen and wood grew stronger behind her, making her want to bolt into the black night.

"Speak not!" A woman with a higher pitched voice said, hidden somewhere in the darkness. "Great danger here."

Between the glow of the light from the encampment behind her and the dim indication of the woods surrounding the camp, Astrid saw nothing as her eyes still struggled to adjust. She shivered at the chill on a breeze that must have come from the depths of the forest, soaked with the scent of pine and earth.

Taking her hand away from Astrid's mouth, a young woman stepped out to face her. The encampment's glow illuminated her face. Looking to be a Midlander, she stood as tall and sturdy as most Northlander women, but her free-falling hair was the color of the bark of an oak tree. Her face was broad and as open as the summer sky. In this light, she looked like a goddess who had the power to split the ground open beneath their feet and fly down into the resulting chasm with ease.

Another woman stepped out from the shadows, petite and wearing her thick, bushy dark hair only to her shoulders. Most likely a Southlander. Her gaze darted constantly, reminding Astrid of a high-strung chipmunk in search of food and on the constant lookout for predators. "Follow," the petite woman whispered.

Astrid realized both women spoke with a different type of accent. Few women outside the Northlands spoke Astrid's language. Typically, she could count only on tradesmen who made their wages by traveling widely to sell their wares to speak the Northlander language. What possible reason would these women have to know it?

Both women slipped quietly away from the edge of the encampment and into the shadows. Astrid followed. Although accustomed to making her way quietly through the woods in daylight when lizards were likely to strike, she'd rarely tried to navigate through them at night. With almost every step, Astrid managed to step on a fallen leaf or twig. The resulting crunch or snap made her feel as clumsy as a herd of cattle bumbling through the forest. *Please don't let them find us because of me.*

But with cries continuing to rise from the increasingly well-lit encampment behind them, no one followed. They traveled throughout the night on foot, winding along narrow paths made by animals, crossing small brooks, and finally crossing a field toward a simple cottage. As they approached, the petite woman let out the soft call of an owl. Moments later, a similar call carried on the wind across the field back to them.

Still moving with caution, the two women led Astrid to the cottage, where another woman stepped out to greet them. Although her eyes were now fully adjusted to the night, Astrid could only recognize her as a woman because of her shape and her voice. "Is her?" the new woman said. Again, Astrid detected yet another type of accent.

"Yes," the Midlander said, sighing in relief. "We set fire and she get out."

Astrid spun to face her in surprise. "That was you? The fire in the encampment was your doing?"

The new woman dropped to one knee in front of Astrid. "Is good you join us. Is good to know you at last."

Astrid frowned, not understanding why the woman was on her knee or who she thought Astrid might be. "How do you know who I am?"

The Southlander stood by the kneeling woman and placed a hand on her shoulder. "How not? He train us. He tell us how to know you. How to find you."

"He?" Astrid's confusion grew by the moment.

The Midlander stood in front of Astrid, reaching out to touch her as if to make sure she was real but drawing her hand back in sudden shyness. "Vinchi," the Midlander said. "Our teacher."

Astrid's heart raced. Vinchi. The Southlander with whom she had stolen Margreet from her dangerous husband. Although he made his living teaching men and boys how to use swords and daggers, Vinchi reluctantly had taught Astrid and Margreet how to use weapons against men, not lizards. They'd parted on harsh terms, angry at each other. But now Astrid remembered her fondness for him and his genuine love for Margreet. These women couldn't mean Vinchi had trained them, too. Why would he do such a thing? "I don't understand."

The Midlander stood straighter as if pride stretched her spine. "We are the Iron Maidens." Smiling, she added, "We now serve you."

CHAPTER EIGHTEEN

Exhausted, Astrid soon fell asleep on one of the benches lining the perimeter of the cottage's single room. As if sinking into the depths of the ocean, she slept soundly and didn't wake until long after the sun had risen. Stretching herself into consciousness, her back ached from sleeping on the wooden surface. She became aware of the soft light pouring through the hole in the roof above the hearth, filtered by the rising smoke. In the distance, lambs bleated. The hefty scent of porridge tickled her nose.

The Midlander woman who had clamped her hand over Astrid's mouth at the Krystr encampment now squatted in front of a cauldron hanging over the hearth fire and stirred the cooking porridge. Like Astrid, she wore men's pants and a shirt. For good measure, she wore a light vest with her belt over it. A sword hung at her side.

In the Northlands, men typically carried a weapon from the moment their feet hit the ground each morning until the moment their head hit the bed at night. One never knew when a village might be invaded or a stranger might strike, and common sense dictated keeping a weapon within arm's reach at all times.

But Astrid had never known any woman other than herself or Margreet to follow this practice. Not until now.

Astrid sat up.

The Midlander looked up and grinned. "You sleep well."

Astrid yawned, feeling sound and whole. "I always sleep well when I feel safe."

The Midlander nodded. "We keep you safe. I am Thorda."

"I'm Astrid."

Thorda laughed.

Astrid shook her head at her own foolishness. "But you already know who I am."

Still giggling, Thorda scooped a hearty portion of porridge into a wooden bowl and handed it to Astrid.

Blowing on the porridge first to cool it, she held the bowl to her lips and took a tentative sip. The first mouthful made her feel even better than her good night's sleep. Thorda had used rich, aromatic Southland herbs and spices to flavor the food and give it some kick.

Thorda walked to the threshold and whistled loudly. She knelt in front of the cauldron and scooped porridge into several more bowls. Did she think Astrid had spent the past days starving?

Quickly, the cottage filled with a dozen young women of all shapes and sizes. Most looked to be Southlanders, but two reminded Astrid of Taddeo—Far Easterners with gem-colored eyes, light skin, and lilting accents. She soon learned Jewely was the Southlander she'd met outside the Krystr encampment, and Efflin was the one who had greeted them at the cottage last night. Some of the women spoke the Northlander language in varying degrees, with Thorda being the most fluent.

The women gathered around Astrid, their eyes lit with excitement. She asked, "Did you learn my language so you could speak with me?"

"Yes," Jewely said happily as she swirled her porridge in its bowl. "Vinchi tell us you not learn how to speak to us."

Efflin pointed at Astrid. "Is stubborn."

Astrid flinched, aware that she had indeed been too stubborn and proud to learn Margreet's language and had never spoken with her properly. Vinchi was right when he told these women about Astrid's stubbornness.

"Worry not." Thorda winked. "We do not care." Snapping her fingers, Thorda placed her own bowl of freshly poured porridge on the bench and then rummaged beneath it. Moments later, she held up Starlight, careful of its sharp blade as she offered its hilt to Astrid. "Yours?"

Relief overwhelmed her. She put her bowl down while standing and extending her other hand toward her favorite weapon and lifelong friend. When she curled her fingers around its grip, she felt as if she were embracing DiStephan, grateful to be back in his arms. "You were there when they chased me through the cornfield."

Thorda nodded. "We learn when it is good to fight and we learn when it is good to run." Her face lit up as she smiled slyly. "Or hide."

Sliding Starlight back in the sheath attached to her belt, Astrid felt balanced and whole once more. "You were there. You saw everything. You're the one who took my sword."

The young women surrounding her beamed. Efflin said, "Keep sword safe. Is good?"

"It's brilliant," Astrid said, grinning as she looked into the eyes of each woman. "It's the most wonderful thing you could have done for me." She paused, adjusting the sheath as she sat down again. "But who are you and why are you here?"

Thorda frowned, her brow crunched in puzzlement. "Last night, hear me not? We are Iron Maidens. We now serve you."

"Yes," Astrid said, sipping more porridge. "But how did you meet Vinchi? Where do you come from?"

Excitedly, the other women began talking at once and in various languages, each eager to tell the tale. Thorda stood and motioned for silence. "We are from everywhere. Merchants take news of Vinchi wherever they go. They say he teaches women how to fight. He teaches more now. Men and women." Thorda straightened herself to stand tall. "We were first women. And best."

Astrid looked down at her porridge, afraid her eyes might water and not wanting the women to see.

Vinchi. He'd spent his life teaching men and their sons how to fight, refusing to see the value a weapon could have in a woman's hand. And now he was training women and girls. Was this how he chose to keep Margreet in his heart? Was it how he managed to keep his memory of her alive?

The animosity she'd harbored for Vinchi melted away. Astrid smiled and raised her head. Gazing at the young women surrounding her, she saw Margreet's smile and determination and courage on their faces. Vinchi hadn't just taught them to fight. He'd taught them to be like Margreet.

For the first time, Astrid realized Thorda's shirt was embroidered with a small symbol of a Keeper of Limru, like the pin Astrid wore. She looked around the room, aware that every woman wore that emblem. Margreet had been the last Keeper of Limru. Once again, Vinchi honored her memory.

Astrid said, "I'm so glad to know you. All of you."

"We serve you," Jewely said as all of the Iron Maidens glowed with pride.

"I don't understand. I'm a dragonslayer. I travel and work alone.

I'm delighted to meet you all, but why would Vinchi send you to serve me?"

Jewely spoke in a hush, as if danger lurked nearby. "Krystr men. Bad men. Everywhere."

Fear sank like a stone into Astrid's stomach. Just last night she'd had her first encounter with a Krystr camp and barely escaped having her body tattooed blue and being turned into a writhing naked thing with empty eyes, in danger of being reduced to something only good for the pleasure of men. She thought she'd seen enough of Krystr followers last year, but the darkness of their hearts now seemed much deeper than she'd ever imagined. She remembered the large cowhide map she'd seen in Mandulane's tent, showing in blood the areas his Krystr army had already conquered. "Then it's getting worse."

Efflin nodded. "Is horrible. Is why we leave home. Is why Vinchi teach us."

A lump formed in Astrid's throat. If he were in the cottage this moment, she would embrace him like a brother. *I hope I see Vinchi again. Someday.*

"Worry not," Jewely said. "Northland is strong. Southland is soon strong. Together they press Krystr army."

Astrid frowned, confused.

"Is crush," Efflin said, correcting Jewely. "Soon is crush Krystr from Southland and Northland."

A sudden worry shook Astrid to the core. She asked the question even though she already knew the answer. She simply didn't want to believe it. "Would the Krystr followers dare to go north?"

"Yes." Thorda set her jaw in grim determination. "But Iron Maidens get in their way."

CHAPTER NINETEEN

After a fitful night's sleep, Mandulane awoke to the scent of smoke and burnt wood. The early light preceding dawn made the interior of his tented bedroom glow like the embers of a spent fire. A few of his blue tattooed dancers draped across the lower half of his bed like dogs, pinning his legs under the bed covers. Flexing his feet, he realized they'd nearly gone numb. One of the girls snored loudly. Outside, men shouted.

Mandulane preferred to wake up slowly and gradually. Today he felt as if he'd been jarred out of a peaceful sleep. Annoyed and cranky, he decided to make everyone pay for his discomfort. Wriggling until he freed his legs, he kicked the sleeping dancers off his bed and on to the dirt floor. When they had the audacity to cry out, he jumped to his feet, standing naked before them with his fists raised. "Leave." Mandulane spoke in a soft voice with chilly currents suggesting the danger of a hidden undertow.

One dancer obeyed immediately, scrambling to find her way out of the tent and quickly followed by two others. The girl who had snored still lay on the dirt floor, shaking her head as she struggled to come awake.

Mandulane didn't enjoy raising his voice. It seemed such an unnecessary and ungainly thing. But stupidity angered him, and this girl exhibited a clear degree of it. He took a step toward her and spoke so softly that it was little more than a whisper. "Leave now."

She froze for a moment like an animal that realizes it's being hunted. Showing an uncharacteristic flash of wisdom, she averted her gaze and murmured, "Yes, my lord." Rising swiftly to her feet, she stumbled out of his sight.

Mandulane smiled. She'd stood so quickly that all the blood had probably rushed from her head, leaving her dizzy and disoriented. If he'd wished, he could have taken her down like a wolf overpowering a deer. On one hand, he hated to miss any opportunity for fun. On the other, these were times that begged for his close attention to detail.

He shouted for his dresser as he pissed into a pot stored discretely in one corner, placing a lid on it when finished. Like many mornings, he reminded himself of how far he'd come in life. He had a faint memory of his parents and siblings as well as a stronger memory of his village being attacked by brigands who burned his family cottage and everyone inside when he'd gone off in the woods to gather mushrooms. Even at such a young age he'd had the good sense to stay hidden, watching the entire village go up in flames. The few who escaped a fire-some death had been captured and most likely sold as slaves. He'd found his way to a land baron's estate where he joined other workers in tending crops and animals. The baron's stinginess often left the workers hungry while he and his family feasted. Years later when Mandulane had grown into a young man, the first Krystr clerks wandered onto the baron's property and he welcomed them in a showy act of shallow kindness. The clerks offered to join his workers in the fields in exchange for daily meals. The baron agreed, not realizing the clerks had manipulated him into handing his workers over as a captive audience.

For days and weeks and months the clerks craftily spoke of the new god, his remarkable powers, and how he inevitably would conquer the gods of all other nations in the world. Mandulane kept his silence, all the while observing the way the clerks cast their words over his fellow workers like a net over a school of fish. It took time, but the clerks succeeded in converting the workers and then staging an uprising that left the baron and his family stoned to death and his wealth in the hands of the clerks, who offered to manage it in the name of the god Krystr.

As a child gathering mushrooms in the woods, Mandulane had learned to keep quiet and observe, waiting to make the right move at the right time as a way to stay alive. As a young man he witnessed the power of words and incessant persuasion, immediately recognizing a sure-fire path to riches and power.

After the deaths of the baron and his family, Mandulane soon accepted the vows of the clerk and figured out how to rise within this new and puzzling system. A year after he became an assistant to the Krystr Lord, Mandulane quietly murdered the man in such a way that threatened all others and took his place. The previous lord had become sloppy and lazy, making it only a matter of time before someone would kill him. Mandulane happened to be the one who succeeded first and no one dared try to stop him from claiming what he believed was rightfully his. Because he was quick to kill anyone who appeared to think of challenging him, no one dared to cross Mandulane.

And one of the benefits of his new power happened every morning when his dresser brought in an array of clothes, many captured from murdered landowners or traveling merchants.

More than almost anything else in life, Mandulane loved to dress in fine clothes and costumes to remind himself that he had the ability to conquer any hardship or problem.

Naked, he perched on the edge of his bed as his dresser staggered into the room under the weight of an armful of outfits, which the dresser carefully placed on the bed next to Mandulane.

The mere sight of his treasured clothes brightened Mandulane's spirits. He quickly forgot the crankiness brought on by this morning's rude awakening. Smiling, Mandulane said, "Show me."

A small but spry man from the Southlands, the dresser picked up a pair of long, bright green pants and a brown tunic, holding them in front of his own body. "We acquired these last week from a merchant coming from the North."

Mandulane grimaced. "Well, that explains it then. That is how the Northlanders dress. I have no desire to look like a common woodsman."

"This is Northlander dress, but they're not woodsmen, they're—"

"Next."

The dresser tossed the unwanted outfit on the floor and selected a new outfit from the bed. "Here we have a slim black underdress covered by a looser fitting purple robe. It gives you ease of movement—"

"I know. I wore it last week." Mandulane paused. "Save it in case we have a more formal dinner next week."

Nodding, the dresser folded the outfit with care and placed it on a nearby bench. He picked up the next outfit from the pile. "Ah… this is quite lovely. The pants are a creamy linen, the tunic likewise, and the outer coat is red silk. I suggest you pair this ensemble with black boots."

For a moment, Mandulane's heart raced. He could easily imagine himself cutting a dashing figure in this outfit. He leaned forward and nearly swooned at the smooth touch of the red silk outer coat. "Far East?"

"Yes. We encountered a merchant who spent the winter there."

"Leave this and take the rest."

As the dresser laid out the outfit and a fresh set of underclothes, he said, "I take sorrow in your loss of the dragonslayer. She should not have escaped."

Mandulane sighed as he stepped into his undergarments, turning his back to allow the dresser to lace him into them. "And sooner than I expected. But I sorrow not. I expect we will meet again, most likely quite soon."

The dresser grunted as he tugged the laces into place. "With due respect, how can that be possible?"

Mandulane smiled again at the beauty of the clothes awaiting him on the bed. One benefit of following Krystr was the excuse it provided for handling women and making certain they acted on a man's request and behalf. "Haven't you learned that all things are possible? Including the domination of a girl who calls herself a dragonslayer."

CHAPTER TWENTY

Taddeo, Wendill, and the other dragons living on Tower Island stood in the middle of its courtyard on a day when the bright, clear sky promised the inevitability of summer. At the same time, the crisp wind reminded them that spring had yet to end. The dragons took the shape of people, and the stone tower rose behind them, blocking out the sun and casting a long, chilled shadow over the flagstone yard. Cattle lowed from the nearby pasture and the air carried the scent of baking bread from the farmhands' cottages that stood between the fields and the tower.

The dragons had taken their time arranging the sacred structure in the middle of the courtyard. First, they moved the Scaldings' wooden furniture out of the tower. Breaking it into large pieces, the dragons carefully formed a circle and made sure to place the largest pieces at the center and the smallest outside. Next, the dragons placed unbroken bowls around the outer edge of the circle and filled them with seawater gathered from the harbor. Although the poison that had contaminated Tower Island made it impossible for them to enter the sea, they were able to scoop water into the containers as long as they made no attempt to touch it themselves.

Taddeo nodded to Wendill, who slowly transformed into a large slate-colored dragon. Like an overgrown lizard, his belly scraped the flagstones as he walked crablike on bowed legs toward the arrangement of wood serving as the bones of a request for help. With each step, the back of his paws scraped against the stones before he flipped them forward, claws gleaming and sharp.

When Wendill sighed, his belly heaved like the bellows of a blacksmith. Easing down to the ground, he rested his elongated head on folded paws, spittle dripping from the dozens of sharp teeth inside his jaw. As the other dragons watched, Wendill turned to stone, resting like a marker in front of a monument.

"Fiera, we call upon you for assistance," Taddeo said. "Behold the bones of the gateway we have created for you and the threshold upon which we beg you to enter."

For the next several moments, nothing happened. The cattle continued complaining from their grassy fields. Birds chirped from their nests in crevices high in the tower. The sun shifted slightly, and its warm rays cast down upon the circle of wood in the courtyard.

Wisps of white smoke emerged from the central pile of wood, swirling casually among the empty spaces between each piece. Like dogs, the wisps seemed to investigate and sniff each broken piece.

The seawater in the bowls surrounding the sacred circle began to tremble as if some giant creature walked upon the land, causing it to shudder.

The white smoke puffed itself larger and brighter from the innermost wood, filling the air with an acrid scent.

Taddeo sneezed, and his eyes watered.

Without warning, the smoke exploded, replaced by enormous flames that rose as high as the tower. The bonfire burned strong and bright, illuminating the entire courtyard and chasing away the shadow that had chilled it. Nonetheless, every dragon except Taddeo, and Wendill—still in his rock form, shivered.

The bonfire roared for several minutes, flaming violently within the perimeter marked by the bowls of seawater. Its heat felt like dozens of hearths crammed into a small space. Finally, the flames diminished until they formed the shape of a woman.

Standing in the center of smoldering ashes, her skin shone alabaster white and her long black hair curled like smoke. She wore a long flame-colored gown that swirled around her legs in the slightest breeze. Orange, red, and yellow sparkling gems encrusted the gown's bodice and high standing collar. With a disinterested sigh, she stepped out of the ashes and onto the threshold of Wendill's rock body.

Taddeo extended his hand to her, smiling.

Taking hold of his hand, she wrinkled her nose and stepped daintily and barefooted onto the flagstones, oblivious to Wendill rising up out of the rock behind her. "What stinks?" she murmured.

"Hello, Fiera," Taddeo said. "It delights me to see you, too."

CHAPTER TWENTY-ONE

Astrid and the Iron Maidens traveled into the Midlands on foot. Spring eased toward summer, a reminder that several weeks had passed since Astrid had first met the Maidens and that they'd spent much of that time walking throughout the Midlands. But because they headed North, every day felt the same. Despite occasional showers, the skies often shone bright and clear, while the temperature stayed balmy. New grass and budding tree leaves warmed the landscape with the yellow green of new spring growth, while lavender, snowy white, and butter-colored flowers dotted the plains, their heady sweet scents mingling with the crisp clean air lilting from the mountain pines.

The Midlander maidens suggested a longer route allowing them to wind through valleys and around a stretch of mountains sure to slow them down. Unlike the Northlands' jagged and towering mountains, those in the Midlands suggested a gentler nature. The Midland mountains looked like giants nestled against the ground, sleeping an indefinite nap. The broad roads winding through the surrounding valleys made for easy trekking.

Like Astrid, the Iron Maidens continued to dress like men, tucking their long hair under jaunty caps and keeping their weapons sheathed at their sides. From a distance, most people assumed they were a group of boys out on an adventure.

Unused to having company as she traveled, it took a week or so for Astrid to adjust to the constant chattering of her new companions. As far as she could tell, the Iron Maidens hailed from several different countries, and they clumped together in groups of two or three, each group conversing in its native tongue. Overwhelmed by all the languages and knowing she had no knack for learning them, Astrid experienced loneliness at first, even though surrounded by other women.

Then Thorda decided she needed to become more fluent in the

Northlander language and took it upon herself to convince Astrid to tutor her while they walked. With Thorda as a walking mate by day and sharing meals with all of the Iron Maidens, Astrid soon felt the loneliness fade, replaced by a sense of camaraderie and purpose. That sense grew stronger when she joined them every day for their early morning weapons practice. Astrid immediately recognized Vinchi's drills and fell back into the habit of practicing techniques designed to fight men instead of lizards.

And as Thorda learned more of the Northlander language from Astrid, she took the opportunity to learn more about Thorda, who had tended crops alongside her family for a landowner who had treated them well.

"What types of crops did you raise?" Astrid said one day as they walked a road flanked by grassy fields.

Thorda paused, gazing to each side. Mountains rose in the distance to their right, but farmers tending plowed fields sprouting new growth stretched to their left. Smiling in recognition, Thorda pointed at two different kinds. "Those."

Astrid squinted, as if that would help her recognize the new crops, but they looked the same to her. Laughing at herself, she said, "I worked in a smithery and never noticed much about crops. I don't know what they are."

Thorda pantomimed shucking something and then holding it horizontally and eating.

"Corn!" Astrid cried in recognition. "It's covered with a green husk and it's yellow and white and sweet."

"Corn," Thorda said, concentrating on the new word. "Corn."

"Exactly. What's the other kind of food you raised?"

Thorda paused, puzzling out an answer. When the wind kicked up, blowing from the mountains, her face lit up. Thorda raised her arms straight above her head. When the wind blew again, she let her arms drift with it.

Now it was Astrid's turn to be puzzled. "I don't understand."

Thorda became more fluid, letting her entire body move with the wind.

"Is it wheat? You're showing me the way wheat waves in the wind like the ocean?"

"Yes!" Thorda brightened again. "We use it to make bread."

"Yes, that's right. It's called wheat."

Thorda took a few moments to repeat this new word, too.

Astrid paused. She wanted to be thoughtful of Thorda's experience with the Krystr army but she also wanted to learn from it. She trod as mindfully as she could. "Was it Mandulane who killed your master?"

Thorda's eyes darkened. "No. His men."

"Mandulane sends out smaller groups of men? Is it like a first attack to make another attack easier for Mandulane?"

"Yes. Mandulane has big army. He murders hope."

Astrid took a deep breath. After being in his camp and looking into the eyes of his women tattooed blue, she had no problem understanding Thorda's meaning. Small groups that initiated first attacks on landowners probably succeeded in most cases, like Thorda's. After killing the landowner and his family, these small Krystr groups could easily control the farmers and other workers. By the time Mandulane arrived with his massive army, anyone entertaining the idea of revolt would likely give up such thoughts and cave in to Mandulane's rule.

An unexpected metallic ringing made Astrid come to a sudden halt. "Stop!" she called out to the Iron Maidens. "Quiet!"

Although some of the women didn't speak the Northlander language, they'd learned a few simple commands from Astrid. Within moments, they stood still and listened.

There it was again: the rhythmic singing of hammer upon anvil, floating in the air like the scent of flowers.

"There's a village up ahead, and they have a blacksmith." Astrid beamed, already looking forward to talking shop with a fellow blacksmith. "Maybe we can spend the night."

Without thinking, Astrid immediately dropped one hand to the pouch hanging from her belt, squeezing the pouch's exterior until she felt the comforting sharp edges of the stone of darkness hidden inside. If the village was a large one, they might also have an alchemist.

Fee and Glee had told Astrid her own sword Starlight held portents about the stone of darkness. They'd said something about not knowing if it was like the sunlight breaking through clouds or a coming darkness or both. Mandulane's men had attacked before the alchemist sisters could tell Astrid what she wanted to know about the stone, although she now knew more about her family, especially her grandfather, Benzel of the Wolf, who had been the first dragonslayer. And the sisters had confirmed what Astrid had long suspected of her brother. Without their father's knowledge, their mother had conceived Drageen by sleeping with another man, leaving Drageen with none of Astrid's dragonslaying blood.

But what was the stone of darkness and what did it mean?

Astrid had to find out. Maybe the portents in Starlight's blade would divulge a way to defeat Mandulane and his men.

Astrid remembered how Fee and Glee had warned her not to let anyone know she possessed the stone. As much as she had grown to care for the Iron Maidens, Astrid also believed the alchemists had been wise to caution her. She relaxed her grip on the leather pouch and cast a casual glance among the Iron Maidens.

As far as Astrid could tell, none of them had seen her telltale grip of the stone of darkness inside the leather pouch.

CHAPTER TWENTY-TWO

Hours later, Astrid and the Iron Maidens made their way cautiously into a large, bustling Midlander village. Like most towns in this region, the village rested in a flat, open space surrounded by fields of grain and vegetables. However, large thickets of oaks, aspens, and evergreens threaded through the entire village, resulting in a maze of nooks and crannies hiding cottages from view. Astrid suspected when the village had first been established, its founders either cleared an existing forest or transplanted parts of a forest into the town.

The comforting scent of smoke from a blacksmith's fire permeated the air, and Astrid smiled as she inhaled. Most of the villagers labored in the surrounding fields. The village was quiet, except for the honks of ducks and geese and the ringing music of the blacksmith's hammer.

Turning toward the Iron Maidens, Astrid said, "See who you can find and ask if there's enough room for us all to spend the night. Thorda, come with me and we'll talk to the blacksmith. The rest of you search through the village. Anyone who speaks the Midlander language, make sure you keep company with those who don't. Stick together."

The Iron Maidens split up and headed in different directions. Thorda kept pace with Astrid as she walked toward the sound of ringing metal. Scanning every cottage doorway in sight, she stopped when she noticed a small puff of bright yellow smoke spill out of one open doorway, followed by a teenage boy who coughed as he stumbled outside. "Are you all right?" Astrid called out.

Looking up in surprise, the boy nodded. Clearly, he understood the Northlander language.

And by the appearance of the yellow smoke, Astrid guessed he had just come out of an alchemist's cottage, probably his mother's.

"Go on without me," Astrid said to Thorda. "See what you can find out from the blacksmith."

Thorda frowned. "Do you not wish to meet him now?"

"No. It can wait. I'll be there in a few minutes."

Thorda glanced from the boy to Astrid to Starlight. Finally, she sighed, seeming to assume Astrid would be safe without Thorda by her side. She walked away without looking back.

After meeting Fee and Glee, Astrid had felt more wary about approaching alchemists or anyone who knew them. Although Fee and Glee had posed no harm, their knowledge of the Scaldings served as a reminder that Astrid already had something for which many people would be willing to kill. Two years ago, the events at her home village of Guell and her experiences with Mauri and DiStephan and brigands had resulted in an abundance of bloodstones cut out of the soles of her feet. She knew from her brother Drageen that with the help of an alchemist, the bloodstones could be ground and added to liquid. Anyone who bathed in the bloodstone liquid was protected by it for a certain time. Any blow delivered against protected skin would bounce or glide off, leaving no damage.

Astrid dreaded the thought of Mandulane learning of her bloodstones, secretly buried in the yard of her smithery. Although others in Guell knew the bloodstones existed, no one else knew where Astrid had hidden them. And if Mandulane were to get his hands on her bloodstones, he could easily conquer every country on the map she had seen in his tent.

Astrid shook off her sudden impulse to shiver. What if the stone of darkness held a power as great as that of her bloodstones? More than ever, she decided to proceed with caution, even with a boy who seemed on the verge of getting in trouble with his mother for playing with her potions.

The boy coughed and rubbed his eyes while Astrid drew near. His straight brown hair had a shaggy cut and threatened to cover his eyes. He stood slightly taller than Astrid, his body in the awkward stage between child and man, lean with young muscles showing promise of growth. Freckles dotted his nose.

"Is your mother at home?"

The boy shook his head and pointed toward the field. "She's out there."

For a moment, Astrid felt a strange foreboding, as if something had shifted out of place. Odd for an alchemist to be working the fields but not completely unheard of. "You speak well," she said, shaking off the peculiar feeling.

"Mother's a Northlander, like you." The boy sneezed loudly, his body shaking from the force of it.

"Gods keep you safe," Astrid said automatically. She thought the idea of a sneeze allowing one's spirit to momentarily escape the body and be vulnerable was nothing more than a superstitious belief, but she often said the blessing just to be on the safe side.

"Too late for that," the boy murmured, brushing his hair out of his eyes. He looked at the ground.

"What?" The foreboding grew stronger, and Astrid shifted her weight uncomfortably from one foot to the other, reminding herself that she had Starlight to protect her.

The boy sneezed again, twice this time. "Mother's due to work all day. She'll come back for evening meal. You can see her then."

Astrid reconsidered the situation. The practice of alchemy often came more naturally to women than men, but she'd heard of some male practitioners. Maybe the boy's mother wasn't the alchemist in the family.

"And your father?"

The boy shrugged. "Died some years ago. It's just me and Mother." He grabbed the end of one sleeve of his dark tunic and shook it hard. He repeated the motion with the opposite sleeve. Each time, a small cloud of yellow dust shook free and drifted away on the wind.

Astrid pointed at the final dust cloud. "Does your mother know you play with such things?"

For the first time, the boy looked directly at her, taking a moment to size her up. "It's not play," he said. "Alchemy's actually quite hard work to learn if you want to get it right."

Taken aback, Astrid found herself speechless.

The boy brightened and extended a handshake. "Albrecht's the name. I take it I'm the one you're looking for."

CHAPTER TWENTY-THREE

Astrid followed Albrecht inside the cottage he shared with his mother and perched on a stool while the boy attempted to straighten up a room that looked as if a windstorm had torn it apart. Unlike Fee and Glee's tidy and well-organized cottage, Albrecht's home was cluttered and cramped. A large iron pot hung over the smoldering hearth, wisps of smoke rising through the small ventilation hole in the roof. Two straw pallets for sleeping lay on the floor by the wall behind the hearth. Piles of clothes, spoons, measuring cups, and bottled potions crowded the surfaces of the wooden benches lined up against the other walls. Unrolled scrolls filled with drawings and diagrams criss-crossed the floor, making it impossible to walk without stepping on one.

Albrecht tiptoed in the tiny spaces between them until he reached the hearth, plunking himself down on a flat stone at its edge. "Tell me why would a pretty miss like you be looking for an alchemist. You need a love potion?"

Astrid remembered what Fee and Glee had told her: For your own protection, repeat nothing of what you see or hear today. She also remembered every alchemist who failed her during the past year. It was time to try a new approach. "No. I need to understand the power of stones."

Albrecht picked up a piece of straw resting atop the stone next to him and stuck it in his mouth to chew. "What about it?"

"How do you tell a stone's purpose?"

"You start with the color. For example, snowstones are white, the pure color. You use them for good intents. Flamestones are yellow, the warm color. You use them for warm things like love potions." He paused to look her up and down. "Are you sure you don't want a love potion? You look like you could use one."

"I'm sure," Astrid said evenly. "What about other colors?"

Albrecht chewed on his straw some more. "Blue and green stones are cool to the touch. You use them for things like cooling a fever or a feud or rivalry. Red, of course, you'd use in battle."

Bloodstones. Of course.

For a moment, his gaze shifted to the sheath holding Starlight on Astrid's belt. "And black is for darker purposes."

Astrid swallowed hard, uncomfortable with this new information. "What type of dark purposes?"

Albrecht removed the straw from his mouth and used his fingers to splay the edge he'd chewed. "Nothing a miss like yourself need concern herself with."

Feeling her nerves get the better of her, Astrid looked down and clasped her hands in her lap. "Having knowledge can be as useful as having a sword. It doesn't mean you'll use it unless someone attacks you."

"True."

Astrid looked up to see Albrecht stand and reach for a small bottle of yellow powder. Sitting back on the flat stone, he un-stoppered the bottle, shook a small amount into the palm of his hand, and twirled the splayed end of the straw in it, his own spit coating the straw allowing the powder to stick. "What are you doing?"

Without looking up, Albrecht said, "Protecting my mother and myself." He threw the straw on top of the fire.

The powder ignited, and the straw exploded. A thick red smoke cascaded up through the roof and throughout the cottage.

"From what?" Astrid called out, pulling Starlight from its sheath and backing up until her body blocked the doorway. Blinded by the red smoke, she was certain she heard Albrecht moving inside the cottage. She felt compelled to keep him from leaving until she could determine if he meant to harm her or the Iron Maidens.

When the red smoke dissipated, the hearth fire sparked white like an overheated and ruined piece of iron being struck by a hammer. The fire crackled and popped as hundreds of white sparks grew larger and jumped toward Astrid. She held up the flat of Starlight's blade to protect her face, and the sparks sang as they bounced off the sword.

"Tell me," Astrid called out, still unable to see much of the rest of the cottage through the lingering smoke. "What are you afraid of?"

The deflected sparks sizzled on the floor, winding into each other and taking the form of a huge snake. Still sizzling, it slithered toward her and rose up in the air until it looked her directly in the face. Without warning, it struck at her.

Taking a step back, Astrid struck a diagonal blow and lopped off its head, which fell on the floor and shattered into black ashes. A fountain of new white sparks sprang from the flopping body, forming two new heads.

"Tell me!" Astrid shouted in desperation. When Albrecht didn't answer, she shifted her grip of Starlight's hilt from both hands to one hand. Not knowing what else to do, she reached into the pouch at her waist, felt around for the stone of darkness, and pulled it out. Facing the growing snake made of white sparks, she held Starlight in one hand and the stone of the darkness in the other.

A surge of anger and resentment rushed through her. Who was this boy to assume she meant harm to him or anyone else in this village? Why should he be so stupid to jump to such a foolish conclusion? Who was he to attack a dragonslayer?

A shudder reverberated through the cottage like the ripples from a stone thrown into the middle of a lake. Something invisible shimmered its way through the remaining smoke and the snake of sparks. With a sound like raindrops plopping on a thatched roof, the snake collapsed into a pile of ashes. The red smoke cleared. In a far corner, Albrecht sat on the floor huddled in a ball with his arms wrapped around his legs. Staring at Astrid, his skin paled and his eyes widened. "Please don't kill me!"

For a moment, Astrid thought, *It would serve him right.* Then, startled by her own reaction, she said with sincerity, "Of course I won't kill you. All I want is for you to tell me what you know. And why did you fight me? What are you afraid of?"

"Them," Albrecht stuttered. Tears spilled from his eyes. "The ones I signaled."

Astrid resisted the urge to shiver as a chill ran through her. "You signaled? With the red smoke?"

Albrecht nodded.

The red smoke had plumed up through the hole in the roof over the hearth, probably rising high in the sky. Gripping both Starlight and the stone tighter, Astrid said, "Who did you signal?"

Albrecht swallowed hard and sniffled. "The Krystr soldiers. They camp a short ride to the East."

CHAPTER TWENTY-FOUR

Astrid's mind raced. Krystr soldiers made camp a short distance from here and the boy alchemist had just signaled them. They could infiltrate the village soon.

Albrecht was young but he seemed to be skilled with potions. He was also frightened and willing to talk. Even though time ran short, this could be her best opportunity to understand what kind of power she held in her hand.

Striding quickly toward the boy, Astrid thrust the stone in front of his face. "What is this? What is it for?"

He froze for a moment, staring into the heart of the stone. Another tear ran down his face.

"Tell me," Astrid said. "Quickly!"

"I told you," he said. "Dark colors have dark powers."

"What kind of power? Did I use it just now? Is it protective?"

"I don't know." The boy hesitated, looking down. A look of shame crossed his face. "Perhaps it was me, not you. I was scared. I lost my focus."

"And the stone?"

"I've never seen anything like it. I don't understand it." Albrecht paused. "Someone old might know."

Astrid pressed her lips together, even more furious that the Krystr soldiers had attacked Fee and Glee, the only alchemists who seemed to understand the stone and its purpose. She didn't know if the women had vanished or been killed, but she held little hope she'd see them again.

And now more Krystr soldiers would arrive at the village at any moment. Why was it so impossible to learn about the dark stone that had emerged from the bottom of her foot?

She wove her way through the maze-like paths of the village. Cottage doors slammed shut and bolted, leaving no one in sight.

Astrid shivered with dread. What if the Krystr soldiers had already come and waited around the next corner? What if…

Astrid stumbled out into the open center of the village where they'd first arrived. She caught sight of Thorda and the other Iron Maidens. Astrid ran toward them. Thorda met her halfway.

"We must go," Thorda said. "We must be quiet."

Astrid nodded. "The boy sent a signal to Krystr soldiers. He said their camp is nearby. They'll be here any minute."

Thorda's lips pressed together grimly. "We take this time to run."

The sound of hoof beats filled the air, and dust rose just above the surrounding treetops.

Astrid paused, taking notice of the size and shape of the clearing where they stood and the trees and bushes surrounding it. "No. We'll hide instead."

CHAPTER TWENTY-FIVE

A dozen Krystr soldiers rode into the village from which the red plume of smoke had risen, sending a signal of distress that had been agreed upon weeks ago with the villagers. Too many savages still resisted, roaming the countryside and wreaking havoc for the good and respectful who had already proven their faith and loyalty to Mandulane and the Krystr god.

The ride had been short and the horses were well rested and ready to run. The stink of smoke still hung in the air, and the leaves on the trees shivered from the fresh wind that blasted through the clearing, kicked up a swirl of dust.

The soldiers halted their horses and dismounted. Unscar's heart warmed with anticipation. Just last winter he'd been one of those savages toiling on his father's small farm, constantly under the older man's critical eye and victim to his harsh tongue. *Stop being such a lazy lout, Unscar. Everyone else in this family accomplishes twice as much in a day, Unscar. Why can't you be good for something, Unscar?*

But all that had changed with the arrival of a handful of Krystr soldiers and clerks, who tromped among the crops and halted each worker, telling them the story of the Krystr and the way the world was changing to embrace this new god. Of course, Unscar hadn't hesitated to put down his hoe for the chance to take a break and meet new people and hear new ideas. The hired workers had done likewise, but everyone else in Unscar's family had resisted. Unscar recognized power when he saw it, so he figured if his folks or siblings didn't have that ability it was their own fault when the soldiers killed them. No one in his family had ever stood up for him. Why should he stand up for them?

Because Unscar had demonstrated his newfound loyalty to the Krystr, one clerk took it upon himself to promote the boy from field hand to soldier. Still swelling with pride and the joy of seeking adventure instead of weeding fields of barley, Unscar trembled with anticipation as he jumped from the saddle to the ground. The past months had been rewarding, but he yearned for real conflict. He loved the idea of proving himself right and others wrong, especially with a gang of soldiers to back him up.

But as he prepared to draw his sword, his leader tossed the reins to his horse to Unscar, saying, "Take care of the animals."

"But you need me!" Unscar protested, holding on to the reins as if they were dead snakes. The leader shot a dark look at him. He quickly silenced himself. Unscar had already suffered explanations of why he had to do what he was told and how he could benefit. He didn't want to be told again. Instead, he accepted the reins of all the horses until the animals surrounded him. One snorted at him while the others tugged on the reins, looking longingly at new spring grass, just steps away.

While the other soldiers drew their small swords and shields and disappeared into the maze-like paths that wound through the village, Unscar sighed. It would be easier to let the horses have their way than let them jostle him. Still holding onto the reins, he let the horses lead him to the grass. He spotted a nearby tree branch. If he could tie off a couple of horses, he could then look for other makeshift hitching posts.

Before he could make his way to the branch, a woman stepped out from behind the tree and smiled at him.

Unscar paused, smiling back. "Hello, miss." He then noticed her odd choice of clothing, which was a man's pants and tunic instead of a dress. And her long hair hung loose, flowing with the wind.

His blood chilled. She was a savage woman who refused to tie up her hair and wear the clothes denoting her position as a lower being and servant to men.

Something hard struck him behind the knees. Unscar cried out. His legs buckled and made him drop to the ground. Moaning, he curled up his chest to his knees and wrapped his arms around them, but it didn't make him feel any better.

"Quickly!" the savage woman called out.

Someone stuffed a small wad of leather in his mouth, stifling his voice. At the same time, many hands grabbed him, rolling him onto his belly, grabbing his arms, and tying them behind his back with thin leather ties, the kind most people kept handy.

The hands were small, not anywhere as large as his. And even though they treated him roughly, nothing they did was severe enough to harm him.

Excitement rushed through his veins. Most women never seemed to notice him, and now many women were fighting over his body. A sense of pleasure washed through him, almost to the point of swooning.

For a moment, he didn't even mind that they were savages.

When the hands released him, Unscar rolled onto his side in time to see a gang of women mounting their horses. For a moment, he felt confused because he thought he recognized one of them. Had he seen her recently in Mandulane's camp?

Their horses!

Unscar tried to shout out a warning to his fellow soldiers, but the balled-up leather in his mouth muffled every attempt. Now feeling angry and duped, he wrestled on the ground as the women rode away, working to pull his hands free of the leather ties. It took several minutes but Unscar finally wrangled one hand free, the leather tie still hanging around the other wrist like a bracelet.

He pulled the balled-up leather out of his mouth and called out loudly for the other soldiers.

As their footsteps raced toward him, Unscar saw the leather opening like a flower in his hand.

Someone had drawn on it.

He held the small piece of leather between his hands, staring at the information drawn in pictures and realizing why he thought he'd recognized one of the women. He remembered seeing her talking to Mandulane, the Krystr lord himself.

The soldiers came rushing back to the clearing. Unscar smiled, understanding the power he held in his hands and how it could advance him in the ranks of Krystr soldiers.

CHAPTER TWENTY-SIX

The air seemed to sizzle with danger as Astrid rode with the Iron Maidens in a pack of horses stolen from the Krystr soldiers. Clouds rose from the horizon and spread quickly, darkening the sky. The roar of the hoof beats of their newfound horses made it impossible for Astrid to hear anything else. She kept her lips pressed together, her mouth already full of the parching taste of dust.

Because the soldiers had numbered fewer than the women, some doubled up on horses. The two Far Eastern Maidens led the pack, sharing a horse. The young women stood shorter than Astrid and looked to weigh as much as a leaf. Their long black hair streamed in the wind until one held her hand high, signaling the women to stop. When all horses came to a halt, the woman holding the reins spoke rapidly in her native tongue.

Astrid squinted as she listened, as if that might help her understand a language she knew nothing about. She thought the woman's name was Banshi, and the Maiden sitting behind her was Kikita.

When Banshi paused for breath, Kikita translated. "A woman said an empty village lies ahead."

Astrid's eyebrows rose. Kikita had stayed mostly silent until today. Astrid had no idea she was so fluent in the Northlander language. For a moment she felt suspicious of the Far Easterner but quickly brushed the thought away. Vinchi had trained these Iron Maidens and she trusted his judgment. Maybe Kikita had spoken the Northlander language before and Astrid hadn't noticed.

Thorda translated Kikita's words into Midlander, the language most of the women understood and used to communicate with each other.

"How do we know it's empty?" Astrid said. "What if Krystr soldiers are waiting there? Who told Banshi this?"

A slight smile tugged at Kikita's lips. "A woman from that village." Kikita nodded back in the direction from which they'd come. "I was with Banshi. The woman told us both. I believe she was being true."

Thorda spoke up. "What if we walk into trap? What if soldiers come from West?"

"They don't," Astrid said. "The boy. He said the Krystr soldiers were camped to the East."

Thorda frowned. "You believe him?"

She had a good point. The boy could have lied to Astrid.

On the other hand, he'd acted as if he were the one in control, almost as if he'd felt sorry for Astrid and the Iron Maidens.

If there was one thing Astrid had learned during the past two years, it was the importance of making a decision instead of wasting time dithering and worrying. It was fine to take time to consider the options but taking too much time could mean losing all of them.

It was better to make the wrong decision than to make no decision.

Looking at Kikita, Astrid said, "Tell Banshi to lead on. We need to find that village."

❧❧

After riding for hours and taking too many forks in the road to remember, Astrid felt grateful when Banshi finally held up her hand again, signaling them to stop. Thick woods stood on the right side of the road, and on the other side a towering, branchless tree dominated a field gone wild. The ground was flat and leveled as if it had been used for farming within the past few years but had since been abandoned. Banshi chattered excitedly as she pointed at the tree, standing like a gigantic wooden spindle. Its bark was blackened, as if it had been struck by lightning.

Kikita dismounted and took the reins from Banshi. "This is the landmark the woman told us about," Kikita said. "We must go through the woods to find the village." Leading Banshi's horse, Kikita walked along the side of the road for a few minutes. Stopping abruptly, she pointed at the woods. "Here. The path is overgrown but it is still here."

Astrid frowned. As she nudged her horse's sides with her heels to urge it forward, she saw nothing but woods. It wasn't until Kikita disappeared between two trees that Astrid could begin to see the shape of the path.

It would make for a perfect hiding place. No one riding along this road would realize the path existed unless they already knew where to look for it.

While the Iron Maidens walked their horses and followed Kikita's lead, Astrid brought up the rear of the pack. Before guiding her horse onto the path into the forest, she cast a long look up and down the road to make sure she saw no one else.

After an easy walk covering a good distance from the road, the path opened up unexpectedly into a clearing of neat wattle-and-daub cottages circled around a well covered with wooden planks. The surrounding trees provided constant shade and kept the air cool. At first glance, Astrid expected villagers to stream out of their homes at any moment, but she soon realized that would not happen.

Unlike the Temple of Limru where the bodies of the slaughtered had been displayed as a cruel warning to anyone who resisted the Krystr soldiers, a more subtle approach had been taken here. The cottages stood intact, although the small gardens surrounding each one lay unkempt and overgrown with weeds. Some of the thatch roofs looked in disarray and in need of repair.

A rope had been strung between two cottages, hung with laundry that had dried but never collected.

With a growing sense of dread, Astrid dismounted, handing her horse's reins over to Kikita. The other Iron Maidens remained mounted, their faces reflecting the same kind of concern that gnawed at Astrid.

She took each step as if a bear trap might suddenly emerge from the ground and clamp its iron teeth around her leg. In the trees behind the cottages, birds chirped and squirrels complained at the unexpected company of the Iron Maidens.

Astrid neared the rope line that hung at eye level and came to a sudden halt, studying what had become obvious and trying to make sense of it. Within moments, she murmured, "Oh, no."

Clothes had been sewn onto the rope, but not in a random fashion. Dresses hung shoulder to shoulder by shirts sewn to pants, with shoes lined up neatly below. Splatters of blood had drenched all the clothing and then dried.

She saw no ashes, no bone, no skin. She saw no sign that people had once lived in this village.

Except for the clothes they had worn, now arranged and attached to the rope as if the people who wore those outfits had been yanked out of them.

Chapter Twenty-Seven

While the other women investigated the cottages and searched the overgrown gardens and fields for food, Thorda helped Astrid gather wood. After checking the wind to make sure it blew away from the road from which they'd come, they sat down in front of the hearth of the largest cottage with all the wood they'd collected.

"What do the Krystr soldiers want?" Astrid said, arranging the kindling in the same way for building a blacksmithing fire.

Thorda hesitated for a moment as if searching for the right words. She handed more kindling to Astrid's outstretched hand. "They want land. Food. Wealth. They take it."

Astrid nodded at Thorda's confirmation of what she'd seen inside Mandulane's tent. "They have a map. I recognized the Northlands, Midlands, Southlands, and the Far East but there were other countries on the map I've never heard of."

"You saw the world," Thorda said.

"I think so. It looks like they plan to take as much as they can from the entire world."

"We stop them in Midlands. They cannot take from Northlands."

"And if we can stop them from getting to the Northlands, they'll be weaker. We can fight them and reduce their numbers. We can at least make it more difficult for them to steal from the world. Maybe we can even drive them out of the Midlands or stop them altogether."

The women worked in silence for a few minutes, now arranging larger pieces of wood above the kindling.

"Mandulane and the Krystr soldiers claim their god is the true god," Astrid said. "But that's just an excuse for them to take what they want."

"Yes. They tell story. They make men feel good. Men want to be soldiers."

Astrid knew she shouldn't have been surprised. Last year she and Margreet had struggled to contain themselves at a mansion where Krystr clerks joined the household for the evening meals. Other women had cowered in fear, staying silent and meek. Astrid had been relieved when Margreet decided to watch Vinchi teach the master's boys how to fight and learned to fight herself with Astrid as her partner.

For the first time, Astrid realized she knew very little about the Krystr religion itself.

"What do the clerks preach?" Astrid put the finishing touches on the arranged wood and then withdrew a piece of flint from the pouch hanging from her belt. "Who is the Krystr?"

"They say people were fishes. Long ago."

Astrid sat back on her heels, astonished. "What?"

Thorda shrugged. "Long, long ago. They say we lived in oceans."

Still astonished, Astrid said, "As fish."

Thorda nodded. "God Krystr took man fish and…" She hesitated, not knowing the words she needed. Instead, she pantomimed. Extending her legs in front of her on the ground, Thorda pointed at them. "Tail." She then chopped with a flat hand at the empty space between her legs. Pointing at them, she said, "Now legs."

A chill ran through her body. Astrid shivered. "Are you saying they claim their god took fish out of the sea and turned their tails into legs?"

"Yes." A grimness slackened Thorda's face. "But only men. God Krystr took men out of ocean and onto land. Women fish stayed in ocean."

No. This can't be good.

Out loud Astrid said, "If the female fish stayed in the ocean, how does that explain the fact that women exist?"

"Men want pleasure. They go back to ocean and take pleasure from women fish. But men want pleasure on land." Once again, Thorda made a chopping motion between her extended legs.

Astrid's stomach churned, making her feel sick. "The men split the tails of the female fish and took them up on land so they could…"

"Have pleasure."

Astrid stared at Thorda, seeing her own queasiness on the Iron Maiden's face. Swallowing hard, Astrid found it hard to speak. "When I was in Mandulane's tent, there were several women who danced. They were naked, and their bodies were painted blue. And the look in their eyes…" Astrid paused, willing herself not to shudder. "They were empty. I think they were only there to be used by Mandulane or his men."

Once more, Thorda nodded. "They take pleasure. They take everything."

Thorda's words shook Astrid to the core. She remembered the horror and shock she'd felt when Margreet had been killed in front of her eyes.

An old familiar longing crept up the back of Astrid's throat like a lingering sickness. It came from the same anger she'd felt at Vinchi for Margreet's death, even though he'd done everything within his power to help her. It came from the same disgust she'd felt when her friend Mauri proved to be an enemy. It came from the same hatred she harbored toward her brother Drageen for manipulating her and destroying her happiness.

All of Astrid's feelings came crashing together toward a new target: Mandulane and the Krystr soldiers.

She focused on the flint as she struck it above a handful of kindling she'd kept aside, cupping her other hand around it even though the air was still inside the cottage. Within minutes, the flint sparked enough to ignite the kindling. Gray smoke curled up. She breathed softly on the tiny flame until it burned brightly. Quickly, Astrid placed her handful of new fire onto the kindling on the hearth and watched the beginning of a strong and steady fire.

"They take pleasure," Astrid said, repeating Thorda's words. "They take everything."

The fire roared suddenly, as if it had a mind of its own.

Astrid crossed her arms, heartened to see Thorda's face more clearly in the firelight. "Let's see what we can do to stop them."

CHAPTER TWENTY-EIGHT

The stone stairway spiraled and twisted, and with the doors open at the bottom and top of the tower, fresh salt air buffeted the steps as it rushed and swirled, looking for a way to escape. Every so often the wind howled, wrapping itself tighter and faster around the stairway. Its stone felt cold to the touch, penetrating quickly to the bone.

Wendill sat on one step, not far from the doorway at the top of the tower. The stairway spiraled into a vast darkness below, and the walls in this part of the tower narrowed so much that if he spread his arms like wings he could touch them. Fascinated, he watched tiny flames shimmer and dance from Fiera's fingertips across one step several feet below.

The step writhed, shaking itself with a moan and released a puff of white powder.

Fiera coughed, waving the powder away from her face. But the flames darting from her fingertips ignited the floating powder, which took the shape of a set of teeth and bit her. Fiera shrieked, pulling the bitten hand toward her chest while swatting the powder back into a harmless cloud with the other.

Looking up at Wendill, she said, "I cannot tolerate this type of working condition."

Wendill shrugged. "It's the only one we've got."

Fiera groaned as she shook her hand. "These steps are poisoned through your fault, not mine."

Taking offense, Wendill said, "I was trapped inside a rock when—"

Ignoring him, Fiera continued. "The poison is dreadful, but what do you expect when the alchemist who made it did so with the intent to murder someone?" She glared at Wendill as if it were his fault. "Compound that with the fact that the one who was murdered chose to be involved in the deaths of hundreds of innocent people, and it's quite a mess." Fiera shuddered, pointed an uninjured finger at Wendill. "I don't know what you were thinking when you decided to integrate with these people. They're absolutely dreadful."

Well. She's got me there.

Out loud he said, "What's done is done. And not all of them are dreadful. I'm rather fond of the dragonslayer."

"Sacrilege!" Fiera shouted.

"It's but a term," Wendill said. "She doesn't slay us. She kills lizards."

"Still," Fiera said, examining her bitten hand. "I hear she's horrible."

"It isn't true," Wendill said. "She has her grandfather's spirit."

"Well, it's all led up to this. My hand is hurt and useless. I can accomplish nothing more today than a nice nap. Where shall I do so?"

Wendill stared at Fiera's hand. It looked fine. No skin had been broken nor could he see any swelling. Reaching down toward her, he said, "Let me see."

Fiera cradled her own arm as if it were broken. "No. Enough damage has been done. I need no more." She sniffed as if offended. "Simply show me to my bedroom."

"But it's still morning."

"And I'm exhausted!" Fiera forgot about cradling her arm and used it to point to the top of the stairway. "Look at how much I've done already!"

Wendill didn't have to look. "You've healed a dozen steps so far."

"And it's horrifically difficult and dangerous and deadly work!" Pausing for effect, Fiera looked down dramatically and then shrieked. "My dress! It's ruined!"

Even though she pointed at a place on her skirt, Wendill saw nothing wrong with it.

"It's from having to kneel on stone." Again, she shot an accusing glare at Wendill. "My knees and shins will be bruised for months!"

Wendill took the complaint to heart. He hated feeling cold and hard, but he had to admit it was the nature of stone. "I will find something to give you comfort when you work. We have a great appreciation for your help."

Fiera sighed heavily. "I know." As if from memory she recited, "It is wiser for us to work together than apart."

"If you cannot work, you cannot work. But it would help us for you to communicate with one of our own."

Fiera raised a questioning eyebrow.

"If we build the fire, you can use it to talk to her." Wendill made no attempt to make it sound like a question. They both knew he spoke the truth.

Fiera smiled sweetly. "I suppose there's time for that before my nap."

CHAPTER TWENTY-NINE

The next morning, like most mornings, Astrid woke before any of the Iron Maidens. For the sake of safety, they'd slept huddled together like a pack of wolves inside the cottage left in the best condition by the Krystr soldiers who had decimated this village. Knowing she'd likely be the first one awake, Astrid had slept with her body blocking the front door. If anyone or anything tried to invade the cottage at night, she would be able to warn the others.

Astrid sat up, yawned, careful not to wake anyone. In a far corner of the room, Thorda snored gently. Pale sunlight beamed through the cracks in the door and the shuttered windows, and she marveled at the other women's ability to sleep in any condition other than pure darkness because she rarely could do so herself. The night had been unusually warm, and the women had agreed to let the hearth fire burn itself out. Its woodsy scent filled the air, still stale from the cottage being closed for weeks or months or possibly even years, despite the small opening in the roof for the smoke to escape.

Rising slowly, still careful not to the wake the others, Astrid winced at the stiffness in her muscles from having slept on the cottage's dirt floor. She'd left Starlight in its sheath on the ground by the wall, just an arm's length away. She picked up her weapon and attached it to the belt around her waist. The door creaked on its hinges as she opened and shut it behind her, but no one stirred. She stretched, easing the kinks out of her body, and yawned again. She turned, looking for the brightest spot on the horizon and finding it between two cottages. Just as she suspected, the sun hadn't come up yet. A low-lying fog rested on the grass between and behind the cottages. Astrid smiled, enjoying her favorite time of day. She loved the quiet and the gentle light.

After finding a place to relieve herself behind the cottages, Astrid walked back toward the center of the tiny village. A rabbit nibbled grass growing through the cracks of the well's stone wall. Looking up in terror at the sound of Astrid's leather shoe as it crunched against a dead leaf, the rabbit paused long enough to assess the situation, and then bounded in the opposite direction.

The square-shaped well stood waist high, and a few wooden planks covered its mouth. Astrid drummed her fingertips lightly against the wood. When they arrived yesterday, Thorda had advised against drinking from the well. Everyone had a leather flask of fresh spring water, and they'd very likely come across a stream or river today as they traveled toward the Upper Midlands.

Knowing Thorda was right, Astrid removed the cover anyway, staring into the depths of the water inside the well. She folded her arms on the top of the wall and rested her chin on top of her wrist. Had it only been a year since she'd seen Norah rise up from the well at Limru?

Astrid didn't like thinking about her childhood, when she and Norah had been caged together. The Scaldings had forced the young dragon Norah into a situation where the only way she could survive was to chew on Astrid and drink her blood. Being entrapped for a few years had left Astrid covered from head to toe with scars, which she hid years later, once she'd grown old enough to shift into the shape and appearance of her choice.

She'd spent years thinking about her own pain, never imagining what it must have been like for Norah. Even worse, two years ago, when Taddeo had freed Norah from Tower Island, she'd been so weak that she'd devoured Astrid's best arm in order to survive.

Astrid dipped her fingertips into the well water, shivering at its frigid touch. Norah could have killed Astrid when they were trapped on Tower Island. Instead, Norah had taken only what she needed from Astrid to keep herself alive. Now, Astrid thought about the pain Norah must have felt all those years ago, as well as the strength it must have taken to be in constant hunger so that Astrid could live.

"You gave my arm back to me," Astrid whispered to the water inside the well. "I don't understand how it was possible. I only know I'm grateful."

The well water rippled as if someone had dropped a stone in its center.

Something touched Astrid's fingertips, still resting on the water's surface.

Gasping, she jerked her hand back. She took a few quick steps away from the well, as timid as the rabbit that had darted away moments ago.

It can't be Norah, Astrid told herself. *Norah lives at Limru now.*

Astrid crept toward the well, holding her breath as she peered into the it.

Its water stood perfectly still, as if nothing had disturbed it.

A sudden thought occurred to Astrid. "DiStephan?" she whispered.

The water remained still, but the low-lying fog rolled from the cottages and the woods behind them, heading toward the well like spokes being placed into the hub of a wheel. Astrid looked up from the well, startled by the sight.

The fog collected next to her, taking the shape of a familiar ghost.

"DiStephan," she said with relief. "I haven't seen you since I met the Iron Maidens." Feeling a flush of guilt, she said, "I've been busy with them since the Krystr soldiers took me to Mandulane, and we've been running ever since."

The faint, foggy shape of DiStephan's face smiled slightly and nodded in understanding.

"But you've been with me?" Astrid said, now leaning at ease against the well.

The ghost nodded again. But his expression shifted as the fog drifted within the shape he took, like smoke captured inside a bottle. Frowning, he pointed at the cottage where the Iron Maidens slept. His lips moved rapidly, but only silence filled the air.

"What is wrong? Are we in danger?"

DiStephan first shook his head to signal no, and then nodded to signal yes. He pointed at the door of the cabin, then jabbed his finger at it.

"I don't understand. What are you trying to tell me?"

The door opened, and Thorda stepped out.

Surprised, Astrid shrieked.

Thorda stopped dead in her tracks, staring at Astrid.

Turning to face DiStephan, Astrid's mind raced as she tried to figure out how to explain the presence of his ghost.

But the fog he'd used to take shape now swirled innocently at Astrid's feet, dissipating as the sun broke above the horizon.

CHAPTER THIRTY

With ax in hand, Thorda hurried toward Astrid, casting a watchful gaze across the open center of the village, the cottages, and the woods behind them. "Why scream?" Thorda asked, keeping a tight and ready grip on the handle of her ax.

Astrid looked down, watching the dissipation of the fog that DiStephan's ghost had used to take shape moments ago. She always recognized his concern for her but felt confused by his message. When she'd asked if they were in danger, why had he first indicated they weren't and then jabbed an accusing finger at the door of the cottage where the Iron Maidens slept, indicating they were in danger, after all? How could both be true at once?

"I'm sorry," Astrid said, staring at the dirt with the hope that DiStephan might have drawn some sign in it to make his message clearer.

But all she saw were the footprints left by herself, Thorda, and the other Iron Maidens.

Looking up at last, Astrid said, "I'm sorry. You startled me. I thought I was the only one awake."

Thorda nodded at the horizon, where the rising sun poured light into the pale pink sky above. "Time to go."

"I'll gather food for breakfast."

Thorda grabbed Astrid's shoulder before she could walk away. "No," Thorda said quietly, her face looking drawn and weary despite her having just woken up. "Time to go now."

"Why?"

"We stay, easy to find us."

"Of course," Astrid said, thinking it through. "The longer we stay in any one place, the sooner Mandulane and his men will find us. We have to keep moving, except to sleep."

"We rest in Upper Midlands. We rest in safe place."

"You're right." Astrid smiled. "Let's get everyone up and ready to go."

Within a short time, the Iron Maidens hurried to gather their weapons and wits, most of them still groggy from waking after a fitful night's sleep.

Soon, they gathered by the well, ready to leave, although their head count was one short.

Dismounting her own horse, Astrid made a final sweep through the small village, making sure they'd left nothing behind and looking for the last maiden. In case soldiers traveled the road nearby, the women agreed to keep their voices low.

Finally, Astrid opened the door to the cottage where they'd slept, startled to find Kikita kneeling in front of the hearth, full of dead embers from last night's fire. Hands spread apart over the ashes, thin strands of smoke wove between Kikita's fingers as if she were examining newly spun thread.

Astrid blinked. The fire had died hours ago. Without fire, there could be no smoke.

When she looked again, the smoke had vanished. Kikita stood, toeing the embers. "I wished to make sure no sparks were left. There is no need to risk wild fire that could burn down the forest."

Astrid remembered DiStephan's ghostly finger. If the door had been open when DiStephan had taken his form from the fog, he would have been pointing at the exact spot where Kikita now stood.

Smiling, Kikita breezed past Astrid and quickly climbed to sit behind Banshi on her horse.

The unmistakable scent of smoke filled the air.

Suppressing a shiver of sudden fear, Astrid followed her outside to join the rest of the women.

When she walked past the bloodied clothes left hanging on the line, a gentle breeze made them move. Astrid said, "I saw a pile of old clothes in one of the cottages. We should take them. Our clothing is wearing thin and we could use what's been left behind."

Already mounted on her horse, Thorda cried, "No!"

Ignoring Thorda's protest, Astrid dismounted and went to fetch the clothes, surprised when Kikita joined her side to help.

CHAPTER THIRTY-ONE

Fiera focused on the small fire she'd just ignited as Taddeo and Wendill stood nearby and watched. They'd led her inside a peculiar structure within the tower, which Taddeo explained had been used by the Scaldings' alchemist when the family controlled Tower Island. Old scents of herbs and spices still hung in the air. The room itself hung like a goiter from the inner wall of the tower, and a narrow stone stairway led to it from the main circular steps that connected the top of the tower to the ground level. Inside and out, the room's smooth, polished walls, floor, and ceiling curved gently, making it sphere-like. As Fiera knelt before the small fire, she shivered at the cool touch of stone against her skin.

"Do you see anything?" Taddeo asked. His fingertips tapped anxiously against his crossed arms.

"Hush," Fiera said. "How can I possibly concentrate when you're talking?"

Looking up, she saw Taddeo open his mouth to protest, then quickly press his lips together in a tight grimace. *Good. It's likely been far too long since he's needed anything from someone who can put him in his place.*

She resisted the urge to smile, even when she heard Wendill's soft footsteps pacing nervously behind her. Fiera gave all her attention to the small fire, letting her hands drift above and around its heat to give it shape while the wind howled and sucked the gray smoke through the doorway and up the tower.

Fiera closed her eyes, shutting out the world. She allowed herself to connect with the comfort of the flame, barely staying aware enough to maintain her own shape instead of bursting into fire herself. She sensed the kindling and wood, longing to feed directly from it. Longing to become unpredictable and wild and filled with life-giving heat.

She stifled a cry when she sensed the connection on the other side, even though she intentionally sought it. In another land across the sea, the colleague whose help they sought tended a similar fire. With her eyes still closed, Fiera visualized the request and sensed an understanding and intent to provide what she needed.

Time had no meaning in this state. Afterwards, Fiera never knew if minutes or hours or weeks had passed. She only cared about what she accomplished during that time, happy when she succeeded and devastated whenever anything unanticipated happened.

When her hands tingled, Fiera opened her eyes, grinning at last when she saw wispy tendrils of black smoke intertwining with her fingers, stretched wide apart. She nearly giggled with delight at the smoke's gentle touch, wrapping it around her hands like newly spun linen thread. It wound around her wrists and forearms. When she'd extracted all the smoke from the fire, she leaned over it and spat into its heart. The flames popped and sizzled, then extinguished themselves, leaving nothing behind but a few charred embers.

Becoming aware of her surroundings again, Fiera heard Wendill's pacing come to a stop. Of course, they'd both watch closely now. They'd only heard of such things that dragons like Fiera practiced and had never witnessed in person.

She prepared to thrill them.

Fiera stood up with a regal air, moving with grace and purpose. Sweeping her smoke-laden arms across her body, she cried out, "Manifest!" as she pointed her hands toward an empty spot in the center of the room.

Threads of smoke un-spooled from her hands and arms, first pooling on the stone floor and then rising to form the shape of the dragonslayer she'd requested.

The smoky shape became solid, and the dragonslayer looked at Fiera in surprise.

Not quite in unison, Taddeo and Wendill sighed with relief.

She looked the figure up and down, finally saying, "I presume you are the dragonslayer known as DiStephan."

"What have you done?" the ghost cried out, staring at them all in surprise. "Astrid…the Iron Maidens…they're in terrible danger. There's a traitor among them!"

Chapter Thirty-Two

Sitting astride his horse, Unscar studied the drawings on the small piece of leather one of the savage women had balled up and crammed into his mouth. By the time he and the other Krystr soldiers had walked back to their encampment, the sun had vanished and dusk crept across the horizon. He needed light to find the landmarks denoted on the tiny map he'd been given.

The soldier in charge of the encampment had jumped to conclusions and mistakenly praised Unscar for his cleverness in deceiving the savage women, first by stealing the map from them and then keeping it safe by letting them tie him up. Unscar had worried he'd appear cowardly, but all the other soldiers agreed that only a fool would try to fight so many women who carried weapons and knew how to use them. Surely a man so clever should take the lead in hunting these women down and delivering the punishment they deserved.

Only Unscar knew the truth: he'd been attacked and bound by the women first. One of them had slipped the map inside his mouth. But why should he admit the truth? Only he could recognize one of those women as a traitor to her kind and a friend to his. That knowledge gave him power, and Unscar wasn't fool enough to give that power up to anyone.

Unscar cradled the precious map in both hands. He saw no reason to reveal the truth that he'd been ambushed and hog-tied by women half his size. He deserved to benefit from the ordeal.

What he hadn't counted on was benefitting so quickly and directly. By showing the map to the soldier in charge and pointing out to him that it showed where the women intended to travel, Unscar's superior promoted him on the spot. The commander would lead most of the soldiers on their planned route, while Unscar would lead a few soldiers to follow the path shown on the map. Unscar suspected his commander feared Mandulane and what might happen if the commander failed to cover all possibilities. If Unscar failed, the commander would look good by having followed the plan dictated by Mandulane. But if Unscar succeeded, the commander could take credit for having taken the initiative of sending expendable men on a potentially fruitless mission while covering important ground elsewhere.

Now, in the middle of the countryside, a handful of soldiers dismounted to rest the horses they'd taken from the villagers while Unscar stayed mounted, pored over the clues on the map, and compared them to his surroundings. A soft breeze blew his fine hair across his eyes, and Unscar tucked it behind his ears. He wrinkled his nose at the dust from the road kicked up by the breeze. This region had seen no rain in a week or so, and the dust he'd inadvertently inhaled had a stale taste. Nonetheless, the pastures flanking the road managed to sprout new grass, and well-fed sheep bleated happily in the distance. Even though the clouds above gleamed white and thin in the bright sunlight, Unscar worried they might portend an oncoming storm.

He had to figure out where they were in accordance with this simple map. Only then would he understand where to go.

His horse shook its head and walked to the side of the road, where it dropped its mouth to nibble on flowering weeds.

"Fine," Unscar said irritably. He dismounted quickly, leaving the horse to eat in peace as he plopped to sit in the middle of the road. He shut out the chatter and laughter of his men, who drank from their flasks and took chunks of cheese and bread from their pouches. Let them eat. Unscar had more important things to consider than lunch.

He returned his attention to the one part of the drawing he understood for sure on the tiny map: a handful of triangular images clearly meant to denote the tents in the Krystr encampment. There, below, was a cottage with smoke rising through the roof, clearly representing the village where the savages had ambushed him once he'd been left alone with the soldiers' horses. The series of roads leading beyond the encampment and village looked simple enough, but Unscar couldn't tell which ones were true roads used by men and which ones were narrow footpaths used by villagers or animals.

A soldier leaned over Unscar's shoulder and said, "Maybe it'll help if you turn it sideways." Laughing, the soldier offered a small chunk of cheese.

Unscar grumbled but took the cheese and gnawed on it as the

soldier walked back toward his colleagues, still giggling. Making sure no one could see, Unscar took the soldier's advice and turned the tiny map sideways. *That doesn't help at all*, he thought, and then snorted. For a moment, he inadvertently inhaled a bite of cheese, terrified to realize he couldn't breathe. Letting the map fall to the ground, Unscar pounded his own chest until the cheese came loose, wheezing and struggling to regain his breath.

His heart raced. Unscar let go of the terror of his brush with choking to death, and he chewed the cheese slowly and thoroughly before swallowing it. For a moment, a flame of rage overwhelmed him. He considered the possibility that the soldier who had given the cheese to him may have meant to kill him.

Nonsense, Unscar told himself. *It was your own foolishness and lack of attention.*

At that moment, he saw the map had landed near his feet, right side up and tilted at an angle so that it took the shape of a diamond instead of a square. And the chunk of cheese he'd been eating had landed on top of the map, blocking out the entanglement of roads that confused him. Somehow, that simple difference made the map come to life in Unscar's eyes. All of a sudden, he understood the relationship between the encampment and the village and the roads leading from them into the Upper Midlands. And in understanding that relationship, he realized where he and his men were on the map and where they needed to go next.

Smiling, Unscar picked up the cheese and took another bite, careful this time to chew it well as he studied the map. *Yes. It all makes perfect sense now.*

After swallowing and brushing the last bits of cheese from his hands, Unscar picked up the map from the ground and stood, telling his men to mount up and get ready to ride.

CHAPTER THIRTY-THREE

Hundreds of miles away, the sun brightened the skies above Guell, Astrid's home village, and sparkled along the dangerous waves of the sea between the shore by Astrid's empty cottage and the rocky outcrop of Dragon's Head. Lizard eggs the size of a man's fist lay scattered throughout its nooks and crannies, warmed by the sun. Soon they would hatch, and the young lizards would stay on Dragon's Head in safety. Lizards used Dragon's Head only as a place to deposit eggs because no people lived on the outcrop. It couldn't support any kind of growth or food other than the lichen and tiny crabs that provided plenty of nourishment for the newly hatched. If adult lizards lived on Dragon's Head, they would eat the young lizards without hesitation.

Spring came slowly to the Northlands and even more slowly to Dragon's Head, where the sea wind blew harsh and cold, even though the sun heated up the rocky ground quickly. Sea birds cried as they coasted on spread wings above, rarely tempted to land on Dragon's Head. The bite of a newly hatched lizard would kill a bird instantly. A handful of dead birds dotted the outcrop, a warning to others that might like the look of unprotected eggs. The eggshells, too, were poisonous to anything that tried to eat them.

None of this mattered to Drageen, Astrid's brother. Darkness surrounded him, the result of having been consumed into the rock where the dragon Wendill had been trapped for decades.

There is no justice! Drageen thought for the thousandth time. Had it been possible, he would have ground his teeth or pounded a fist into an open hand or stamped his foot hard on the ground to express his frustration. But he felt no ground beneath his feet. In fact, he couldn't feel his feet or his hands or his teeth.

He wasn't entirely convinced his body still existed. He couldn't see or hear or speak or feel.

Oddly enough, his sense of smell and taste seemed to be intact.

Although sometimes he wondered if it might be nothing more than his memory of smells.

At the moment, he smelled mostly the rich, dank scent of earth and stone, with a slightly chalky aftertaste. Sometimes he thought he tasted sunlight, which had a gentle and pleasant tang. Sometimes he felt convinced he tasted the salt of seawater crashing in waves on Dragon's Head or the fresh taste of rain from the heavens above.

He wished he could experience it all himself instead of trying to remember what the world was like.

Mostly, he hated the absence of time. He had no inkling how long he'd been trapped inside Dragon's Head. Had it been days or weeks or months? Resigned, he suspected the most accurate answer was years.

I should have known better, he thought, again, not for the first time. *But who would have thought she'd align herself with dragons? How could I have guessed they'd come to her aid? What were they thinking?*

Drageen relived the events in his thoughts once more, looking for a way he could have prevented such a horrific outcome. He had instructed his alchemist to poison the girl Mauri, capture her spirit, and use it to track down Astrid, who he needed to produce blood-stones for the protection of himself and the Scalding territories. But the dragons had interfered, bringing them to Dragon's Head, where he had fought Astrid, who could never have defeated him without the help she received from the dragons and spirit girl. And if that hadn't been bad enough, he'd forgotten the ancient curse placed upon Dragon's Head by dragons and his family until it was too late. Even then, how could he have anticipated that he'd be the one to be absorbed into Dragon's Head?

If he could have felt his head (which he suspected no longer existed), he would have shook it in woe. No matter how many times he examined the details, he couldn't find a way in which he could have captured Astrid and the bloodstones ready to emerge from her body. All his well-designed plans had fallen apart, and the worst possible outcome had come to pass. His responsibility had been to lead the Scalding family and protect their land and people. He had failed in the worst possible way, and he blamed Astrid.

He hated her with the core of his being.

Normally, at this point, Drageen imagined fire coursing through his veins and strove to remember the iron-like smell of blood.

For the first time since he'd become trapped inside Dragon's Head, Drageen lost heart. He didn't have the will or the drive to put so much energy into hating his sister.

Had it been possible, Drageen would have heaved a long and heavy sigh.

A flash of memory came back to him, something he hadn't thought about in a very long time. He remembered telling Astrid about her responsibility to the family and her duty.

She had said something about not being asked. Of course, it was true but also necessary. If he'd asked Astrid for help, it would have been impossible to put her into the state of chaos needed to purge the bloodstones from her body.

Drageen realized no one had ever asked him if he'd be willing to sink into the depths of Dragon's Head and live a life of nothingness. The curse demanded a Scalding to replace the dragon should it be set free, and Drageen had *not* volunteered. He'd had no desire to set the dragon loose, anyway. He resented having had no choice in the matter, especially when he was the one to pay the price.

Astrid paid a price, too, he realized. *A very high price.*

That thought shook Drageen free of the doldrums. If he could have sensed blood running through his veins, he convinced himself it would be boiling. *Why does Astrid matter?* he thought angrily. *What about the impending invasion? If I am not there, who will protect the Northlands?*

Chapter Thirty-Four

After departing the abandoned village, Astrid and the Iron Maidens rode through the gently sloping hills of the central Midlands. The day remained bright and warm. The evergreen scent of the forest drifted through the air, intermingling with the heaviness of freshly turned earth in the fields. A few times they passed fields dotted with seed sowers, throwing in wide arcs as they walked slowly and methodically among the freshly turned rows.

Late that afternoon, the women rode into a small village, where they made arrangements to sleep in a farmer's pasture that night. While the maidens took charge of the horses and bargained for food, Astrid followed the comforting metallic ring to the local smithery. She found a solidly built man drenched in sweat as he pulled the iron head of a hoe from his smithing fire, laid its glowing orange edge on his anvil, and hammered several well placed blows until the color began to fade. He reminded her of Temple, the man who had bought her when she was a child and trained her as his apprentice.

Astrid smiled with a sudden wistfulness. She missed the constant heat and smoke of a smithery, as well as the feel of a perfectly balanced hammer in her hand. She missed reading the malleability of the iron by its color and how quickly she could shape it into something useful. For a moment, envy washed through her.

Without looking up, the blacksmith picked the hoe head up with a pair of tongs and plunged it into a nearby bucket of water to quench it. "What do you need?"

Astrid took a deep breath, hesitating to ask a question that could stir trouble. "I'm wondering if there's an alchemist nearby."

The blacksmith looked up, and his eyebrows rose as he took in her appearance.

Astrid braced herself, so accustomed to her way of life as a dragonslayer that she had to remind herself that a woman wearing men's clothes and a sheathed sword startled most people.

Not wanting to interrupt the rhythm of his work, Astrid pointed at the quenching bucket.

Shaking himself back to the task at hand, the blacksmith swirled the hoe head in the water for a moment and then withdrew it, taking several moments to study the results.

Astrid couldn't help but peer at it, too. "That's good work," she said. "Nice and solid and sharp."

He placed the finished hoe head on a bench and crossed his arms. He faced Astrid. "I've heard stories of a blacksmith who became a dragonslayer. A girl, they say."

Astrid nodded. "That would be me." She showed him her hands, which were relatively clean in comparison to his sooty and grimy skin. "But it's been much too long since I've smited metal."

"And why would a dragonslayer who was once a blacksmith be looking for an alchemist?"

Astrid wondered if she'd made a mistake. If this man decided she meant trouble or could bring it to this village, she could be driven out before nightfall, along with the Iron Maidens.

But the stone of darkness hidden in her pouch haunted her day and night. What if it held the kind of power that could help them keep the Krystr soldiers out of the Northlands? After seeing Mandulane's camp and encountering the men he commanded, Astrid worried about protecting her home of Guell, her friends, and all of the Northlands. She needed all the help she could find, even if it meant taking risks like this.

"I oppose the Krystr invasion," she said. "And I seek like-minded people who can help me."

The blacksmith considered her for a long moment. "Take my advice. Never say those words again. Especially not in Krystr territory."

Astrid froze, well aware of the tools he had at hand that he could easily use as weapons. She didn't want to draw her sword and hoped he wouldn't make it necessary.

Casting a quick glance beyond Astrid, the blacksmith said, "Follow me."

Startled, Astrid wondered for a moment if she should walk away instead. But as the blacksmith checked to make sure his smithing fire was well contained and his weapons put in their place, she felt as if she were with her own kind. She decided to trust him.

Walking past the anvil and through the small smithery yard, Astrid followed the blacksmith into a cottage. At first, it reminded her of her own cottage back in Guell, simple and sparse. But then she noticed a faint odor of unusual herbs and spices. As her eyes adjusted to the dim light inside the cottage, she noticed several boxes tucked underneath the benches lining the walls around the central hearth.

The blacksmith faced her with crossed arms, keeping an eye on the open doorway behind her. "I learned smithing from my father and alchemy from my mother. What do you need?"

Recognizing his risk in confiding in her, Astrid reached into the pouch hanging from her belt, found the stone, and pulled it out for him to see. "What can you tell me about this?"

For a moment, the blacksmith seemed to be made of rock, staring at Astrid and the stone without moving a muscle. Finally, he took the stone from her as gently as if it were made of eggshell and held it up to the light. "What happened to you?"

Startled, Astrid said, "What?"

The blacksmith turned the stone in his hand, examining every angle of its rough shape. "What sorrow have you suffered? Who has died before your eyes?"

Astrid's heart sank. Temple had died many years ago, leaving her as the only blacksmith in Guell. DiStephan had died a few years ago, but she hadn't seen it happen. However, she'd witnessed far too many other deaths, from those in Guell to Mauri. But the worst of all had been Margreet, because Margreet had come so close to defending herself and creating a new life. More than anything else, Astrid blamed the Krystr followers for Margreet's death, and a growing rage made her hate them for it. Barely able to speak around the lump in her throat, Astrid said, "I've seen far too many deaths."

"Important ones? Important to you?"

Astrid nodded. "Yes."

The blacksmith looked away from the stone of darkness as if breaking free from a trance. He shoved it back at Astrid, gesturing for her to put it away. "Heed my advice. Destroy this thing and forget it ever existed."

Chapter Thirty-Five

Unscar leaned against the covered well, lost in thought as he watched his men scour the abandoned village. One moment he found himself standing in sunlight, the next in shade. Looking up, he saw a large, dark cloud had passed in front of the sun, casting a shadow on them all. Feeling an unexpected chill, Unscar shivered. *It's a sign. Something bad is going to happen.*

Then he almost bit his tongue, relieved he hadn't been foolish enough to speak those words out loud. Portents were the beliefs of the old ways and the old gods. Krystr had no use for signs or omens of any kind.

But old habits were hard to break.

Unscar felt as if he noticed his surroundings for the first time, even though he'd been looking at all of it since they'd arrived. He became aware of the disrepair of the thatched rooftops of the wattle-and-daub cottages. He gazed upon the overgrown and weedy gardens that now grew wild. But the sight of the clothes on the laundry line strung between two cottages disturbed him the most.

Simple dresses hung on the line, as well as tunics and pants attached together at the waist. The colors had faded, and the line sagged so that dirt had soiled the hems of the dresses and pants. Every time a breeze kicked up, the clothes billowed as if ghosts wore them.

"They slept here," one of the men called out as he stood in the open doorway to the most sound-looking cottage.

Unscar hurried over to enter the cottage, anxious to get out of the sight of the billowing clothes.

His man pointed at the hearth in the center of the cottage. "That's from a recent fire."

Unscar walked briskly to the hearth and knelt in front of it. The ashes looked fresh enough. "Did you find anything here?"

The man shook his head. "Nothing."

Unscar frowned. The simple map the woman had stuffed into his mouth had led him here. The landmarks on the map were clear and accurate. This had to be the right place, and the ashes confirmed someone had been here as recently as last night. But now what?

"Sir?" The man hesitated in the doorway, waiting for instruction.

"Look everywhere," Unscar said, striving to keep the disappointment out of his voice. "Search every home and the grounds around it. Check the well. Look at the clothes on the line. She must have left some clue behind."

Nodding his understanding, the man darted away, calling out directions to the others.

Unscar sighed. They'd ridden through most of the night, pausing only long enough to catch a few hours of sleep. He felt certain they'd gained ground and could catch up with the barbarian women soon, if only he could discover the direction they'd taken.

He sat on the ground, staring at the ashes in the hearth. Maybe there had been no discussion. Maybe they had left with the intention of making their decision as they traveled.

Unscar gazed at the walls and the benches lining them. The cottage was mostly empty, except for a few cooking utensils and vessels and straw mats for sleeping. Inspired, he jumped to his feet and raised each mat, looking intently beneath each one. Nothing.

Taking a slow walk around the room, he examined each bench, looking to see if she had scratched a message into a wooden plank. Again, nothing. When he reached the wall on the opposite side of the hearth, a loud noise outside made him look up sharply. Through the doorway, he saw one man drop to one knee and rub his foot as if he'd stubbed his toe.

As his vision shifted from the doorway back to the interior of the cottage, Unscar froze. Here, on the opposite side of the hearth, flat stones had been wedged into the ground vertically to contain the hearth fire. Images drawn with fresh ash covered the largest stone, and now he could see it because he'd walked behind the hearth and now looked at it from the back. He crept forward slowly, as if any sudden movement might destroy the delicate-looking map. Studying it, he felt the relief of instant recognition. He needed no more than a few minutes to decipher and memorize what he saw.

Unscar smiled. If his estimation was correct, he and his men could catch up with the barbarian women tomorrow.

Chapter Thirty-Six

The next morning, Thorda drew Astrid aside while the Iron Maidens arose and prepared themselves and the horses for another day's journey. Although now on the verge of summer, the air had chilled sharply overnight, and their breath hung visibly in the air. New clumps of yellow-green grass, now covered in frost, crunched beneath their feet as they walked away from the pasture where they'd slept the night before, its earthy scent still clinging to their skin and clothes.

"We come to the Upper Midlands tomorrow," Thorda said. "Maybe a day after."

"Do you know men who will fight against the Krystr soldiers?" Astrid said, rubbing her hands together before they grew numb from the unexpected cold. Dawn spread pale light across the horizon. Glancing up, she saw no clouds in the sky. With any luck, the sun would bake into their skin soon. "Or do many of them side with Mandulane?"

Thorda grimaced. "No one likes Mandulane in Upper Midlands. Men join and fight with us."

"Good. As soon as we've recruited enough, I'll cross the sea to the Northlands and—"

"No!" Thorda's forehead creased in distress. "We need you. You fight with us."

"But the Northlanders know little about Mandulane. They don't know he plans to invade and take over the Northlands. Someone has to warn them. Once they know, I'm sure they'll unite to defeat Mandulane."

Thorda looked more worried by the moment, now wringing her hands like a fishwife. "We need all people with weapons to fight. Mandulane has many men."

"And Vinchi has trained you well. I've traveled through parts of the Upper Midlands. It seems to me there are many men who look like they can fight well."

Thorda shrugged.

Astrid wondered for a moment if she was simply scared of Mandulane and his men. She'd never been able to shake the memory of the blue-tattooed women in Mandulane's tent and the emptiness in their eyes. Astrid had been on the verge of becoming one of those women had the Iron Maidens not created a diversion allowing her to escape. Didn't she owe them more than running off to the Northlands and leaving them to fend for themselves against the Krystr soldiers?

But then Astrid thought of Guell and everyone who waited for her to return. She longed to see her friends again. And the thought of Mandulane setting a single foot on Northland soil made her feel ill.

"I'll stay with you until we're sure you have numbers large enough to stand up against Mandulane," Astrid said. "I won't leave for the Northlands until that happens."

Heaving a sigh of relief, Thorda nodded her appreciation.

Hours later, the small road they traveled wound into a forested area. With open fields behind them and a canopy woven by towering trees in front of them, Astrid signaled the other women to halt their horses.

Astrid inhaled deeply but detected nothing more than the heavy scent of pine and earth after a fresh rainstorm. Still, something gave her pause, and she wished she knew why.

Dismounting, she held onto her horse's reins. She turned slowly in place to examine the landscape surrounding them. Fields and meadows stretched toward mountains as far as she could see in every direction behind and beside them. They hadn't encountered another road for hours, and retracing their steps could lead them directly into the arms of the Krystr soldiers.

If we travel through fields or meadows, the footing is likely to be unsure, and one or more of the horses could pull up lame. Even if we navigate the terrain successfully, we'd end up facing a hike through the mountains and would have to abandon the horses. How far could we travel safely without them on the other side?

Turning back to face the forested path, she saw the woods stretch out on either side of the road. They couldn't walk around the woods. The only choices were to travel through them, risk hiking through the distant mountains, or turn back.

"Dismount," Astrid called out to the Iron Maidens. "And keep a tight rein."

Casting worried glances at each other, they took the advice and followed Astrid into the wooded road. Leaving Banshi to lead the horse they shared, Kikita hurried to walk by Astrid's side. "What troubles you?"

Keeping her gaze on the forest now surrounding the road, Astrid said, "I don't know." Her eyes narrowed at a stretch of fallen leaves from last autumn, brown and brittle, up ahead by one side of the road.

Suddenly, a lizard emerged from the trough it had dug before covering itself with those leaves. About 10 feet long, it raced toward the women, its legs stubby and bowed but quick.

The horses reared and shrieked in terror. Some of the maidens froze in fear as their horses galloped back the way they'd come, while others tried to control the reins they still held, without much luck.

Only Kikita, who quickly took Astrid's reins into her own hands, succeeded in calming her horse by placing a gentle hand on the bridge of its nose and gazing solemnly into its eyes, as quiet as the eye of a storm.

Astrid drew Starlight from its sheath and called out, "Go back!"

Frantic, the Iron Maidens raced back toward the light of day, although Kikita managed to mount Astrid's horse and ride it away as the lizard bolted directly at Astrid, seemingly having eyes for no one but her.

Before Astrid could deliver a blow, the lizard surprised her by rearing on its hind legs and running forward on them until its front paws slammed on top of her shoulders. The force knocked her to the ground and Starlight out of her hand.

The lizard's foul breath filled her mouth and nose. It gazed into her eyes, its yellow tongue flicking like flames against her face as the escaping maidens shrieked in the distance.

CHAPTER THIRTY-SEVEN

The road leading into the forest loomed ahead. Unscar reined in his horse and signaled the handful of Krystr soldiers riding behind to stop. Something didn't feel right.

Since childhood, he'd always been sensitive, especially with regard to animals. Whenever any farm animal became pregnant, Unscar could forecast its time of birth simply by laying his hands on the mother's head and gazing into her eyes. Although he had fewer opportunities, he discovered he could perform the same task with women, which had made him popular among them. Every spring he foretold the precise day on which the birds that flew away before winter would return. He sensed the best time for tilling the land and planting seed. He understood the fickleness of the weather and always wore the clothes best suited for the temperature, no matter how much it shifted during the day.

And sometimes he knew when danger lurked around the corner.

One of the soldiers rode up next to him. "This road leads straight to the Upper Midlands. No need to worry about brigands or thieves. We've eliminated or recruited most of them."

Unscar stared at the forest stretching ahead of them, cutting across the road like a knife beheading a chicken. He glanced to either side, noting the overgrown fields and meadows flanking them as well as the mountains in the distance. From the ashes used to draw upon a hearthstone in the abandoned village they'd left yesterday, he was convinced the barbarian women had taken this road. Taking a harder look at the landscape surrounding them, he knew they hadn't headed toward the mountains. The terrain would take time and effort to cross, and the women on their horses—rather, on the horses they'd stolen from Unscar and his men—would likely be in view, even from a distance.

"I don't worry about brigands or thieves," Unscar said.

"What then?"

"I don't yet know."

The soldier shifted uncomfortably on his saddle. "Would you have us wait all day until you do?"

Unscar couldn't explain his sensitivity to this soldier or anyone else associated with Krystr or Mandulane. They'd consider him to be as barbaric as the women they pursued. They'd likely hang him or burn him alive, as he'd seen them do to other Midlanders.

Unscar willed his face to be as still as an iron mask even though anger flashed through his veins. If this soldier dared to be insolent, let him suffer whatever danger waited. "Go ahead. Lead the men into the forest."

The soldier paled, apparently startled and unprepared for Unscar's order. "Me?"

"Why not? Whoever captures the women can take credit for it." Unscar hesitated and then smiled warmly. "I will commend you to Mandulane myself, and I'm sure your reward will be plenty. I will keep a good distance behind you to make certain they're not in hiding."

Nodding, the soldier waved for the others to follow. He kicked his horse's sides, urging it into a trot toward the road ahead, darkened by the canopy of treetops.

Unscar stayed put, and his horse snorted as it shifted from foot to foot, taking a few steps back.

Soon, the soldiers shouted to each other, dismounting and tying their horse's reins to trees at the edge of the forest.

One of them called out to Unscar. "We've found them. They're all dead."

Drawing their weapons, they stood in the sunlit road and stared into the shadows lying ahead. Gradually, they took slow steps into the dark, becoming murky images in the distance.

For a moment, Unscar wanted to ride away, far away, maybe even beyond the Midlands and the Southlands and build a new life for himself in the Far East.

Nonsense, he told himself. *Other Krystr soldiers or clerks found the barbarian women first. They must have left their bodies out in the open to rot as a warning for anyone else traveling these roads.*

Unscar reminded himself that he'd come too far to put his future at risk. He'd survived the Krystr invasion and already rose in the ranks. Who would be foolish enough to throw that away?

Sighing, he dismounted, leading his horse as he walked toward the trees where the soldiers had tied their own mounts. Apparently, he'd been with the Krystr soldiers long enough to lose his sensitivity to the world around him, which was probably for the best. Clearly, they faced no danger. It must have just been nerves that got the better of him, making him dream of a nonexistent threat. He approached the mouth of the forest. Unscar squinted, barely making out the figures of his men as they walked among the dead left on the shadowed and wooded road.

Memories of the time before the Krystr soldiers invaded his family's territory rushed back to him. His father, constantly complaining that Unscar accomplished nothing more than proving himself as a worthless son. His mother, pointing out his laziness and unwillingness to help the family plant and tend and harvest the food they needed to survive. His brothers, always tattling to their parents whenever Unscar slipped away to nap or relax away from accusing eyes. Everyone in his family hated him and threatened to throw him to the wolves if he didn't shoulder his responsibilities.

Angered by those thoughts, Unscar gripped the handle of his ax so hard that his entire hand went white.

Who had been slaughtered by the Krystr soldiers because of their foolishness in resisting them? His entire family.

Who had not only survived but thrived in the midst of the Krystr followers? Unscar.

And who now had the opportunity to prove himself a mighty warrior who deserved to advance to the highest rank?

Grinding his teeth, Unscar let the anger he'd felt all his life toward his family roll over him. His brothers always showed him up, making him feel worthless and miserable. No one had ever let him shine. Instead, he'd always felt ground beneath their feet.

As he walked purposefully along the sunlit road toward the point where it became enshrouded by the forest, Unscar resolved to take this chance to prove himself. Not to his old family of self-congratulating idiots, but to his new and faithful family of Krystr followers. He'd show them his true worth, and the soldiers under his command would sing his praises when he delivered them safely back to camp.

One of the soldiers screamed, and the others shouted.

Unscar's horse wrenched the reins free from his hand and galloped down the sunlit road, away from the forested area. The other horses, still tied to trees at the edge of the forest, whinnied in panic and struggled in vein. Quickly, he pulled his ax from his belt. Still squinting, he made out soldiers running in the shadows and still figures on the ground but nothing else.

One of the soldiers ran out of the shadows and into the light, his clothes torn and bloody. Terror had left his face blank. Empty-handed, he'd apparently lost his weapon. Stumbling, the soldier cried out as he fell on his hands and knees.

A dragon clambered out from the darkened road, sank its teeth into the screaming man's leg, and dragged him back into the shadows.

Chapter Thirty-Eight

Unscar froze, watching in horror as the dragon dragged one of the Krystr soldiers under his command back into the shadowed depths of the forested road. Despite the warmth of the sun on his skin, Unscar trembled as if he'd been buried in snow. *This can't be happening.*

He reached the edge of the shadowed road, letting his eyes adjust to the darkness ahead. A tremor ran through him as if the ground beneath his feet had shaken, and he struggled to remain steady on his feet.

Heaps of clothes lay scattered across the shadowed road. Clearly, the dragon had feasted on them, leaving little left. His men stumbled among the clothes, and to Unscar's dismay, they fought fruitlessly against an army of dragons. Everywhere he looked he saw enormous tails thrashing and glistening ivory teeth gnashing. His men struck their weapons against dragon skin to no avail. Sharp iron edges slid off the animals' natural armor like a careless step placed in the mud.

Stepping into this fight would be suicide.

Within moments, every soldier on the shadowed path collapsed, either dead or moaning in pain, unable to move. One spotted Unscar, who still stood on the road's sunlit edge, and reached one hand toward him. "Help me," the soldier said, barely able to whisper.

The dragon nosing him looked up at Unscar, staring greedily. The animal seemed to weigh the benefits of attacking him.

Mesmerized by the dragon's eyes, Unscar held his breath as if that somehow would make him invisible. The intelligence in the dragon's eyes terrified him more than any creature he'd ever encountered. The dragon knew it was in charge. Killing Unscar would be easy. But having already devoured the barbarian women and overpowered Unscar's soldiers, would these dragons need one more?

Unscar glanced into the shadows, spotting two other dragons before returning to stare at the one closest to him.

Only three dragons in all? Unscar would have sworn there had to be at least twenty. He swallowed hard, keenly aware of the tightness of his throat. Perhaps the others had slithered into the woods in some sort of hunting tactic. Maybe they were circling behind him now, preparing to entrap him.

Sure enough, the trees by the dragon nearest him rustled. He cried out, holding his ax in front of his face, ready to fight. The dragon eying him took a step closer.

"Smoke!" a woman's voice called. "Stop!"

Unscar would have sworn that the look in the dragon's eyes sagged into disappointment. It halted and cast a look at the trees from which the voice had emerged. Had he still worshipped the old gods, what he saw next would have caused him to drop to his knees in reverence.

A breeze nudged the branches of the canopy above the road, and soft light dappled onto the figure of a woman dressed in the colors of the earth and woods. As the light danced around and through her, Unscar realized he was looking at a ghost. Gripping his ax even tighter, he called out, "Be gone, shadow demon!"

The dragon that had considered attacking him now crept toward the ghost, positioning itself as if ready to protect her. Unscar didn't know of a bond between ghosts and dragons, and this new insight disturbed him.

The ghost mocked him. "Do you know who I am?"

Unscar squinted. Now he recognized her. "You were the woman who slayed dragons. And now they have slayed you and your barbarian women!"

"And now your men. You will be next unless you do as I say."

He let the ax drop to his side. His men had already proven that weapons were useless against dragons. And an ax could certainly do no harm to a ghost or convince it not to harm him. "What do you want?"

"Tell Mandulane what happened here today. Tell him the line where you now stand is the line he must never cross. I now command all dragons, and I will make sure they kill any Krystr soldier who dares cross this line into the Upper Midlands or the Northlands. I will make sure they find and kill Mandulane himself, wherever he hides." The ghost paused, seeming to fade as the breeze and light lessened. "And if you fail to deliver this message, I will make sure they find and kill you, too." Then she dissolved into the woods, visible no more.

Choking back a scream, Unscar scrambled to untie and mount the nearest horse. Leaving the others behind, he kicked his heels into the horse's sides, despite the fact that it ran away from the shadowed road the moment it found itself free.

Chapter Thirty-Nine

A chilly wind whistled through the winding stone stairway inside the tower of Tower Island. Outside, seabirds shrieked as they circled above the tower. The drafty air smelled like the salt-drenched sea. Seated on a stair step, DiStephan shivered. "This makes no sense," he muttered to himself. "I'm two years dead, but somehow I always feel alive when I'm with your kind."

"That's what they all say." Fiera stood facing him several steps below. Keeping her eyes closed, she let her hands drift and sway like bellowed flames. The whistling wind lifted strands of her hair so that it surrounded her head like a crown. "Men, I mean. Women tend to fear me, but put a man before me and I'll have him mesmerized in moments."

DiStephan rubbed his face with his hands. Anywhere else, he'd feel nothing. But for some reason, any time he found himself in the presence of dragons he felt real and whole again. But perhaps it boiled down to nothing more than finding it easier to remember the touch of his own skin.

"I need to be with her," he said, louder this time. "She needs me more than you."

Fiera gasped as a sudden whoosh of air fanned her, seemingly brightening her hair and causing her skin to glow warmer. She rubbed the palms of her hands together until white smoke spilled from them. Opening her eyes, she pushed the smoke in front of her until it pooled on top of the step below DiStephan's feet. She looked at him expectantly.

DiStephan crossed his arms in defiance.

"She has the metal girls," Fiera said.

"The Iron Maidens," DiStephan said, correcting her. "They don't know there's a traitor among them. Not to mention there's hardly any of them next to the Krystr soldiers. Have you seen Mandulane?

He's a madman!"

"I am aware of him and his men," Fiera said in a tone icy enough to extinguish herself. "Why do you think we're here?"

"Because you're using me."

"That is not why we're here, and you know it."

"But Taddeo used Astrid to set Norah free." DiStephan's eyes narrowed with cruel accusation. "Just like Drageen used her to create bloodstones."

"And what about your bond with Taddeo? What about the sacred bond between dragon and dragonslayer?"

DiStephan sat up straight, offended by her inference that he'd shirked his word. "That bond is for me to protect you and your kind by killing lizards that threaten people. It's for me to prevent people from killing true dragons by taking the role of dragonslayer. It's for me to convince others that dragons are so deadly that only a true dragonslayer can kill them. It's for me to convince people who see you in your dragon form that I will kill you so they can sleep at night without having to worry about tracking you down and doing the deed themselves."

Fiera spoke pointedly. "And it is an honor for someone like Taddeo to trust you."

"Yes, of course." DiStephan struggled to keep his patience with her, reminding himself that she could snuff him out like a candle, destroying him forever. And if that happened, Astrid would truly be alone. He had to reason with Fiera with the hope of convincing her to let him return to Astrid's side.

Astrid assumed a lizard had killed DiStephan, never dreaming that he had died at Taddeo's hand instead.

"I died for the sake of helping your kind," DiStephan said. "And in return Taddeo promised me I could stay with Astrid and watch over her. You have to let me go back to her before it's too late."

"Are you going to make it necessary for me to explain again why you're here?"

For a moment, sparks seemed to ignite from Fiera's eyes, reminding DiStephan that even though he was a ghost, he faced one of the most powerful creatures in existence. "No, Ma'am."

Fiera tapped her foot and crossed her arms, nodding at the white smoke still pooled on top of the step.

DiStephan stood and then stepped down into the white smoke.

Sizzling, the smoke wrapped around him, covering DiStephan from head to toe. It squeezed him until he gasped for breath, even though he had no need for air. Light-headed, he sank to sit on the step on which he'd previously rested his feet, reaching blindly for the stone with his hands to steady himself. When his ghostly hands touched the cold stone, he felt as if hundreds of threads sliced through his body, leaving him shocked at the sudden and excruciating pain until the familiar voice of another ghost whispered in his ear.

"Forgive me," the faint voice of Mauri said as it rose up from the step on which the white smoke had pooled.

"Of course," DiStephan said, meaning it. He wished he'd never witnessed Mauri's betrayal of Astrid, but in the end it was Mauri who saved Astrid from being murdered by her own brother. "I forgive you."

Although DiStephan rarely encountered other ghosts, he knew enough to tell the difference between the true presence of a ghost and the remnants it left behind. He'd seen Astrid free Mauri's spirit two years ago, and he knew Mauri no longer existed in this world. Instead, the violence done against her had trapped part of her essence within every step of the winding stairway within the tower, and there were hundreds of them. Fiera had brought him to Tower Island because she needed one ghost to free the remnants left behind by another.

As Taddeo had explained, the remnants left by Mauri's ghost blocked the gateway that he and the other dragons needed to leave the surface of this realm and return to their home. The dragons had come here for a reason. They'd come to learn about people and to understand the decisions people make. And now the dragons readied themselves to leave.

The threads cutting through DiStephan's ghostly body spun together until he nearly fainted from the phantom pain.

Then the white smoke cleared, transforming the step beneath his feet into a pale pink stone. The phantom pain vanished, and DiStephan collapsed.

Behind him, a dozen pink stone steps glittered as a thin beam of sunlight shone through the open doorway on top of the tower. Beneath him stretched hundreds of gray steps.

"Well," Fiera said with a heavy sigh. "That was quite exhausting. I do believe that's enough for one day."

As he watched her flounce down the steps, DiStephan wished he had the ability to sleep. As long as he kept his ghostly form in this realm, it forever kept him awake.

A few steps above him shifted shape until Wendill rose out of them and walked down to sit next to DiStephan. "Come now," Wendill said. "Be of good cheer."

"I wish none of you had ever come here," DiStephan said. "I'd still be alive and killing lizards. And everyone else would be safe and sound."

When Wendill draped a friendly arm around DiStephan, the ghost at first tensed up, startled by the dragon's touch and then wondered if he should feel honored by it.

"But that is not what happened," Wendill said lightly. "Taddeo determined we needed to learn about people before deciding what to do about you. You must admit it is quite fair. And even if you do not like the current state of affairs, you must admit things could be far worse."

DiStephan snorted. "How could things possibly be worse than they are right now?"

Wendill hummed for a few moments. Finally, he said, "Without us, none of you would be alive."

DiStephan sighed in resignation. As always, the dragon spoke the truth.

Chapter Forty

Astrid watched Unscar ride away from the shadowed forest until he disappeared into the horizon. Then she kept watching for another hour. Finally, the gentle touch of a hand on her shoulder startled her back to the task at hand.

Thorda's brow creased with concern, and she squeezed Astrid's shoulder. "Men are dead. Dragons eat them. Time to leave."

Astrid gazed at the shadowed road. The lizards made quick work of the Krystr soldiers they'd killed. In the past, Astrid would have been horrified at the plan she'd proposed once she realized the lizards they initially encountered were ones whose lives she'd saved near Guell. Suspecting they might be true dragons, she'd slain an adult lizard bent on devouring them and then traveled with them until they went their own way and ended up in Taddeo's care. She'd even named them: Smoke, Fire, and Slag. And now they were juveniles, their bodies the same length and weight as her own, not counting tails.

Her jaw tightened as she clenched the muscles in her face, a habit she seemed to be developing in the presence of Krystr followers. She'd always believed in peace and hated any kind of bloodshed, but something had changed when Margreet died. Margreet's death hadn't been necessary. No one would have been harmed if Margreet had lived. And yet that choice had been taken without her consent.

Astrid had learned how to accept death when it came in the form of disease or accident. But she refused to accept death when it came by murder. It stirred an anger deep inside. Margreet should still be alive. She should have moved to Guell with Vinchi and perhaps even married him. Margreet should have met all of Astrid's friends and neighbors: Lenore, Randim, Trep, Donel, Beamon, Kamella, and all the blacksmiths and their families. Every time Astrid had returned to Guell or woken up inside her own cottage in her home village, there had been a moment when she groggily wondered what Margreet was doing and looked forward to seeing her.

And then Astrid would remember that Margreet had not only died, but Astrid had set her spirit free from this world. Astrid would never see Margreet's face or hear her voice again.

That's what made it easy for Astrid to watch her young dragons rip and tear the Krystr soldiers into pieces. If not for Krystr and all his followers, Margreet would still be alive. Astrid had no pity for anyone associated with her death, even those who knew nothing of it. As far as Astrid was concerned, all Krystr soldiers and followers were the same.

They were monsters.

"Astrid?"

Realizing she'd been lost in her own thoughts, Astrid looked away from the carnage and back at Thorda, who looked even more worried now. "Fine," Astrid said. "Tell the Maidens we're leaving." She frowned. "But we should burn the clothes first."

The clothes they'd brought from the deserted village where they'd spent the night had sparked Astrid's plan. After the initial panic of thinking dragons were attacking them, the Iron Maidens had kept their distance while Astrid found herself entwined with her long lost friends. Once the young dragons calmed from their initial excitement at seeing Astrid, she and they became aware of distant hoof beats.

Still keeping their distance, the Iron Maidens had watched as Astrid heaped the clothes in piles on the shadowed road. Astrid had worried that the dragons might merely greet the Krystr soldiers in the same way Smoke had jumped on Astrid with joy. But once the Krystr soldiers arrived, she had no need to worry. The dragons attacked the men immediately, leaving no doubt in her mind that these were in fact true dragons and not lizards.

Surprised but grateful, Astrid saw Kikita carrying a burning stick toward the feeding frenzy. The Far Eastern Maiden had the best knack for making fire, but Astrid felt startled by the ease with which Kikita moved among the feeding dragons to set the heaping piles of clothes on fire. As she passed by Smoke, the dragon paused to give the Maiden's hand a friendly nudge.

Astrid expected Kikita to scream or cry or run away in terror. Instead, Kikita smiled as Smoke returned his attention to the glorious feast of men spread before him.

"Gather up their horses," Astrid told Thorda. "Now every

woman will have her own horse, and we can sell the spare ones when we reach the Upper Midlands."

In the same moment, Astrid and Thorda looked at the direction from which the Krystr soldiers had come, making sure the one who had escaped was truly gone for good.

CHAPTER FORTY-ONE

Leaving the dragons behind to feed, Astrid and the Iron Maidens untethered the horses belonging to the dead soldiers and rode for the rest of the day through the forest without incident. Trees and bushes crowded both sides of the road, still darkened by shadows. A stone's throw ahead, a chipmunk sat on its haunches and chewed on an old acorn left over from autumn. Without warning, a hawk swooped over the women's heads, its wings hunched as it glided with its legs and talons extended. Grabbing the unsuspecting chipmunk, the hawk then beat its wings and flew to the nearest treetop.

Astrid watched, swallowing hard.

"Bad sign," Thorda said, riding next to her and shaking her head. The road was wide enough for two horses, and they led the pack, keeping the pace at a walk. "Bad omen."

"I don't believe in omens," Astrid said, convincing no one but herself. As they passed under the tree where the hawk had come to rest, thirty feet above them, Astrid craned her neck to watch it, even though the raptor paid no attention to her.

"No time to sleep," Thorda said with resolution.

"What?" Astrid shifted her attention from the hawk to the Maiden.

Thorda glanced quickly at the treetop and then shivered. "We cannot go back. We must go to Upper Midlands. But it must be fast. We cannot be slow."

"Why? Because you think we've seen a bad omen?"

Thorda nodded. "The gods warn us. We must listen."

Astrid sighed. As far as she could tell, the gods Midlanders like Thorda worshiped were similar to those in the Northlands. But unlike many Northlanders, Astrid had never put much faith in the gods. She'd witnessed many people pray to them for help and either receive nothing or stumble upon a lucky coincidence. The Northlanders placed a great deal of credit upon luck, believing the gods bestowed a certain degree of luck on each man and woman at birth, but Astrid believed luck to be a matter of happenstance.

At the same time, she believed in respecting the beliefs of people like Thorda and the other Iron Maidens. From what Astrid could tell, they seemed to be good people who cared about others. And for all Astrid knew, maybe Thorda's belief in bad omens could help them evade the Krystr followers.

Astrid snorted in disgust at the thought of them. She had seen enough in Mandulane's camp to be convinced they were little more than men who manipulated others to get what they wanted, and Astrid had no respect for such people. She wished all the gods of the Northlands and Southlands and Midlands and all the rest of the world would rise up and demolish such wretched people. Remembering Margreet, Astrid wondered for a moment what it would feel like to stand among the gods and raise her sword to help them. She pushed the thought away, now remembering the argument that had driven her apart from DiStephan. She'd been horrified when he'd slaughtered lizard hatchlings, and then a year later when she stumbled upon a dragon's nest she hadn't had the heart to kill them, even when she didn't know if they were dragons or lizards. Of course, she still didn't know for sure, but...

"Astrid?"

She looked over at Thorda and noticed lines of worry creasing her face. "What?"

Concern threaded through Thorda's voice. "Be you all right?"

Astrid smiled. "I'm fine. But I think you're right. We should only make brief stops to rest until we reach the Upper Midlands."

As they rode forward, the hawk let loose a piercing cry behind them, sending shivers down Astrid's spine.

CHAPTER FORTY-TWO

For an hour Unscar rode his horse as hard and fast as he could, keeping his eyes staring straight ahead and never daring to look back. Once convinced he'd left the shadowed road far behind, he felt safe in the bright sunshine dousing the vast countryside of rolling meadows and fields. Unscar reined his horse near a stream where they both could quench their thirst. Sliding from the saddle, he watched the horse wade ankle-deep into the water and drink. But Unscar fell to his hands and knees and vomited onto the grass.

"I'm sorry," he said to his horse, which ignored him. "I didn't know there'd be dragons or shadow demons. I didn't know they'd murder everyone."

The horse continued to ignore him, raising its head to stare at something on the other side of the river. Unscar followed the creature's gaze and saw nothing.

He crawled to the edge of the bank and rinsed his mouth out several times before drinking, but the horrid taste still lingered. He covered his face with his hands and cried. For the first time since Mandulane and his Krystr soldiers had invaded his homeland, Unscar missed his dead family and the simple life he'd once lived.

Late that afternoon, Unscar reined his horse to pause at a fork in the road. The road on the right would take him back to Mandulane's camp, where he would have to report the horrors of seeing his men killed and eaten by dragons as well as his encounter with the ghost of the girl who called herself a dragonslayer. What would Mandulane do to him? Unscar had witnessed soldiers flogged and beaten to death for lesser offenses. Mandulane might make an example of him, maybe even testing new torture techniques on him.

The road to the left would take him into the Eastern Midlands and beyond that into the stretch of mountains separating the Midlands from the Far East. Unscar had once known traders who traveled across those mountains and told stories about a fabled land full of magical landscapes and creatures. They said the language could be challenging to learn because it shared no commonalities with the languages of the Northlands, Midlands, or Southlands. Traders described the Far Easterners as an odd and distant people. Running away to a new country seemed a strange but appealing choice to Unscar. It would provide the opportunity to start his life over. He could become anyone he wanted without having to worry about anyone from his past haunting him. Weariness weighed heavy on him from the conflicts brought about by the Krystr invaders, and he longed for a new adventure.

At the same time he couldn't push the sight of his dying men out of his head. They'd trusted him, and Unscar had unwittingly sent them to their deaths. Although he couldn't call any of them his friends, they had willingly followed him even though he'd won the right to lead ahead of more experienced and maybe even more deserving soldiers.

What right do I have to let their fates go unknown? Their families and the other soldiers will want to know what happened to them. And Mandulane might appreciate knowing where there are dragons and that the girl who failed to slay them is dead.

Setting his jaw in grim determination, Unscar took the road to the right, leading back to the commitment he'd made.

By nightfall, Unscar reached Mandulane's camp. Exhausted, he dismounted, handed his horse's reins to a servant boy, and put in a request for an audience with Mandulane. Unscar had just joined the outdoor encampment circled around an open fire to eat supper when a messenger brought word of agreement for an immediate meeting with Mandulane. Eying a cauldron full of roasted meat and potato stew, Unscar's stomach rumbled as he turned his back on the opportunity to fill his belly and walked to Mandulane's tent instead.

Unscar immediate regretted his haste when he entered Mandulane's tent and saw his master resting atop a pile of furs and bright gold and red pillows, surrounded by dozing women with skin colored blue. Obviously, everyone here had already supped and now relaxed to let digestion do its work. Unscar repressed a sigh, not wanting to appear any more pathetic than he already felt.

"I hear you returned alone," Mandulane said as he petted one of the women lying next to him. "Where are the rest of my men?"

Unscar cleared his throat. "Dead, Sir."

Mandulane cocked his head to one side, puzzled. "How can that be?"

As much as Unscar wanted to stare at his feet in shame, he forced himself to look Mandulane directly in the eye. "We found the barbarian women dead, piled up in heaps. I sent the men ahead to make sure they were dead. But dragons came out of the shadows and killed them all."

"Dragons," Mandulane sighed. "I keep hearing there are few if any left, and yet they seem to find my men. How do you explain that?"

Unscar shrugged. "I remember far more dragons from when I was young, but dragons still exist. The dragonslayers haven't killed them all yet. This time of year they travel North. Maybe we got in their way." Unscar paused, considering his options. He could walk away and forget the rest of it happened. But the shadow demon had said she'd make sure the dragons would kill him if he didn't deliver her words to Mandulane. "There is something else."

Mandulane raised a questioning eyebrow. "Pray tell."

Unscar cleared his throat again, stalling. "The dragonslayer girl was dead, too. I met her shadow demon. It told me to relay a message to you."

Mandulane's face tightened with concern. "What message?"

"She said she guards the Upper Midlands and Northlands. She forbids us to enter. She claims all the dragons listen to her and do what she says. I'd say it's true because I saw it happen with my own eyes."

Surprisingly, Mandulane relaxed, smiling. "What else did this ghost tell you?"

"If we don't stay out of her territory, she will have the dragons kill us. She said no matter where you hide, they can find you and kill you."

Mandulane laughed long and hard, waking up some of the women next to him who had fallen asleep. "Everything she said is a lie."

Unscar frowned. Mandulane's response to the threat made no sense. "I don't understand."

But instead of explaining himself, Mandulane simply kept laughing so hard that tears rolled from the corners of his eyes.

CHAPTER FORTY-THREE

A few days later, the air took an unexpected chill. The wind blew hard and cold, sending last fall's dead leaves scampering like mice across the road in front of Astrid and the Iron Maidens. Looking up, Astrid frowned at the ever-growing presence of low-hanging dark clouds that blocked the sun. But when the wind shifted for a moment, she took heart at the scent of salt.

That meant they must be near the coast. In that case, they'd reach the Upper Midlands sometime today. And once they set foot in the Upper Midlands, they'd be safe from Mandulane and the Krystr followers.

Astrid took in a deep breath of relief. During the past few weeks the only bright spot had been meeting Thorda and the other Iron Maidens. The rest of it, from encountering Mandulane and his blue women, to finding no answer to the purpose of the stone of darkness she still kept in the pouch hanging from her belt, had felt like a nightmare. Although duty still bound her to follow the dragonslayer's winter route and kill any lizards she encountered, Astrid couldn't wait to head back to the Northlands and her home in Guell and see her friends again.

Maybe the Iron Maidens could come with me.

Astrid held onto that thought for a moment as the memory of plans to return to Guell with Margreet and Vinchi made her long for the days when Margreet still lived.

I should have killed him when I had the chance, Astrid thought, remembering the brief opportunity she'd had to put an end to Gershon, Margreet's murderer. Instead, she'd suppressed her intense hatred of him the same way she'd learned to rein in her feelings about other people in order not to change the way they looked, honoring the unwritten law of the Northlands that while people always had the right to change themselves, they must not impose change upon others.

Still missing Margreet, Astrid glanced at the Iron Maidens riding near her. *I won't let them die*, Astrid promised herself. *I know they can fend for themselves, but if they need help I will be there for them. And maybe someday they can come to Guell.*

Of course, they couldn't for now. Just a couple of days ago, Thorda had made it clear the Iron Maidens intended to stay in the Midlands and fight the Krystr soldiers to prevent them from taking over more territory. Astrid had promised to stay with them until they'd recruited enough men from the Upper Midlands to stand and fight with them. Once their numbers were strong enough, Astrid planned to cross the sea separating the Upper Midlands from the Northlands and spread the word to warn all Northlanders of what might come if the Iron Maidens and Upper Midlanders failed to keep Mandulane and his men at bay.

Astrid became aware of what sounded like a heated argument behind her. Looking back over her shoulder, she noticed Kikita and Banshi talking in their native Far Easterner language. Turning to look ahead again, she caught Thorda's worried gaze.

"What's wrong?" Astrid said.

Thorda shook her head. "I do not know their words." Thorda kicked her heels into her horse's sides, riding in front of the other women and stopping to block their progress. To Kikita and Banshi, Thorda called out, "What problem?"

Kikita spoke for both of them. "We disagree. Banshi insists we should continue to the Upper Midlands. I believe we must reconsider."

"Reconsider?" Astrid said. "Why?

Kikita pointed to the skies above. "Look at the omen."

For a moment, it seemed as if all the Iron Maidens held their breath at once, staring up at the threatening clouds that looked close enough to touch.

The clouds reminded Astrid of the way Fee and Glee had transformed into shadowy smoke and vanished first through the floorboards of their cottage and then out the smoke hole in their roof when Krystr soldiers invaded their home in search of the alchemists. Had they died and turned into smoke? Or had they somehow escaped?

Could it be them? Astrid wondered, touching her pouch and feeling for the stone of darkness inside. The women had been on the verge of explaining the stone and its use when they'd been attacked. *Have they come back to help me?*

Thorda shrugged. "It means nothing. Just clouds. Sometimes clouds come before summer."

"No," Kikita said, looking to Astrid as if for confirmation. "These clouds are peculiar. It is a sign, and we must heed the warning given us."

Banshi spoke up, gesturing first at the sky and then at the road ahead. Although no one but Kikita understood her, everyone knew what Banshi wanted.

"If we wait, the Krystr soldiers find us," Thorda said with conviction. "We go to Upper Midlands."

"Who made you the leader?" Kikita said.

Thorda and the other Maidens who understood the Northlander language looked at Kikita in confusion. "What?" Thorda said.

"You may have been one of the best swordswomen when we studied with Vinchi," Kikita said. "But you are not our leader. The most experienced one among us is Astrid. Therefore, she is the leader. She must make the final decision."

Astrid looked from Kikita to Thorda, wondering how the Midlander would respond to the Far Easterner's declaration.

Thorda pressed her lips together in frustration for a moment, and then turned to Astrid. "Do we wait or go?"

There it is. Whether I want the honor or not, I seem to have become the leader.

She gazed up at the sky for a few moments, as if looking at it long enough would allow her to gain new insight. But the clouds simply kept rolling, seemingly oblivious to the women, even though Astrid still wondered if they might be nothing more than Fee and Glee watching over them. And maybe even guiding them.

"We keep going," Astrid said.

Kikita looked away in disappointment. Watching Kikita's reaction, Banshi smiled.

Chapter Forty-Four

A few hours later, the women spotted a coastal town in the distance.

"Hagentown," Thorda said to Astrid when they and the rest of the Iron Maidens dismounted and gathered to decide how to move forward. "It is lowest town in Upper Midlands."

"But it's by the sea," Astrid said, confused.

Thorda shook her head. "Not sea. Long lake opens to sea."

It took Astrid a moment to realize she knew what Thorda meant. DiStephan had often told Astrid about these lands and had mentioned a lake running through the Upper Midlands and emptying into the sea.

Banshi spoke passionately, gesturing ahead.

"She believes we should waste no time," Kikita said quietly as she looked down at the ground.

"Tell her the leader disagrees."

Kikita looked up sharply, and the hint of a smile tugged at one corner of her mouth.

"We don't know if the men in this town will believe we can fight. They might laugh at us." Astrid looked at the women circled around her, pausing to give some, like Kikita, time to translate her words into whatever language they understood. "The worst thing we can do is ride into town and claim to be warrior women. We must think of a reason why a group of women would travel together and present ourselves that way."

Thorda frowned. "Lie to men who can help us?"

"Not lie," Astrid said. "Let's present ourselves in a way that won't make them dismiss us. Let them believe what they want to believe about us at first. If we take time to learn who the best men are, it gives us a better chance of convincing them we can fight together."

"What will they think when we ride into their town dressed like men and bearing weapons?" Kikita said.

Shouting something Astrid couldn't understand, Banshi strode back toward her horse, mounted, and raced toward Hagentown.

"No!" Astrid called out, but Banshi kept riding.

While Kikita dashed to mount her horse, Astrid faced Thorda. "Keep the others here. If we don't return by sunset, leave this place without us." Making sure no one followed, Astrid jumped on her horse and rode to catch up with Kikita and Banshi, coughing as she breathed the clouds of dust kicked up by their animals.

As they neared the edge of town, lined with stone walls separating the village from the outer fields of grazing cows, Kikita urged her horse to overtake Banshi. Astrid caught up with them. Banshi cried out, trying to grab the reins of her own horse out of Kikita's hands.

But as Astrid neared them, something at the edge of the Hagentown caught her attention.

Just ahead, the road led into the town. Dozens of men and women thronged the streets in the distance, and their own chatter made them oblivious to the presence of the women on the outskirts of town. However, a small gathering of women engulfed in white cloaks made their way slowly through the crowds.

The sun broke through the parting clouds, shining brightly on the townspeople.

In the unexpected sunlight, the blue legs of the white-cloaked women glowed brightly.

CHAPTER FORTY-FIVE

"They're here," Astrid said, her throat tightening in horror. "Mandulane's Krystr soldiers have taken over the Upper Midlands."

Kikita looked up sharply, following Astrid's gaze. "I don't see any soldiers."

"Look at that group of women in the white cloaks. Look at their legs. Those women belong to Mandulane. Or his men. Or both." Astrid frowned. As always, she longed to help his women, but she'd learned they didn't respond to any help she'd already offered. She didn't want to give up on trying to reach them, but now wasn't the time.

Astrid looked at the Far Eastern maidens and saw Banshi still leaning in a vain attempt to take her horse's reins back from Kikita, whose face paled as she stared at the women in the distance. "We must retreat," she said softly.

"Yes," Astrid said. "Now."

They rode back toward the Iron Maidens, Kikita leading Banshi's horse, the other Far Eastern women protesting all the way. Pulling up alongside Thorda, Astrid said, "We have to go somewhere else. They've already invaded this town."

Thorda's face sagged. "Hagentown is gate to all of Upper Midlands. There is no other way."

Astrid pressed her lips together in frustration. "We have to go somewhere. Anywhere." She cast a worried glance over her shoulder. "They may have seen us, Thorda. We should move fast."

Thorda nodded sharply, making up her mind. "We can ride on lake beach but on other side." She pointed at the shimmering lake lying to the west of Hagentown. "This side belongs to Upper Midlands. Other side belongs to Outer Midlands where land is harsh and few people live." Thorda pointed down the road from which they'd come. "We go back. Path from road takes us to Lake of Wolf. Follow lake and it takes us to sea between Midlands and Northlands."

"Fine," Astrid said. "Let's ride."

❧

As the women backtracked, Banshi continued complaining and pointing behind them toward Hagentown. She became more upset when they turned onto a path leading toward the lake.

Astrid held back as the Iron Maidens rode single file onto the small path, waiting for Banshi and Kikita, who would be last in line. "What's wrong?"

Kikita sighed. "She makes no sense. I've told her over and again that Hagentown isn't safe for us, but she won't listen. She keeps insisting we go back."

Startled, Astrid turned her attention to Banshi. Pointing behind the woman, Astrid said, "Krystr."

Impassioned, Banshi babbled at Astrid, who understood nothing she said. Kikita interrupted, arguing with equal passion.

"Keep moving," Astrid said, gesturing for the Far Eastern women to follow the other maidens onto the path.

Still holding the reins to Banshi's horse, Kikita urged her own to walk forward, forcing Banshi to follow.

Astrid took a final look in the direction of Hagentown. Either no one had noticed them on the road leading into the village or no one cared. Either way, all that mattered was putting as much distance as possible between the Iron Maidens and the men who would happily destroy them.

❧

Traveling the narrow path made Astrid nervous. The roads they'd used until now had been wide enough for the women to ride close together. But this seemed to be a path worn by local animals, winding aimlessly through the thick trees. Branches crowded each side of the path, scratching arms and legs easily. A faint scent of fish permeated the breeze blowing from the direction of the lake, but for a moment Astrid thought she tasted the tang of salt at the back of her throat. Was the lake made of seawater?

With every minute that Banshi kept complaining, Astrid grew more worried. She'd already called ahead to Kikita to ask her to quiet the other woman but to no avail. Astrid could barely hear herself think but worried more about Banshi giving away their presence on this clandestine path. If someone in Hagentown had noticed them,

Krystr soldiers might be in pursuit at this very moment. Although the women traveled west of the road leading to Hagentown, anyone on it would surely hear Banshi's sharp voice rising above the forest.

Why wouldn't she be quiet?

Suddenly, Banshi succeeded in yanking her horse's reins from Kikita's grip. Banshi kicked her heels into her horse's sides and bolted out of sight.

Kikita turned around, looking as surprised as Astrid felt.

Walking her horse up into the empty space left by Banshi, Astrid saw another path branching off from theirs. Pointing at it, she said, "There!"

"Where is she going?" Kikita said in astonishment.

Banshi screamed.

"Stay here!" Astrid said to Kikita.

Astrid swung one leg quickly across her horse's back then dismounted by jumping to the ground. Dashing onto the branching path, she yanked her leather gloves from where they were tucked under her belt and shoved them on her hands. She first noticed Banshi's spooked horse backing up frantically, having no room to turn around. Diving into the brush at the side of the path to avoid the panicking animal, Astrid saw the Iron Maiden a short distance ahead.

Banshi cowered as an adult lizard twice the size of her horse lowered itself to the ground, eying her with delight as it thrashed its tail from side to side.

CHAPTER FORTY-SIX

Wrapping her hand around Starlight's grip, Astrid cried out as she thundered forward, trying to draw the lizard's attention away from Banshi.

Pale light dappling through the forest leaves gleamed off the scales covering the animal's body, shining gray and lavender and white. Its nostrils flared slightly as it breathed in Banshi's fear. Wood cracked loudly as it thrashed its long tail between the surrounding trees.

Astrid neared them. The lizard's warm and pungent breath hovered in the air between it and Banshi. Still yelling, Astrid drew Starlight from its sheath. With the flat of the blade, she raised the sword above her head and delivered a downward blow that smacked the lizard's nose, intending to stun it.

Startled, the reptile flinched and its gaze darted toward Astrid.

"Go back!" she called out to Banshi. Even though she knew the woman wouldn't understand her words, Astrid hoped she'd grasp the meaning and run.

The lizard charged Astrid, its bowed legs moving surprising swift despite the way it dragged the backs of its paws against the ground with each step forward. The spittle hanging from its jaw swayed and its eyes seemed hungry.

Having fought lizards in all kinds of conditions and terrains, Astrid quickly evaluated her options. This narrow path barely parted the dense trees and bushes of the forest. She had no place to run.

But at her side stood a tree with a few low-hanging branches spiraling around the trunk like stair steps. Keeping a tight grip on Starlight, Astrid hauled herself onto the lowest branch and then hopped onto one branch after another, winding her way up and around the trunk as she heard the lizard crashing through the underbrush beneath her.

With a quick glance, Astrid saw the animal positioned perfectly with its belly still dragging on the ground and its head facing away. She shifted her gloved hands to grip Starlight by its blade and then stepped off the tree branch. Landing on the lizard's back, she shoved the tip of her sword through the vulnerable and unprotected back of its neck, pinning the creature to the ground.

She held on tightly to the blade. The lizard struggled beneath her, almost wrenching free of the sword while it struggled to free itself. Finally, after what seemed like an eternity, the animal sighed and collapsed. She kept her gloved hands on the blade, waiting to feel a heartbeat make it tremble, but none came.

Slowly and carefully, she pulled Starlight free of the lizard's neck, wiping the blood off with a cloth she kept in the pouch hanging from her belt. Kneeling on the lizard's back, Astrid took her time, drying the polished iron carefully before putting it back in the wool-lined sheath.

Footsteps crashed through the brush ahead of her, coming from the main path the Iron Maidens had taken. Kikita came into view first, followed closely by Thorda. "Banshi," Kikita said. "Where is she?"

"What do you mean?" Astrid said, feeling a sudden tug of worry. "Didn't she run back?"

Thorda cried out, pointing at the lizard.

Astrid rose from where she still knelt on the lizard's back and jumped to the ground. Following Thorda's shaking finger, Astrid saw Banshi pinned under the dead animal's paw.

CHAPTER FORTY-SEVEN

Astrid jumped to Banshi's side. The lizard had trapped the woman beneath one of its front legs when Astrid had killed it. The bowed leg draped across Banshi's back, seemingly cradling her in the crook behind its knee.

Careful to avoid the sharp curved talons on the creature's paw, Astrid touched Banshi's neck, grateful to feel it throb lightly as the blood coursed through the woman's veins. "She's alive," Astrid said in relief. Looking up at Kikita and Thorda, she said, "Why didn't she run back to you?"

Banshi spoke quietly. All of the women jumped in surprise. Astrid looked to Kikita to translate.

"Vinchi trained us to fight men," Kikita said quietly. "The dragon frightened Banshi. She'd never seen one before, and she found herself so terrified that she couldn't force herself to move."

The brush rustled as more of the Iron Maidens walked the narrow path toward them.

"Come and help!" Astrid called.

She directed the women to crowd around her, making certain they all steered clear of the lizard's talons. Together, they grasped and heaved the lizard's leg up in the air, allowing Kikita enough space to haul Banshi out from underneath its heavy weight.

"Lower it slowly," Astrid told them. "Be as mindful letting it down as you were when you picked it up." With the other women's help, she eased the animal's leg back onto the ground.

"Astrid," Kikita said. "I believe everyone should stay where they are until you see this."

Frowning, Astrid squeezed her way out from the women crowded around her, needing to step behind a tree to get to the place where Kikita had pulled Banshi out from under the lizard's dead body. As Banshi's eyelids fluttered, Kikita pointed to her arm. Banshi's torn shirt revealed a bleeding gash below her elbow.

"The dragon bit her," Kikita whispered. "She will be dead within days."

❧

Astrid's mind raced. This couldn't be happening. Not to one of the Iron Maidens.

"It might not be a bite," she told Kikita. "She will only die if its spittle gets into the wound."

Astrid remembered what had happened several weeks ago. Something surprising and unexpected. She resisted the urge to touch the pouch hanging from her belt. How could it be wise to reveal a secret about a power she didn't understand?

Again, Banshi spoke, looking up at Kikita.

The back of Astrid's throat tightened, and for a moment she could hardly breathe. She remembered Margreet and the words she'd spoken that Astrid had never understood. She missed the unlikely friendship in which they'd discovered themselves and how it ended too soon. Vinchi had loved Margreet and he still loved her by training other women to protect themselves against a cult that threatened to destroy their hearts and minds and spirits. How could Astrid let an Iron Maiden die?

"Don't give up hope," Astrid told Kikita. "Even if the lizard has bitten her, she may still yet live."

Kikita shook her head. "From all I know about dragons, that's impossible."

Wrapping a hand around the pouch that held the stone of darkness, Astrid said, "I was bitten by a lizard weeks ago, and yet I still live. I believe I can save her."

CHAPTER FORTY-EIGHT

Under Astrid's instruction, the Iron Maidens created a make-shift camp at the intersection of the road to the lake and the narrow path that Banshi had taken of her own accord. They gathered bare branches knocked to the ground by past storms and built a simple shelter around Banshi and then covered it with pine branches cut with their weapons. While they worked, the Maidens constantly wiped their hands against their clothes only to end up with both hands and clothes sticky with sap.

Astrid chose to butcher the lizard herself. She'd watched Donel carve up many a beast in Guell, and he'd told her what he'd learned from his father to make the process easy. After borrowing an ax from one of the Iron Maidens, Astrid hesitated, feeling sick to her stomach at the thought of cutting into the lizard.

This thing could have killed Banshi, Astrid reminded herself. *This is my chance to show it how I feel about that, even if it is already dead.*

She felt as if a cold, wintry blast of air rushed through her, chilling her heart and head. Her desire for mercy evaporated. She would not allow anyone or anything to harm any of these women. And now she had the opportunity to provide them with a feast that would shore up their souls.

With cool determination, Astrid struck the dead lizard across the back of its neck with her borrowed ax. As a matter of habit, she cupped one hand to catch the blood and drink it. Few people outside the Northlands ate lizard meat, which meant they never consumed lizard blood and could not shift shape. She'd been surprised to learn that in other countries people could only see themselves and others as they truly were, not as they wished to be seen. And since drinking Norah's water offering at Limru last year, Astrid's shape had locked into place so that everyone saw the smooth skin and whole body she now possessed. She no longer needed to shapeshift or to be around shapeshifters. Even so, she still drank lizard blood. DiStephan had been right when she'd first met him so many years ago: drinking it *did* make a dragonslayer stronger.

When they eat this meat, will the lizard's blood let them shift their shape? Astrid wondered.

Once Astrid had cut all the meat she believed they could use, she recruited most of the Iron Maidens to help her drag the carcass as far down the narrow path as possible. She was happy to let the night predators help themselves to the remains as long as they found the leftovers far from camp.

When the Iron Maidens walked away from the carcass and back down the path, Astrid pulled Kikita aside to ask a question that had nagged at her all day. Speaking softly so no one else would hear, Astrid said, "Why did Banshi run away?"

Kikita looked calmly into Astrid's eyes. "I was as astonished as you. She shared nothing about her decision with me."

"But did she say anything after it happened?"

"I heard nothing but screams."

Astrid gazed in Kikita's eyes and sensed she told the truth. At the same time, Astrid wondered if the Far Easterner might be holding something back. "Is there anything else I should know?"

Kikita shrugged. "I think not."

"Would you speak with her after she has a chance to recover? Maybe tomorrow?"

Kikita smiled. "Of course."

Toward the end of the day, Astrid showed the Iron Maidens how to make the same kind of trench fire she used to forge swords. But instead of creating the trench on a table, they dug it down the middle of the path. She explained this would allow them all to sleep near it and stay warm during the chilly night after roasting and eating all the lizard meat they wanted.

As the meat cooked, Astrid took a few of the Maidens into the woods to search for root vegetables, finding only a handful. Back at the camp, she cut up the vegetables and mashed them, which yielded heavy liquids. Adding lizard blood to the mixture, she created a soup and fed it to Banshi while the other Maidens ate their fill of meat. The same healing broth had once helped Astrid regain her strength, and she hoped it would have the same effect on Banshi.

Having decided to keep the stone of darkness her secret, Astrid refused to leave Banshi's side. Astrid remembered how her own pouch had rested by her bedside when she'd fallen ill from a lizard bite and kept that same pouch near Banshi. Although Astrid had failed to learn the nature of the stone, it obviously had healing powers. The presence of the stone of darkness had to be the only explanation for Astrid's recovery. If it worked for Astrid, surely it would work for Banshi, too.

After eating the soup, Banshi fell into a deep sleep, making Astrid feel hopeful. As the other women ate around the trench fire, she watched carefully for signs that they might develop a sudden ability to shift shape but saw only the way the firelight warmed their faces. Although subdued, the Iron Maidens seemed to regain some strength from the meal, making Astrid feel more confident about the journey ahead of them. She relaxed, happy to listen to their light chatter.

Sometime later, Astrid glanced up to see a startled look cross Kikita's face. Following her gaze, Astrid looked at Banshi.

Astrid frowned, not believing what she saw at first. She shook her head and looked away for a moment. Surely, it had to be a trick of the firelight.

But when Astrid looked back, she realized the flickering light played no tricks. Banshi's skin had turned blue.

Chapter Forty-Nine

"Banshi!" Astrid cried, recognizing the color of death. Without hope, Astrid grabbed the woman's arm as if she could shake the maiden back to life.

Banshi murmured and shifted, her eyelids fluttering slightly.

Shocked, Astrid let go and scooted away from her in fear. When people with pale skin like the Far Easterners died, their color would go very white at first and eventually take on a bluish hue.

"Astrid?" Thorda said, rising from where she sat with the other Maidens around the trench fire to assess the situation. "Be you well?"

Astrid rubbed her fingers together. Banshi's skin had been warm to the touch. But if Banshi hadn't died, why did her skin look blue?

"Look!" Astrid said, pointing at Banshi. "Look at her!"

The Iron Maidens who understood the Northlander language turned and stared at the resting Banshi while the others looked about in confusion.

"She rests," Thorda said evenly. "She is the same."

"No! Look at her skin!"

The camp fell silent except for the crackling fire. Thorda's face softened with concern. "You rest. Sleep now."

Astrid crawled slowly back to Banshi's side and placed her bare forearm next to the maiden's face. "Look at the color of my skin and look at the color of hers."

Kikita stood and walked behind Thorda, placing a reassuring hand on her shoulder until Thorda resumed her seat by the fire. "Astrid has faced many difficulties today," Kikita said in a soothing voice.

Astrid drew back her arm, feeling anger bubble up. Kikita saw the truth as easily as Astrid. Why wouldn't she admit it?

Kikita squeezed her way behind the Iron Maidens until she could kneel by Astrid's side. "They don't have your ability," Kikita whispered to her.

"We've all had lizard meat tonight." Surely Kikita knew that consuming lizard's meat and the blood it contained gave people the ability to change how they looked. If Banshi wasn't dead, either she changed her skin color despite being barely awake—or one of the Iron Maidens changed it by the way they perceived her. And because none of the Maidens had shown any sign of change after eating, it seemed none of them had the power to change anyone.

But Kikita had looked at Banshi in a peculiar way before Astrid had brought attention to her condition.

"You see it as plainly as I do," Astrid said.

"Like the Northlands, the Far East practices the consumption of dragon meat."

"But they've just eaten lizard meat. Why don't they see the change?"

"Only those who taste dragon blood in childhood can change."

Astrid frowned. "That's not true. I have friends who knew nothing of shapeshifting until they began to eat dragon's meat."

Kikita shrugged. "Perhaps the food Northlanders eat makes them different. Or your climate. Or perhaps we have greater differences than we imagine." She shrugged again. "In the Far East, and perhaps in the Midlands and Southlands, once adulthood is entered, consuming dragon's meat has no effect."

Astrid's understanding of the world trembled, as if she were caught in an earthquake. "How is that possible?"

"How is it possible for a caterpillar to turn into a butterfly? For glow worms to light up like stars at night? For a lizard that has lost its tail to grow a new one? It is the nature of the world."

The light from the trench fire danced in Kikita's eyes. A piece of burning wood cracked loudly, and an ember in the heart of the fire burst, sending sparks shooting up toward the sky. The floating bits of ember glowed bright yellow and floated in an arc toward her.

As Astrid watched, the sparks spiraled around Kikita's head and nestled in her hair. Their glow softened from yellow to orange. Although her hair emitted wisps of curling smoke, it did not catch on fire.

I know you from sometime before, Astrid thought about Kikita. *Why do you seem so familiar to me? Why do I feel I remember you?*

"I did not change her," Kikita said. "Therefore, she must have changed herself."

Astrid shook her head. How could that be possible? "But Banshi sleeps. How can anyone change when they sleep?"

"I do not believe she changed knowingly or with purpose."

Astrid grew more confused by the moment. "Then what does this change mean? Why would her skin turn blue?"

"I've been wondering why Banshi felt so compelled for us to enter Hagentown. Why she broke away from us. Could she have planned to go back to Hagentown? I cannot imagine where else she would have gone if the dragon had not stopped her."

"Hagentown? But I saw Mandulane's women—" Astrid stopped as a new realization chilled her to the bone. "They have blue skin."

Kikita nodded. "The same blue skin that Banshi now exhibits." She sighed heavily. "I believe her current state and the dragon blood she consumed have made it possible for the truth to surface through her appearance. I believe she must be one of them."

"Ask her."

Kikita hesitated as she considered the sleeping woman then cleared her throat. "Banshi."

When she didn't respond, Astrid said, "Banshi, wake up," and then shook her gently.

Still, Banshi failed to open her eyes.

Frowning, Kikita laid a hand on Banshi's forehead. Her face creased with concern, Kikita held her fingers next to Banshi's nostrils.

Looking up at Astrid, Kikita whispered, "She's dead."

CHAPTER FIFTY

"She can't be dead," Astrid said, staring at Banshi's still form in disbelief. *I gave her the healing soup of dragonslayers with lizard meat and blood. It should have made her stronger. I kept the stone of darkness near her. If it saved my life, it will save hers.* Astrid shook her by the shoulders, but the woman weighed limp and heavy in her hands. "Banshi!"

Still seated around the trench fire they'd made in the middle of the narrow path, the Iron Maidens' conversations faltered. They looked up at Astrid's outcry.

Kikita placed a gentle hand along Banshi's neck. "She's cold. Her skin is cold."

Frantic, Astrid tried to prop the unresponsive woman up in her arms, but gravity pulled her back to the ground. "You can't be cold! You can't be dead!"

"Dead?" Thorda repeated. The Iron Maidens who spoke the Northlander language translated the single word for those who didn't. All of them stared at Astrid in disbelief.

"No, she's not dead," Astrid murmured while she took Banshi's face in her hands and forced the woman's eyes open.

But Banshi's dark eyes held nothing but emptiness.

Taking her by the shoulders again, anger rushed through her veins. Shaking the unresponsive body, Astrid cried, "Wake up!"

She looked up in surprise when Kikita placed her hand on top of Astrid's.

"It is too late," Kikita said. "We will gather stones for her in the morning and then ride to the lake. Everyone should try to sleep or at least rest. We must put distance between ourselves and Mandulane's men while we can." She gently pried Astrid's hands from Banshi's body.

Unable to sleep, Astrid tended the trench fire all night, feeling stunned and confused. How could it be possible that she let Banshi die? Why had nothing worked?

Kikita had said lizard blood had no effect on anyone outside of the Northlands who tasted it only in adulthood. Apparently, once someone completed the passage from child to adult, the opportunity to gain the ability to shift shape had passed.

That's why giving her lizard meat and the blood it contained couldn't help her. If Banshi didn't eat lizard meat before she became a woman, it couldn't help her. And the healing soup…if it's meant especially for dragonslayers, then the same thing is true. The healing soup is meant for anyone who can shift their shape because all dragonslayers are shapeshifters.

Astrid sighed. Before now she'd never realized all the advantages she had as a Northlander and a dragonslayer.

She'd never seen anyone die so quickly from a lizard bite, although she'd heard of it: DiStephan had seen children die very quickly from a bite, while large men could take up to three days. The Far Eastern women were about the size of a Northlander girl on the threshold of womanhood. That would explain why Banshi's death came so quickly.

But as clouds gathered and blocked the stars and moon from view, one question still haunted Astrid.

How could the ability to change shape make any difference to a stone? she wondered. *If the stone of darkness saved my life, why couldn't it save hers? And if it wasn't the stone that saved my life, why am I still alive after getting a lizard bite that would kill anyone else?*

Astrid cast a casual glance at the Iron Maidens sleeping around the trench fire, making sure no one's eyes were open. She opened the pouch hanging from her belt and felt inside until she found the familiar shape of the stone. Drawing it out of the pouch, she held it up to the firelight and gazed into its depths for answers.

But the stone remained as dark and distant as the clouded skies above.

CHAPTER FIFTY-ONE

The next morning they gathered stones and laid them around and on top of Banshi's body to keep it safe from predators. At Kikita's suggestion, they worked quickly.

The morning dew made every rock's surface slippery and difficult to grasp. Even the stones resting on top of dry, brown leaves revealed wriggling insects when overturned. The wet earth stank of hard minerals and chalk.

Astrid dawdled, searching for stones that looked worthy of protecting an Iron Maiden. Finally, she found a pile of fist-size round stones seemingly polished by a dried-up stream and embedded with bits that sparkled in the sunlight. By the time she returned, a large stack of stones covered Banshi's body. Astrid arranged her contribution on a flat rock covering the dead woman's feet, wishing for the Iron Maiden's soul to find its way quickly to the spirit world.

The women rode for the rest of the morning, thankful to reach the lake's shore when the sun reached its peak. They tied up their horses at a tree line near the shore and set about to collect any sand creatures they could eat or use to lure fish close enough to catch.

Still shaken by Banshi's death, Astrid took off her shoes, rolled up her pants legs, and waded into the clear rippling lake. The water's icy chill made her catch her breath, but she felt grateful for the sudden sense of coming awake.

She turned at the sound of sloshing water. Kikita waded toward her.

"Should we tell the others?" Astrid said.

"Tell them what?"

"What we saw. Banshi's skin turned blue."

Kikita shrugged. "When people die, their skin pales to blue."

"Not that quickly." Astrid gave Kikita a knowing look. "I've seen people die from all sorts of causes, including lizard bites. It takes time for their skin to change color. Banshi was alive one minute and dead the next. No one's skin can change color that fast."

Kikita nodded. "What good would it do?"

"To let them know Banshi may have belonged to Mandulane?" Astrid paused. It seemed there should be an obvious answer, but she could think of none.

"To let them know that one of us turned to betrayal? That a traitor fooled all of us and Vinchi? From the first day of training, we have all stayed together or in small groups. I've seen no opportunity for any of us to be alone with outsiders. If Banshi betrayed us, she did so before she met us."

Astrid shook her head in dismay. "How could anyone do such a thing?"

Kikita took a deep breath, staring across the lake. "People are capable of a great many atrocities."

The sudden cries of the Iron Maidens pierced the air. Astrid and Kikita turned to see the Maidens drawing their weapons, their backs to the lake as a dozen armed men stepped from the tree line, ready to fight.

CHAPTER FIFTY-TWO

For a moment, Astrid, Kikita, and the other Iron Maidens stared in surprise at the men walking toward them, eying the women as if sizing them up. They wore small animal pelts over their simple pants and shirts, as if the chill of spring were too much for them to bear. Each man held an ax or oversize knife in hand.

"Together!" Thorda yelled.

Before Astrid could take another breath, all of the Iron Maidens dashed into an arcing formation, standing side by side within an arm's length of each other, the lake at their backs. Kikita ran forward to join the formation, leaving Astrid standing behind it. Immediately, each woman drew her weapon, ready to fight.

The armed men hesitated as their leader stepped forward and shouted at the women.

"Does anyone know his language?" Thorda called out in North-lander then in Midlander. A few other Maidens translated Thorda's words for those who didn't speak those languages.

Astrid walked forward to join the Maidens' rank, easing her way between Thorda and Kikita and keeping Starlight sheathed. "They aren't Krystr soldiers," Astrid said. "Look at how they're dressed. Look at the way they regard us."

The men's leader took another step forward, shifting his grip on his short sword. Barely taller than Astrid, his hair fell long, dirty, and tangled. His skin looked rough and weathered. He squinted at the Iron Maidens, his gaze falling upon the weapons in their hands and the determination darkening their faces. He asked a question that none of the Maidens understood.

When one of his men took a tentative step forward to follow his leader, Thorda lunged forward, criss-crossing her blade in the empty air.

A warning, Astrid thought, remembering the technique Vinchi had taught to her and Margreet. *Thorda is showing them we know how to fight and we're not afraid.*

The man who had taken the step forward froze then glanced at his leader, who cocked his head in curiosity, gazing at the women as if trying to puzzle them out.

"Step up," Thorda called out.

In unison, the Iron Maidens lunged and criss-crossed their blades in the air, taking their formation closer to the men but still far from striking distance. All of the Iron Maidens now extended their weapons toward the men, showing the edges of their blades, whether ax or sword or dagger. It would take little effort for each woman to cast a deadly blow at anyone foolish to come close.

Out loud, Astrid said, "Are all the commands in Northlander?" She walked to stand between Thorda and Kikita again. Keeping Starlight sheathed, Astrid took a casual stance while keeping a steady eye on the men in front of them.

"Vinchi taught us commands in Northlander so you could understand them and keep up with us," Kikita said.

"Clever idea," Astrid said.

The leader held out a calming hand to his men and called out a question to the Maidens.

Astrid sauntered forward from the line of defense as if she were asking a friend for directions. "Sorry," she called out. "We don't know what you're saying."

The leader pointed at Astrid while calling back to his men. The one who had stepped forward spoke back in an argumentative tone.

"Step back," Kikita said to Astrid. "Stay with us or you'll get hurt." After a moment of consideration, she added, "Better still, get behind us and stay out of harm's way altogether."

Astonished, Astrid turned to look at Kikita. "I'm a dragonslayer. I'm in harm's way all the time. I know how to protect myself."

"From dragons. You don't know as much as Vinchi taught us about protecting ourselves from men who mean us ill."

The leader called out his question once more, this time gesturing with his weaponless hand.

Astrid looked at him. The sunlight glinted off something silver pinning the pelt he wore around his shoulders together.

"Wait," Astrid said to Thorda and Kikita. "Stay here."

Before they could answer, Astrid walked toward the leader,

placing her hand on Starlight's grip.

The men facing her tensed, but their leader called out to them, again gesturing for them to hold their ground.

Smiling, Astrid spoke even though she knew he wouldn't understand her words. "Let me show you something that will make everything clear."

Slowly, she drew Starlight from its sheath. She cradled its blade in her gloved hands, creating a showcase for the men to admire.

Excitedly, the leader pointed to his own brigand sword, calling out to his men, who grudgingly relaxed and put their weapons away. The leader then pointed to the silver brooch pinning the pelt at his neck, as if showing it to them for the first time.

Putting Starlight back in its sheath, Astrid strode confidently to the leader, suppressing her urge to run up and throw her arms around his neck in relief.

Grinning widely, the leader spouted a greeting even though the only thing Astrid understood was her own name.

"Hello, Komdra," Astrid said happily, pointing at his brigand weapon. "How's that sword I made for you?"

CHAPTER FIFTY-THREE

After the Iron Maidens built a fire on the lake's shore, Komdra's men cooked and shared the food they carried with them. As they all sat on the shore and ate lunch together, Komdra chattered constantly to his men, gesturing warmly toward Astrid the entire time. Simultaneously, Astrid told the Iron Maidens of their history.

"We found the island where the brigands sold Lenore into slavery," Astrid said, pausing to let some of the Maidens translate for the others. "Komdra owned her, and no matter what I offered, he didn't want to sell her. Finally, I offered him that brooch." Astrid paused, remembering how difficult the decision had been. The silver brooch took the form of a twisting dragon surrounded by two snakes. When she'd first met DiStephan, Astrid had been a child in the company of a childseller anxious to be rid of her. The brooch had been DiStephan's, and she'd cherished it since the day he'd given it to her. But the brooch was mere metal, while Lenore was flesh and blood. While parting with the brooch had been painful, leaving without Lenore would have been unthinkable.

"And he wanted a sword, so I made one for him." She pointed at Komdra's sword, which he proudly displayed resting upon the knees of his crossed legs for all to admire.

Komdra grinned, proud as he pounded her on the back. He gestured to his brigand sword, half of the size of Astrid's dragon-slayer's sword, and then slapped his hand to his chest as he beamed.

"I imagine," Kikita said, "few men can boast of owning a sword made by a blacksmith who knows the secret of making a dragonslayer's sword. Especially a blacksmith who also happens to slay dragons."

As they continued eating, Astrid struggled to figure out how to communicate with Komdra, who gnawed happily on a roasted chicken leg. "What are you," she said as she pointed at Komdra, "doing here?" She pointed at the ground.

While chewing a mouthful of bird, Komdra chattered happily while he dug one heel into the sand of the lake's shore.

Thorda sat next to Astrid and sipped a cup of broth. "He says what?"

Astrid sighed. "I have no idea."

"Have you ever considered learning someone else's language?" Kikita said, nibbling on a raw potato.

"I have no knack for it. I used to know a few words of Komdra's language, but it's been so long I've forgotten them." Astrid waved a hand at him and his men. "They're from one of the islands off the west coast of the Northlands. No one else speaks their language."

"Islands?" Thorda said in surprise. "Why are they here?"

One of the Midlander Iron Maidens asked Thorda a question.

Astrid studied the variety of faces and languages surrounding her. So many people from so many different lands. It reminded her of the map she'd seen in Mandulane's camp, the map of what appeared to be the whole world, which he planned to conquer. And it looked like he'd succeeded in planting a traitor among them. What if Banshi had been one of Mandulane's women and instead of tattooing her skin blue, he'd sent her to scout the Southlands for people resisting his takeover? What if Banshi had pretended to be one of those people and had met Vinchi? What if Banshi had infiltrated the Iron Maidens with the intent of destroying them by turning them over to Krystr soldiers?

Astrid shuddered at the thought. Surely, the rest of the Iron Maidens had better intents. But the thought of what Banshi might have been lessened Astrid's confidence in the rest of them.

Nudging Thorda, Astrid said, "What did she ask?"

Thorda hesitated as if trying to figure out how to put the answer into words Astrid would understand.

Kikita said, "She wants to know what you and Thorda have said to each other." Smiling at Astrid's surprise, Kikita said, "I speak Midlander, too."

One of Komdra's men rose slowly to his feet, staring at the Iron Maidens. He asked a question.

Thorda and a few of the Iron Maidens cried out in surprise, while Kikita simply raised an eyebrow. Thorda spoke rapidly, her face lighting up with joy.

Leaning toward Kikita, Astrid said, "What's happening?"

Keeping a steady gaze on Thorda and Komdra's man, Kikita said, "He speaks Midlander." When Komdra's man answered Thorda, Kikita held up a hand telling Astrid to hold quiet.

All the men and women seemed to hang onto every word spoken, although most understood none of it. When the initial conversation ended, each group anxiously absorbed the translations.

While the Midlander women passed the information to the other Iron Maidens, Kikita told Astrid what had transpired. "His name is Hevrick. His mother was a Midlander captured by brigands and sold into slavery, so he learned the language from her. Krystr soldiers have overrun the islands."

Astrid shuddered. "But the islands aren't far from the coast of the Northlands. If the islands have been taken over, they'll go to the Northlands next."

Kikita nodded. "Hevrick believes it's part of Mandulane's strategy. The Northlanders are strong and unlikely to be conquered easily. Hevrick thinks it's no accident that Krystr soldiers are taking over the islands and the Midlands at the same time."

Astrid felt light headed. "The Krystr soldiers will attack from the south and the west at the same time."

"Hevrick says they are building their numbers. Once they have as many men as they need, they will attack the Northlands."

"When I was in Mandulane's camp, I saw a map. It showed the territories the Krystr soldiers already control. That happened weeks ago and the map showed only the Southlands and Lower Midlands in Mandulane's control."

"Perhaps they do not have full control of the Upper Midlands or islands yet."

"Then why is Komdra here instead of defending his home?"

Komdra gave Astrid a quick look and a grim smile at the mention of his name.

Kikita interrupted Thorda, speaking in Midlander.

Thorda nodded, letting Kikita pass Astrid's question along to Hevrick, who seemed to give a long and complicated answer.

"He tried," Kikita told Astrid. "But the Krystr soldiers waited to attack until most of the islander men set sail to trade in Northland and Midland towns. When the Krystr attacks began, the few remaining islander men realized their cause would soon be lost. They hid their families in caves on the far side of the island then sailed here in search of help."

Astrid looked at Komdra with new hope. "Have they found any?"

"Hevrick says they search for the Hidden People in hope of guidance." Kikita paused. "Komdra would like to know if we care to join them."

CHAPTER FIFTY-FOUR

That afternoon, the Iron Maidens rode alongside the men on a path through the forest near the lake's shore. All of the Midlander Maidens, including Thorda, clustered around Hevrick and chattered constantly. Even Kikita guided her horse near their group.

Astrid rode alone at the end of the pack. The path spread wide between sparse trees, making it easy to get a good look at the surroundings. The other forests Astrid had traveled through tended to be denser, making it necessary to listen to every noise surrounding her. Hevrick and the Midlander Maidens talked loudly enough to scare off any bears or wolves, and Astrid suspected most lizards would hesitate to attack such a large group of people.

Still, she made a practice of keeping a close eye on their surroundings and an open ear to the sounds behind her. Thin streams of sunshine threaded between treetops and lit the path in patches. Astrid relished the intermittent warmth on her skin.

A sudden crack echoed through the woods. She sat up straight, looking ahead for the source of the unexpected sound.

Kikita had dismounted and stood by her horse at the edge of the path. She drank from a skin slung across her back. When she shifted her weight, a dead branch snapped beneath her foot.

When she reached Kikita's side, Astrid pulled up her horse. "Are you all right?"

Kikita nodded, watching the others forge ahead before getting back on her horse and riding next to Astrid. "Do you trust Komdra?"

Oh. This was a ruse to speak to me so no one else could overhear us. Out loud, she said, "I suppose."

"What has been your experience with him?"

Astrid thought back to the first time she met him. "He bought one of my friends as a slave."

"How did he treat her?"

"Well enough, I think." Astrid pursed her lips, trying to remember. "She seemed to be as healthy and well fed as anyone else on the island."

"How did Komdra use her?"

"As a cobbler. Lenore learned the trade from her father."

"And he used her as nothing else?"

Kikita's question shocked Astrid. "No! Of course not. Komdra isn't like Krystr soldiers. Or brigands." Astrid paused. "Although he's clearly a man who knows how to use a sword and understands its value. I'd say that makes him some kind of warrior when he's not busy farming."

Kikita paused, seemingly digesting this information.

Astrid decided to take her turn asking the questions. "Who are the Hidden People? What do you know about them?"

"Only what I gleaned from listening to the others speak with Hevrick. They seem to be a tribe of spiritual people who guard the lake."

"Guard it?" Astrid said, immediately thinking of Limru and its decimation by Krystr soldiers. "From what?"

"Mandulane, I imagine." Kikita sighed. "Thorda admitted this lake is considered sacred by some Midlanders. From what I heard Hevrick and the other Midlanders say, the Hidden People now move from site to site around the lake to elude the Krystr soldiers."

"And Komdra thinks they can help us? How?"

Kikita offered a wistful smile. "Magic."

Astrid stiffened. She'd always believed in rational explanations and logic. She'd seen plenty during the past few years that stretched her belief to the breaking point, but she still preferred to believe in reason before magic.

Up ahead, Hevrick, Thorda, and the Midlander Maidens laughed together.

For some reason she couldn't quite pinpoint, their laughter made Astrid uneasy.

CHAPTER FIFTY-FIVE

They traveled through the woods surrounding the lake for several days. The spring green color of the leafing trees darkened as those leaves grew fuller and thicker. Summer insects buzzed loudly, the sound seeming to come from everywhere. The air grew warm enough to encourage sweat. As they headed toward the northern shore of the lake, cliffs lined the landscape and narrow waterfalls tumbled over them.

Komdra fell into a routine of leading the pack with Hevrick and the Midlander Iron Maidens in tow. Although the other Maidens initially interspersed themselves among Komdra's men, they soon separated and rode behind them. Astrid chose to be the last rider, often keeping a good distance between herself and the Iron Maidens in order to listen to the land surrounding them. Most lizards had probably made the swim across the sea separating the Midlands from the Northlands but there might be a few stragglers, like the one whose bite had killed Banshi.

Disappointed in the lax attitude Thorda and the other Iron Maidens seemed to have adopted since joining Komdra and his men, Astrid thought, *At least one of us is on the lookout for danger.*

Komdra led the group onto a wide section of the shore near a cliff. Young leafy trees jutted out from crevices in the rock face, seeming to hover in mid-air although their deeply entrenched roots anchored them in the cracks. Smooth, round stones littered the ground between the shore and the cliff, looking like a giant's blackened toenails. The lush sound of churning water filled the air, announcing the presence of a waterfall looming around the next corner.

Astrid exhaled a grateful breath at the chance to stop and fill their skins with fresh water. Once their path turned and brought the waterfall into view, she smiled as the wind blew fine, chilly mist across her face. Following the others' lead, she rode to a cluster of trees near the shore, tied her horse, and tiptoed through the stone-covered stretch of land. Even this far away, the waterfall's mist made the stones slick and slippery, so she walked between them. Unlike the others, she preferred getting water at the base of the fall instead of the stream that trickled from it into the lake.

When Astrid walked away from the group, Hevrick pointed at her and called out as if beckoning her to stay. Thorda piped up, gesturing with her hands until Hevrick shrugged. With every step, the rushing sound of water grew louder, making it impossible for Astrid to hear everyone she'd left behind. She walked slowly, careful to plant one foot steadily before raising the other.

Astrid approached the powerful fall, easing her way close to its edge. Like many waterfalls in the Northlands, it rained down like a curtain in front of the mouth of a cave. When Astrid caught a thin stream of the waterfall's edge into the mouth of her drinking skin, water splashed wildly, drenching her hair, skin, and clothes. She didn't mind. The warm sun would dry her soon enough. The drinking skin bulged full, and she pulled it back, ready to return and join the others where they rested on the shore.

But before Astrid could turn away from the waterfall, she saw a shift in the darkness behind it. She froze in place, giving herself time to gaze through the tumbling water that sparkled in the sun. Perhaps she'd merely seen a trick of light, imagining movement where none existed.

Out of habit, she sniffed the air. This close to the waterfall, she could detect nothing beyond the fresh scent of mist and the heavy earthiness of rock and mud.

The darkness behind the waterfall shifted again. Something was hiding in the cave behind it.

CHAPTER FIFTY-SIX

Astrid froze. She stared through the waterfall and into the cave as her mind raced, considering what might be lurking there. *Do lizards hide in caves? Or could it be brigands? Or Krystr soldiers?*

The roar of heavy streams of water crashing onto the smooth rock ledge at the foot of the cliff filled her ears while rogue splashes clipped her, drenching her clothes. Out of habit, she strained to listen for noises that could tell her if the waterfall separated her from man or beast.

Starlight. She needed Starlight.

Remaining still, Astrid reached slowly until she felt the familiar grip of her sword. Normally, she'd never remove it from the sheath this close to water in order to protect its iron blade. But she had to be ready in case whatever she faced burst through the waterfall, ready to attack.

The Iron Maidens. They can be here in moments. Komdra and his men, too.

Astrid remembered what Thorda had told her when they first met.

We learn when it is good to fight and we learn when it is good to run.

Vinchi had taught them that. Astrid breathed evenly and steadily, feeling a rush of anticipation that she needed to control. At the beginning of any fight with a lizard, her flesh and blood and bones thrummed with excitement and fear and determination. Experience had taught her when to keep those feelings in check and when to let them loose. She needed them during a fight, not before one began.

Again, moving slowly, Astrid held Starlight in front of her body with both hands, pointing its tip toward the waterfall as she took a careful step back, feeling for sure footing before committing.

Light and dark shifted again behind the waterfall, this time quicker and more widespread. Either a very large lizard or many people moved about inside the cave.

Astrid swallowed hard, focusing to keep her hands and Starlight steady. *Don't look back*, she told herself. *Stay focused on the waterfall. Be ready for anything.*

She took another slow step back, reaching with her toes to find solid land, but when she placed her weight on it, her heel slid off the side of a small stone. Recovering quickly, Astrid caught her balance and held Starlight steady.

Calling out to her companions would accomplish nothing. She'd have to cover half the distance between here and the lakeshore before they'd be able to hear her over the roar of the waterfall. Turning around would leave her vulnerable to attack, as would waving her sword in hopes of drawing attention. Astrid knew her best bet was to keep stepping backwards, no matter how long it took.

Stay calm, Astrid told herself, reaching with her foot to take another blind step back. *Stay ready.*

But when she backed into something solid against her back, Astrid froze again.

"What is it?" Thorda shouted next to Astrid's ear.

With a quick glance to her side, Astrid saw Thorda holding an ax in one hand and realized she'd stepped back into Thorda's open arm. Another glance revealed the Iron Maidens, Komdra, and his men creeping up on either side, all with weapons in hand. "I don't know," Astrid said.

Thorda patted Astrid's back and said, "We find out."

Thorda slipped away from Astrid and headed toward one side of the waterfall while Hevrick approached the other. Each crouched in a fighting stance, weapons positioned to strike. Hevrick called out in the Midlander language as if commanding whatever hid behind the waterfall to come out or suffer the consequences.

If a lizard emerged, it would kill one or both of them in seconds. "You're too close," Astrid called in a panic. "Come back!"

Thorda and Hevrick remained in place, either not hearing Astrid or ignoring her.

Moments later, Hevrick stood upright and let his weapon hand fall to his side. He then extended his free hand, accepted by an elderly woman who stepped from behind the wall of water and offered a friendly smile to them all.

Chapter Fifty-Seven

Astrid shifted her position once more on a sheepskin spread out on the floor at the back of the cave. The soft wool didn't disguise the uneven and sharp rocky surface beneath it.

The elderly woman who had first greeted them sat on a simple wooden chair draped with wool scarves dyed in bright yellows and greens and blues. Her long white hair hung in a braid over one shoulder. She wore a plain linen dress decorated with large silver brooches at the shoulders and a heavy blue hooded cloak. Several strands of colored glass beads hung around her neck.

About 30 people surrounded her, all sitting so they faced the Iron Maidens and Komdra and his men.

The elderly woman spoke. Astrid recognized the Midlander language and looked to Kikita, seated next to her, for translation.

"Her name is Spathar," Kikita whispered. "She is the gothi of the Hidden People."

Astrid wrinkled her brow in confusion. "Gothi?"

Kikita paused as if trying to figure out the best translation. "Their chieftain. Their mystic. She has the power to look into the future and divine anyone's fate."

As Spathar spoke and those who understood her paid rapt attention, Astrid's gaze wandered. The cave's walls were smooth and carried sound well, while at the same time seeming to dampen the noise from the waterfall, which Astrid barely noticed. She saw little more than animal skins, Spathar's chair and scarves, and a few cooking tools inside the cave. Either the Hidden People hadn't been here long or they traveled light. Or perhaps both were true.

"She says we have come to a crossroads because of Mandulane and the Krystr soldiers," Kikita said. "The new god honors the way of man. Gaining control through fighting. Direct words. Deeds. Because of this, the new god considers all things hidden to be wicked."

"Does that mean the hidden people?" Astrid felt baffled. "Mandulane is telling everyone that the hidden people are wicked?"

Kikita's expression darkened. "More than that. He says the ways of all women are wicked because those ways are hidden. Men are strong, so they fight. Women are weak, so they have to find other means to get what they want. They work hidden magic. White sorcery."

"White," Astrid said, suddenly understanding. The color symbolized cowardice. It described weak people who resorted to secretive plans to get what they wanted instead of standing up for themselves and asking for it in a direct way. This wasn't the first time Astrid had heard the color associated with women, and she didn't appreciate it. "How would Mandulane and his soldiers like it if we called the Krystr god white?"

Kikita smiled briefly. "The White Krystr? I imagine they'd be enraged. I've heard they believe that women are especially easy to manipulate by magic."

"Manipulate?"

"By evil spirits. And the Krystrs also believe that if men allow themselves to spend too much time in the company of women, the men risk the infection of witchcraft that can flood through women."

Astrid spent a long moment looking at Kikita in astonishment. "No one can be stupid enough to believe such nonsense."

Kikita held her hands up in mock defense. "Do not blame the translator."

The gothi Spathar called out, and a boy led a young goat into the cave. The goat trotted happily next to the boy's side. Handing the rope collaring the goat to Spathar, the boy then turned away and ran as he burst into tears.

"What's wrong?" Astrid whispered.

Kikita shrugged. "Perhaps the goat was his pet."

Before Astrid could blink, Spathar slit the goat's throat with a knife, allowing its blood to spill on the rocky ground between the hidden people and the Iron Maidens and Komdra's men.

Leaning closer to Astrid, Kikita said, "I imagine this is some sort of blood sacrifice to appease the gods."

"I have never studied the gods," Astrid admitted.

Kikita raised a questioning eyebrow. "But surely you must have invoked their help. Perhaps when you were a blacksmith? Perhaps you asked the goddess of air for assistance when building a fire?"

Astrid felt the hair on the back of her neck stand up as she looked into Kikita's eyes, which seemed to hold a depth of amusement. Astrid had sometimes uttered a plea to the higher power of fire or air, usually when she felt frustrated and didn't know what else to do. But Kikita simply must have drawn a practical conclusion. No one other than Astrid knew what Kikita had guessed. Apparently, Kikita excelled at guesses. Before Astrid could answer her question, Spathar's voice rang through the cave.

Astrid looked up to see Spathar now lying prone on the ground next to her chair, her fingertips inches from the spilled blood offering. The hidden people circled around her, knelt, and sang. Astrid looked back at Kikita.

"It is a magic song," Kikita whispered.

Astrid shot her an irritated look.

"No, truly," Kikita said. "They sing praises to the gods to gain their attention." Kikita paused. "You might try it yourself sometime."

Astrid clapped her hand over her own mouth to keep from laughing out loud. She had no desire to offend the gothi or the hidden people, but Kikita's words made Astrid want to giggle. Astrid had witnessed odd things that stretched her sense of reason and suddenly felt amused by those who took such things so seriously.

Spathar chanted slowly, her voice ringing once again throughout the cave.

With a wicked look in her eyes, Kikita leaned slightly toward Astrid. "And now the gothi invites the gods to listen. If you want to ask the gods a question, this would be a good time."

Astrid's eyes teared as she choked back her giggles, and Kikita's gleeful expression only added fuel to the fire. Astrid breathed deeply, determined to regain her composure.

Suddenly, Spathar rose to her knees, shouting. She pointed at Astrid.

The hidden people stopped singing, and everyone turned to look at Astrid as Spathar called out to her.

Sobered and concerned, Astrid turned to Kikita, wanting and not wanting to hear the translation.

Once again, Kikita raised an eyebrow. "The gothi Spathar says you have a question for her."

Astrid shook her head. "No. I don't."

Spathar called out again, jabbing her finger directly at Astrid.

"I think you do," Kikita said. "The gothi says you are hiding something."

CHAPTER FIFTY-EIGHT

The gothi Spathar spoke rapidly to the hidden people, while Thorda translated her words to the Iron Maidens, and Hevrick to Komdra and his men. They all stood and walked toward the mouth of the cave. Spathar then pointed at Astrid once more, her words spoken slowly and plainly.

"She commands you to choose one of us to stay and tell you what she says," Kikita said.

Astrid considered the Midlander Iron Maidens as they walked away.

Thorda paused and looked at Astrid, looking hopeful, as if she expected to be chosen.

Astrid remembered her unease when Thorda had ridden ahead on the path with Hevrick and the Midlander Iron Maidens, all speaking in their native language. Their immediate camaraderie had left Astrid feeling like an outsider and ill at ease. Since that moment, Thorda seemed to have forgotten Astrid existed.

"I choose you," Astrid said to Kikita, who relayed the information to Spathar.

After everyone else had left the cave, Spathar gestured for Astrid and Kikita to approach her. As they stepped closer, Astrid noticed the deep wrinkles creasing the woman's face. Spathar's eyes sparkled bright blue, deep with wisdom. Spathar looked into Astrid's eyes as if searching for information. Easing back into her chair, Spathar pointed to the ground, indicating to the other women that they should sit. As they did so, Spathar spoke firmly, still staring at Astrid.

"She wishes to examine it," Kikita said.

"It?" Astrid said, suppressing a feeling of dread. "What?"

Without looking at Spathar or speaking to her, Kikita said, "You know what."

The stone of darkness, Astrid realized. *It's the only thing I keep hidden, and Spathar accused me of hiding something.*

Astrid reached into her pouch and pulled out the stone.

Spathar nodded and held out an open palm. Astrid placed the stone in her hand.

The gothi stared into the depths of the stone, transfixed for what felt like an eternity. Finally, she spoke and Kikita relayed the message to Astrid. "She recognizes you. She says you are a producer of bloodstones. For that reason, under certain circumstances, you can also produce a stone of darkness, although this is far more rare than a bloodstone. This is something only someone with your lineage can do."

Astrid paused, remembering that Master Antoni had given her a similar explanation for the stone of darkness, even though his information had come from a legend handed down through his family. "My lineage?"

"Your grandfather was Benzel of the Wolf. Benzel Scalding. You have the true blood of the Scaldings."

The back of Astrid's neck prickled. She hadn't heard Spathar mention any of those names, and names needed no translation.

Spathar shook a nagging finger at Astrid.

Kikita hesitated for a moment before turning to Astrid. "The dragon warned you."

Astrid forced herself to remain still and calm. Perhaps Kikita lied about the translation. On the other hand, perhaps the gothi had referred to the Scaldings and Astrid's grandfather without naming them. Alone in the cave with Kikita and Spathar, Astrid decided to use caution in trusting them while feeling compelled to gather as much information from the gothi as possible. How did Spathar know that a dragon had warned Astrid?

Only dragonslayers knew that two different types of dragons existed: lizards and dragons. Lizards were just that: lizards so impressed with themselves that they'd shifted shape into a size that matched their opinion. Dragons were creatures with the ability to shift shape into human form. While lizards were dangerous, dragons were powerful.

Kikita thinks Spathar is talking about lizards. Only dragonslayers know that true dragons exist.

Astrid forced a laugh, unsure how much Spathar knew about lizards and dragons, if anything. "How could a dragon warn me?"

Without waiting for Kikita to translate Astrid's words, Spathar spoke again, keeping a steadfast gaze on the dragonslayer.

"The dragon warned that you must choose who you are," Kikita said. "The dragon said it is not something you do just once, but something you must do with every decision you make. You must choose who you are every day, and you make that choice with every action you take."

Taddeo, Astrid realized. *Spathar is talking about Taddeo.*

Spathar looked deeply into the stone of darkness for a while and then spoke again.

"Never forget the warning of a dragon," Kikita translated. "These are times when it becomes easy to forget the things you know best, the beliefs you hold dearest, unless you knowingly hold onto them tightly. The days of great fear are upon us, and fear can break any man or woman into pieces."

"I'm a dragonslayer," Astrid said with forced evenness, feeling insulted. "I'm not afraid."

This time, Kikita didn't translate Astrid's words for Spathar. Instead, Kikita said, "There are many things other than fear capable of breaking people. Greed. Envy." Kikita paused as if remembering something she'd long forgotten. "Arrogance."

"But I have none of those problems." Astrid thought for a moment. "Could you ask her what the stone is for? I've talked to alchemists throughout the Northlands, Midlands, and Southlands. They either have never heard of the stone or they refuse to talk about it."

"Perhaps you should heed their advice," Kikita said.

"Perhaps you should tell Spathar what I want to know." Astrid pressed her lips together grimly, frustrated with Kikita's interference. Kikita was merely an Iron Maiden. As a dragonslayer, Astrid had far more experience and knowledge about the world. Why couldn't Kikita see that?

Reluctantly, Kikita translated Astrid's question.

Spathar replied with a nonchalant tone, handing the stone to Kikita, who seemed mesmerized as she stared into its depths. She didn't relinquish it until Astrid nudged her with an open hand.

"The stone of darkness is the curse of the Scaldings," Kikita said, still staring at the stone as Astrid cupped it in her palm.

"What does that mean?"

Kikita snapped out of what seemed like a spell. "The Scaldings made a pact with dragons. While all other people feared dragons, the Scaldings befriended them. But to protect dragons from other people, the Scaldings pretended to slay them. It began when Benzel plunged into the ocean in feigned pursuit of a dragon and cut the dragon's arm off, knowing the dragon had the power to regenerate it. Benzel then pretended to chase the dragon onto Dragon's Head and force it into stone. In reality, the dragon willingly took the form of stone to make people believe the Scaldings had the power to control dragons. Therefore, people paid little attention to dragons, trusting the Scaldings to take that responsibility."

"Wendill," Astrid said in amazement, remembering the dragon that had shaken itself free of Dragon's Head when her brother Drageen and his alchemist had taken its place and turned into stone. "The dragon my grandfather pretended to kill was Wendill."

Kikita watched her patiently. Without speaking first to the gothi, Kikita said, "The agreement struck between your family and the dragons is that Dragon's Head is to be used as a symbol of fear. When a dragon is not entrapped there, a Scalding must take its place. People must fear Dragon's Head so that they fear the Scaldings and dragons alike. As long as people are afraid, they will keep their distance from dragons. If people fail to do so, they will encounter a far greater danger than they face now."

Astrid shuddered, enveloped in a sudden sense of dread. She looked at the stone and then back at Kikita. "But what is the curse of the Scaldings? And what does it have to do with the stone of darkness?"

When Kikita asked the question of Spathar, the gothi spoke quietly.

Kikita said, "The curse is the power that comes to you from dealing with dragons. The stone of darkness gives you the power to end the cycle of Dragon's Head."

Astrid took a moment to consider the implications. "But you said this cycle is necessary to make people afraid for their own good."

"Yes," Kikita said. "The stone of darkness gives you the power to end the secret bond between the Scaldings and the dragons. And in doing so, you would put the lives of all people who live in dragon territory—all Northlanders, Midlanders, and Southlanders—in grave danger."

CHAPTER FIFTY-NINE

Still inside the cave with Spathar and Kikita, Astrid held the stone of darkness, weighing as cold and heavy as guilt. The gothi's fingertips brushed the palm of Astrid's hand. Spathar's fingernails felt as sharp as Starlight's edges, and her skin looked as translucent as the dying petals of a white chrysanthemum. The gothi's hot breath lingered in the cave's chilly air, smelling like anise and wine.

Astrid curled her fingers into a fist around the stone. Spathar wrapped her own hands around it and whispered.

Not understanding, Astrid looked into the gothi's eyes anyway, hoping to see something in them that would give her insight. Instead, something Astrid had forgotten flashed out of her memory.

Dragon bites are deadly, Drageen had told her two years ago. *Almost everyone dies, even those descended from a dragonslayer. Only those with the purest dragonslayer blood can survive. Like you.*

Still staring in the gothi's eyes, Astrid realized why she'd been wrong to believe the stone of darkness could have saved Banshi from a lizard bite.

When the dragon bit you, chewed you up, its spit mixed with your blood. It made you stronger. That's why you have the power to produce bloodstones. Only those who truly become like the dragon can produce bloodstones. That's you, Astrid.

Norah, a true dragon, had chewed up Astrid in childhood. A few months ago, Astrid had been bitten by a lizard and assumed she would die because dragons and lizards were entirely different creatures. Her recovery from a lizard bite had been impossible. Unheard of. The only explanation seemed to be the presence of the stone of darkness.

But what if the same bloodline that allowed Astrid to survive Norah's bite allowed her to survive a lizard's bite? Wouldn't that explain why Banshi had died?

The stone inside her fist heated up like a piece of iron tucked into a hot blacksmithing fire. Crying out, Astrid jerked her fist free and opened it.

The stone had vanished. A black tattoo in the shape of the stone had burned into Astrid's skin, much like the way her scars formed the shape of a sword's blade down her sternum and spine. Unlike her scars, the stone tattoo ached as if someone had driven a knife through her palm and left it there. Frantic, Astrid looked up at Spathar. "What did you do?"

The gothi smiled briefly and uttered a few words before walking past the women toward the mouth of the cave.

Kikita said, "She said you're welcome."

"I'm *what*?"

Astrid followed Kikita's gaze as she watched Spathar walk out of the cave and disappear around the waterfall. "Perhaps she has given some type of gift to you. Some advantage that you cannot understand until you need it or use it."

Shaking her aching hand, Astrid said, "At least I can't lose the stone now. Mandulane or the Krystr soldiers can't steal it from me."

"Unless they cut off your hand," Kikita said. "And perhaps that would destroy the stone or make it fall out."

"I don't think it's lodged in my hand. I think it's melted into my skin." Astrid blew on her palm, but that only made it hurt more.

"I have an idea. Come with me."

As Astrid followed Kikita toward the mouth of the cave, she noticed the hidden people had removed their few belongings. They'd left behind only the spilled blood of their sacrificial offering. Apparently, the hidden people intended to find a new place to lie low.

Once they reached the slippery rock ledge between the entrance to the cave and the waterfall, Kikita took Astrid's hand and held it under the falling water. Astrid cried out at the painful pressure against her newly injured palm, but Kikita held it firmly against water. Within minutes, the pain faded.

Astrid looked at Kikita in astonishment. "It feels better."

Kikita smiled. "Cold water is good for burns."

They edged their way around the waterfall, wincing at the brightness of the sunlight. When their vision adjusted, they saw the hidden people and Spathar had vanished. Back on the shore of the lake, Komdra stood and spoke to his men, while Hevrick translated for the Midlander Iron Maidens who then relayed the information to the other women.

Astrid and Kikita headed toward them, the Far Easterner straining to hear Hevrick's words but failing because Komdra drowned him out. Finally, the women reached the rest of their group and stood outside it.

Komdra spoke passionately and gestured with his hands. He pointed at the sun, which now skimmed above the western horizon.

Of course. We're at the beginning of summer. In six weeks' time, the sun will set for only a short time in the depths of night and then rise for a very early dawn. Most of each day will be bathed in light.

After Hevrick spoke, Kikita turned to Astrid. "Komdra talks about joining forces with us. He says Mandulane already controls all of the Midlands and most of the Western islands. The Krystr soldiers head now for the Northlands, but Komdra believes we can get there first and spread the word of their coming."

"That's impossible," Astrid said. "The only way is through the Midlands and across the sea. If Mandulane controls the Midlands, how can we possibly travel through them?"

"There is a narrow waterway from the lake to the sea. The hidden people said they and their kind still protect this waterway. They have boats sheltered away that we can use. However…"

Astrid felt a sudden fear creep down her spine. "However?"

Kikita looked into Astrid's eyes with the grimness of a friend preparing to deliver the news of a loved one's death. "The waterway opens onto the sea where islands line the coast. These islands once were home to the hidden people." Kikita took a deep breath. "Now the islands are home to clerks of the Krystr. The only way to cross the sea to the Northlands is to sail within view of a Krystr stronghold."

Chapter Sixty

DiStephan perched on a step high on the stairway that spiraled through the tower. He sighed heavily, reminding himself that the relationship between dragon and dragonslayer always had been fraught with complexity. Why should today be any different?

Fiera worked her sorcery on the step where he rested his feet, taking her own sweet time as always. At this rate, they'd be lucky to free the stairway by winter.

Without warning, the stairway shuddered beneath DiStephan. He looked up to see his own startled feelings reflected on Fiera's face.

"That wasn't your doing?" DiStephan said.

Ignoring him, Fiera called out, "Taddeo!" Her voice rang with an empty tone throughout the tower, but no one responded.

Another shudder shook the stairway hard enough to make DiStephan grasp each side of the step with his ghostly hands, forgetting for the moment that not even a long fall had the power to harm him.

Irritated by Taddeo's failure to answer, Fiera rubbed her palms together quickly. A tiny spark ignited, floating above her cupped hands. She mumbled irritably to herself.

"What is it?" DiStephan said, growing more concerned by the moment. "What's happening?"

Fiera stared into the floating spark, seemingly lost in it.

Footsteps echoed throughout the tower as Taddeo ran down the steps from above. "Fiera? What are you doing?"

DiStephan scooted to one side of his step, even though Taddeo could have simply run through him. DiStephan didn't like the uncomfortable sensation of anything passing through him and avoided it whenever possible. Turning to look back at Taddeo descending the stairs from the doorway to the top of the tower, DiStephan said, "She won't talk to me."

Taddeo sank down on the step to sit next to DiStephan. Puzzled lines creased his face as he watched Fiera and the floating spark above her hands. "Has a mountain spit forth your fire?"

Fiera shook her head. "No more than the ocean crashing with one of your storms." Her eyes widened as the spark exploded and fizzled out, seeming to read a message delivered by it. "The dragon-slayer," Fiera said. "She embraces the stone of darkness."

DiStephan turned to Taddeo. "You said that wouldn't happen."

Ignoring the ghost, Taddeo leaned forward, staring into Fiera's eyes. "Can you be certain?"

Fiera stared back. "Absolutely."

DiStephan fidgeted. "She'll need help. She doesn't know what the stone is or what it means. You have to let me go to her."

Taddeo spoke, his voice wavering slightly. "That is not possible. Fiera needs you here."

"What about what I need? What Astrid needs?"

Taddeo's gaze cooled as he looked at DiStephan. "What sense does it make to put what you need before what we need? Please explain how that will benefit you and your kind."

Of course, DiStephan thought as he felt the ghost of his heart deflate. *He's right. He's always right.*

Out loud he said, "Isn't there anything we can do to help her?"

"Continue with our work here," Taddeo said while Fiera nodded her agreement. Taddeo paused as if pulling a thought deep from his memory. "And have faith that there are others who would help her when she needs it most."

❧❧

Trapped inside the rocky surface of Dragon's Head, Drageen continued to fume. *What I did to Astrid, is what has happened to me. I trapped her just as the curse of the dragons trapped me inside this rock. But I am the leader of the Scaldings! Who else can protect the Northlands?*

Drageen considered everyone in his clan as his kin, along with the thousands of people who worked their lands in the North and depended on the Scaldings for protection. Bloodstones provided the only source of reliable protection in battle. Anyone who bathed in a concoction made of bloodstones could not be wounded over the course of at least a month, sometimes longer. An army of men bathed in bloodstones could easily win any battle or skirmish in far less time.

But producing bloodstones required a certain degree of purity, and Astrid was the last Scalding capable of creating them. Drageen had always suspected their mother had been unfaithful and that unfaithfulness had resulted in his birth. He'd never learned the identity of his blood father and didn't care to know it. Thank the gods he'd been born into the Scalding clan, the wealthiest and most powerful family in all the Northlands. Only a fool would relinquish the Scalding name.

A slight tremor seemed to pass through the rock encasing Drageen's body or spirit or whatever form he took inside Dragon's Head. It felt like a hesitant shudder, like the body's reaction to an unexpected draft of chilly air. If Drageen had been capable of sitting up and taking notice, he would have. Instead, he became keenly alert.

Is change coming? Drageen wondered. *Is there a chance one of the Scaldings will bring a dragon to entrap here and set me free?*

When he was younger, he'd imagined that someday he might need a bloodstone or two that emerged slowly and naturally from Astrid's body for the sake of fighting the dragons that constantly attacked Tower Island before Taddeo set Norah free. But as more and more merchants brought word of the self-made king and the new religion that savaged the Southlands, Drageen saw the obvious. Astrid's bloodstones represented the only hope of defeating such an army. And the only way to harvest the vast number of bloodstones the Scaldings would need to protect the Northlands had meant creating a horrific degree of chaos to scare the bloodstones out of Astrid's body. Unfortunately, that required destruction and mass murder.

But doesn't saving the lives of thousands justify the deaths of a few hundred? Doesn't saving an entire land from invasion and takeover require sacrifice?

The rocky ground around him trembled again, harder this time. Drageen thought he felt something loosen, ever so slightly.

CHAPTER SIXTY-ONE

Below deck, Astrid sat alone on the wooden floor. They'd followed the directions given to them by the hidden people and found this ship sequestered away in an inlet off the lake sheltered by trees. The planks reeked of musty cloth and old potatoes. Several layers of dust covered every surface, making Astrid sneeze every few minutes. She'd found an abandoned cloak and wrapped it around herself like swaddling clothes to ward off the chill.

Normally, Astrid had no use or time to sulk, but tonight she decided to wallow in self-pity while she could. Thorda and the other Iron Maidens acted smitten with the men who had ventured uninvited into their lives. The Midlander women hung on to every word of Hevrick's translation of Komdra's commands. *Komdra says we should risk sailing past a Krystr stronghold to get across the sea and to the Northlands. Komdra says the only people on those islands are weak and insignificant clerks. Komdra says Mandulane has better things to do than go anywhere near such a place. Komdra says we'll be safe.*

Komdra says, Komdra says, Komdra says.

Why were the Iron Maidens listening to *him*?

I'm a dragonslayer. Komdra has been sitting pretty on his little remote island while I've been traveling throughout the lands killing lizards. He's been removed from our world while I've been fighting in the thick of it. He's encountering the Krystr clerks for the first time while I've—

The memory of Margreet punched Astrid like a fist in her stomach. Less than a year ago, when Taddeo told Astrid her duty included traveling the winter route, she'd refused. Back then, Astrid had wanted nothing more than to protect her own people, meaning Northlanders, but with a special emphasis on the village of Guell. Astrid had wanted nothing to do with foreigners. Let them protect themselves.

Meeting and knowing Margreet and Vinchi had changed everything. Astrid would never have guessed she could love people from other countries as much as she loved her own friends in Guell. But it happened. And it made her want to protect all the lands from the terror of the Krystr soldiers and Mandulane's rule. She wanted to protect the Northlands, Midlands, Southlands, Far Eastlands, and even the Western Islands where Komdra came from. And if the map she'd seen at Mandulane's camp illustrated the truth about the expansiveness of the world, she wanted to protect every land in existence.

Astrid removed the pin she wore near her throat. She cupped it in her hands and studied its tree shape. She remembered Limru and the way the Krystr soldiers had destroyed it and tied the bodies of the Keepers of Limru to the outdoor temple's sacred trees. She remembered the day she'd cleaned up the destruction with Vinchi at her side. She remembered the way Margreet had taken the bones of the dead and set their spirits free.

Fighting back tears, Astrid remembered wanting Margreet and Vinchi to live in Guell alongside Lenore and Randim, Trep and Donel, Beamon and Kamella, and all the others. How wonderful it would have been to be with them all in one place. One safe place.

The Krystrs are to blame, Astrid thought as hatefulness twisted like a serpent in her blood. *Margreet died because of the Krystr soldiers. Because of the lies and wickedness they spread. Because of the people they've poisoned.*

She stroked the surface of the pin with her thumb. The pin of the last Keeper of Limru, now dead.

Astrid thought about the Krystr soldiers and clerks and Mandulane. *They deserve to die. They have brought madness upon the world.*

Astrid put the pin back on. She'd dare anyone to look at it and call her a barbarian for wearing it. The Keepers of Limru had died protecting their gods and beliefs. Filled with determination, she vowed to make sure they had not died in vain.

The ship lurched as if steered into a sudden turn.

The hatch door above banged open, and Kikita's voice called down the stairs from the deck above with fear and urgency. "Astrid!"

Jumping to her feet, Astrid pulled Starlight from its sheath and bounded up the stairs.

Chapter Sixty-Two

Starlight drawn and held tightly in her hand, Astrid clambered onto the deck of the ship, squinting as her eyes adjusted to the light. She took a wide stance to steady herself against the gentle pitching of the ship beneath her feet. A chilly wind whipped across her face, and a spray of sea mist stung her eyes, making them water.

Then she smelled smoke.

The Iron Maidens and Komdra's men shouted as they ran to one side of the ship. Astrid followed, noticing the sun skimmed the horizon, indicating a late-night hour at this yearly season of perpetual twilight.

When her eyes finally adjusted to the light, Astrid felt stunned to see how close they sailed to a long and narrow island dominated by a stone mansion large enough to put any others to shame. Her stomach twisted when she recognized brown-cloaked clerks lined on the beach, torches in hand.

"They see us! We have to sail faster," Astrid said to anyone who would listen.

But no one did. Komdra climbed atop a barrel near the mast and clung to it as he shouted orders. His men scrambled to grip the oars at the ship's sides, and the Iron Maidens followed suit until all the rowing seats filled.

Good. The sooner we get out of here, the better.

Instead, the ship began to pivot toward the island's shore.

"No!" Astrid shouted, running toward Komdra with Starlight still in hand. "What are you doing?"

Komdra climbed down from the barrel and placed a firm hand on her shoulder.

Looking into his eyes, she thought she saw genuine affection as he clapped her back and said something she couldn't understand before shouting more instructions to the men and women.

"This is madness!" Astrid said as she followed Komdra. Spotting Hevrick sitting on the outer side of a bench as he rowed, Astrid tried to reason with the man, forgetting he spoke the Midlander language, not Northlander. "Don't you understand?" she shouted at Hevrick. "All we have to do is sail past the island! They won't be able to reach us in time. There's no need to do this!"

Hevrick gave her a puzzled look for a moment, and then returned his full attention to rowing.

"We'll be ashore in moments!" Astrid called out to anyone who could understand her. "Back up!"

Astrid lost her balance and struggled to stay on her feet as the ship slid onto the island beach, the sand grating loudly below. Before she realized what had happened, clerks climbed over the railing and onto the deck, flaming torches in hand.

Komdra shouted, and his men drew their swords and axes, immediately attacking the clerks.

"No," Astrid whispered. "This can't be happening."

The air filled with shouts, swinging weapons, and the slick scent of blood. Frozen with fear, Astrid clutched Starlight's grip with both white-knuckled hands, keeping its point in front of her in case she had to defend herself. Slowly backing away from the chaos unfolding all around her, Astrid grew numb. Maybe she could hide below. Maybe she could crawl into a corner. Maybe she could—

Kikita cried out, and Astrid turned to see a scowling clerk grab the Iron Maiden by her hair. He grabbed the ax from her hand and aimed its sharp blade at her throat.

Before she realized it, Astrid took a few quick steps and then ran Starlight's blade through the clerk's back.

He paused as if unsure what had just happened. When he looked down at the tip of the sword emerging from his chest, his grip on Kikita's ax loosened, and she snatched it back from him. The clerk pulled himself free from the blade, struggling toward the railing and leaning over it as his blood stained the deck.

With all her might, Astrid shoved him over, satisfied when she heard his body hit the beach below.

For a moment, she looked up and met Kikita's steady and determined gaze.

As shouting and chaos continued with each man and woman fighting the attackers on the ship's deck, Astrid looked for the next clerk to kill.

CHAPTER SIXTY-THREE

Hours later, Astrid stood alone on the island's beach, surrounded by the slain bodies of more than a hundred Krystr clerks. The frigid seawater lapped back and forth across her feet, sunk into the coarse wet sand. Each gentle wave shocked her like a slap across the face, icy and unrelenting.

The horizon glowed with early morning light, and the sun would soon crawl higher in the sky. Already, the air seemed to grow warm, although Astrid felt numb and cold.

Seabirds screamed as they whirled in the sky above the beach. It wouldn't be long before distant carrion birds picked up the scent of death in the wind and hastened to come for the feast.

With a sudden chill, Astrid wondered if any lizards lurked on the island. Looking over her shoulder, she saw nothing but the stone mansion and Kikita standing at its entrance.

No, Astrid realized. *Any lizard living on this island would have come by now.*

Like carrion birds, lizards could detect the scent of a fresh kill from far away. Twice each year, lizards swam across the sea separating the Northlands from the Midlands, so the shallowness of this water's passageway would pose no challenge to them.

And considering that many lizards were likely in the middle of their spring migration, dozens of them could arrive within a few hours.

"We have to leave," Astrid whispered, looking across the water to the wild and untamed Midland shore.

A stirring on the beach caught her attention. Among the slain clerks bloodying the sand and sea, a young man raised his head and gazed cautiously all around him.

Astrid froze when their eyes met across the stark distance between them. The young clerk froze as well, like a spider she'd once caught crawling up her arm as she awoke one morning long ago.

Instead of killing it, she'd blown it off her arm and onto the dirt floor, letting it skitter away.

What have I become? Astrid thought, remembering the blood she'd drawn, suddenly afraid of herself.

Before she could take another breath, the young clerk scrambled to his feet, and Astrid could see his brown robe soaked in blood. He stumbled toward the incoming tide, and threw himself into the narrow stretch of seaway that separated the island from the Midlands mainland.

The young clerk moved as if his life hung by a thread. He'd probably drown within minutes.

Shame washed over her. Astrid turned her back to the seaway. She couldn't bear to watch another clerk die.

Facing the stone mansion, she called out, "Kikita! We have to leave!"

Kikita waved her understanding and vanished inside the mansion.

Astrid walked into the seawater until it reached her chin, begging the water to wash away all the blood. She opened her mouth to wash out the iron taste of it. She scrubbed her arms and clothes on her body, shivering as the water stained red around her. When she couldn't take the cold any longer, she backed up to the beach to let the weak sun dry her.

She didn't want to look at the landscape of death behind her. She didn't want to think about what had just happened. So she kept her feet where the tide could keep washing them clean, minute after minute. She stared at the Midlands shore, keeping one hand resting around Starlight's hilt in case the lizards came.

Several minutes later, Kikita joined Astrid's side. "They will join us soon," Kikita said. "They have been thorough."

"Why did we come so close to the island?" Astrid said quietly. "Why did we provoke the clerks?"

"Opportunity." Kikita spoke in an even tone and without regret. "Komdra learned that Mandulane is secreting Krystr clerks away on islands to protect the hordes of treasure they've stolen. Komdra believes we will need every advantage to defeat them. Gold and jewels will give us finance for the days ahead and weaken Mandulane's resources."

"Is that why they fought? Why they climbed on board our ship?"

"I imagine fighting us might be less daunting than the wrath of Mandulane after failing to protect his wealth."

Astrid stared at the bloodied beach. "Should we do something about the bodies? Burn them? Bury them? Cover them with stones?"

"Komdra says no. He says leave them."

Astrid swallowed hard. "Lizards will find them. You know what will happen."

Kikita nodded. "Everyone knows what will happen."

"And then the carrion birds will come. When the lizards have finished, the birds will fly the bones high up in the air, drop them on the beach, and then eat the marrow out of them when they shatter."

"Komdra knows. He says let it be a message to Mandulane and the Krystr soldiers."

Astrid nodded. She'd thought as much. "We should leave now, before the lizards come."

"I know." Kikita looked over her shoulder toward the stone mansion. "They know, as well."

Astrid heard them chattering and laughing in the distance. Komdra and his men, along with the Iron Maidens. A few had been injured during the battle with the Krystr clerks, but none had died or been seriously injured.

That came as no surprise. After all, none of the clerks had held weapons, unless a torch could be counted as one. They had killed a small army of unarmed men.

As if reading Astrid's face, Kikita said, "They attacked us. They could have let us pass in peace."

"We had time to sail away. We could have simply left them behind."

Kikita sighed. "Yes. And they would have sent word to Mandulane, who might then have cut us off before we could reach the Northlands."

"Or perhaps not."

A throng of Komdra's men and Iron Maidens rushed past Astrid and Kikita, their arms full of colorful cloth and hearty vegetables and silver bracelets, most likely stolen from Midlanders and traveling Northlanders who wore their wealth on their arms. As they piled happily back onto the ship with their bounty, Komdra strolled up next to Astrid. He carried a wooden box made in the same shape of the stone mansion and painted to look like it.

Grinning, Komdra opened the lid to show Astrid and Kikita its contents: silver and gold ingots, coins, and jewelry, as well as precious gems.

Staring in disbelief, Astrid murmured, "That must be worth a fortune."

Komdra giggled like a young girl in love for the first time. Replacing the lid, he placed the box on the sand, careful to keep it out of path of the incoming tide. He removed a silver brooch holding his shirt together at his neck and handed it to Astrid.

"He is grateful to you," Kikita said.

Astrid stared at the silver brooch he placed in the palm of her hand. Made of thin strands of silver, the brooch took the shape of a dragon surrounded by two snakes. When Komdra purchased Lenore as a slave from Drageen's brigands, Astrid struck a bargain to buy back her friend's freedom. She made a short sword for Komdra, the same one he still used today, and sealed the deal when she handed over this brooch at his request. Komdra had seen how much she valued it. Many years ago, the blacksmith Temple had made this brooch for DiStephan in appreciation when the dragonslayer killed the lizard that had killed Temple's daughter. When Astrid first met DiStephan, he'd given this brooch to her as a silent message when the childseller peddled Astrid in Guell. As soon as Temple saw she held the brooch he'd given to DiStephan, the blacksmith bought Astrid. If not for this brooch, Astrid realized she'd never have become a blacksmith, much less a dragonslayer. If not for this brooch, she might have died all those years ago.

Astrid pinned it to her own shirt, next to the Keeper of Limru pin Margreet had given to her after they'd restored that temple.

Komdra nodded his happy approval and then spoke briefly. He picked up his treasure chest and boarded the ship with it.

Kikita followed, gesturing for Astrid to come with her.

But Astrid stood still, Komdra's words still ringing in her ears. Years ago when she'd first met him on his home island, she'd learned a few words of his language. Until now, she'd forgotten everything she'd learned.

Slaughter Island.

From his words and joyful grin, Astrid realized he had taken it upon himself to name this spit of land.

Taking one last look across the water at the wild Midlands coast,

Astrid took care not to focus on the dozens of slain clerks littering the beach when she ran to keep up with the others. A sudden movement in the bushes lining the Midlands coast startled her, as if someone or something had just run through them. Letting her gaze drift across the sea, Astrid realized she saw no sign of the injured young clerk who had thrown himself into the water.

CHAPTER SIXTY-FOUR

It took less than a day for the ship to sail through the narrow passageway between the western shores of the Midlands and the chain of islands off its coast. The passageway then opened up into the broad and choppy sea separating the Midlands from the Northlands. The sun beat down so strongly that Komdra's men stripped off their shirts, revealing muscles that rippled like waves across the sea. Weathered lines creased their brown faces, but their chests and backs were smooth and pale from the long winter now behind them.

Astrid stood at the railing, staring at the rhythmic movement of the sea, feeling its presence while it rocked the creaking wooden boards beneath her feet. Her mouth felt dry from the salt spray she'd unintentionally swallowed.

She stood with the wind in her face to carry away the lingering stench of blood. No matter how hard she'd scrubbed her skin with the seawater on the beach of Slaughter Island, the blood of the clerks she'd killed remained in her hair, her clothes, and the pores of her skin.

Kikita joined her side. "They are ready."

Astrid nodded, and the two women crossed the deck and walked down the stairs to the lower deck. A sudden draft kicked up a stale but pungent scent of horse musk. Even though they'd brought no animals with them, Astrid knew many men often sailed with horses tied up on the lower deck. Although the floor had been swept clean, she imagined bits of hay used to keep the floors tidy had probably fallen into crevices between the planks, keeping the scent embedded in the ship's flesh.

Komdra and Hevrick perched on a couple of barrels, laughing loudly as they seemed to reminisce about better days. They looked up, smiling, as the women walked before them.

"I have a plan," Astrid said. "At this time of year, lizards are entering the Northlands. They are likely finishing their swim across the sea and stepping on shore as we speak. We will land while they are still near the shores. Why not drive them back and use them to guard against the Krystr invasion?"

Kikita stared at Astrid for a moment. "Use them?"

"Yes."

Kikita relayed Astrid's idea. Hevrick translated for Komdra, and both men shared another laugh. After another chain of translations, Kikita turned to Astrid. "They think you've gone mad."

"Nonsense. It's a good plan."

"How do you plan to control the lizards?" Kikita said dryly.

"We could build a great wall to fence them in. Or we could chain and collar them. We could stake the chains to the ground and give them enough lead to cover a good amount of territory."

"It would take the entire population of the Northlands a year to build such a wall. And probably just as long to forge chains long enough for the lizards to roam and strong enough to keep them staked to the ground. I simply do not see how any of this is possible, and neither does Komdra."

Astrid considered Kikita's words. The Iron Maiden probably spoke the truth. As much as Astrid longed to harness the power of lizards and use them against Mandulane and his Krystr soldiers, the task seemed impossible. "Then what are we going to do?"

Komdra spoke solemnly as Hevrick listened and then translated for Kikita.

"Komdra says we should split up," Kikita told Astrid. "Once we arrive in the Northlands, we can form small groups. There are enough Iron Maidens who speak either Northlander or Midlander so that each group can spread the word about the inevitability of the Krystr invasion. Instead of trying to line the coasts of the Northlands with dragons, we can line it with men from throughout the Northlands. We can stop the Krystrs as soon as they attempt to invade."

Of course. Many Northlanders in the southern region speak Midlander. The groups with a Midlander speaker can cover the lower Northlands while the rest of us can travel through the upper Northlands.

"All right," Astrid said. "But tell Komdra one more thing."

Kikita spoke of the decision to Hevrick, and then waited for Astrid to speak again.

"Tell everyone that I will no longer kill lizards and that they should do the same unless they're attacked by a lizard and have no choice but to defend themselves." Astrid took a deep breath. She wondered if she questioned her own decision but spoke it out loud before she could change her mind. "I believe the Northlanders are better served by leaving them at risk of a lizard attack in the hopes that lizards may attack the Krystr soldiers instead."

When Komdra understood Astrid's words, he laughed once more and clapped her back heartily as he replied.

Kikita hesitated before making the translation. "Komdra says you are no longer a dragonslayer but now a slayer of men, like him."

Astrid wanted to say she was merely a blacksmith, but the words wouldn't come. Her hand, the one that had absorbed the stone of darkness, throbbed as an icy chill spread like frost throughout her body.

Komdra was right. Astrid had become a slayer of men.

After all these years had her heritage finally caught up with her?

What if she was no better than the rest of the Scaldings?

What if she'd been right all those years ago when she believed herself to be nothing more than a monster?

A startled cry from one of Komdra's men broke her concentration, and Astrid looked up to see a foreign ship cutting off their path.

The foreign ship bore the wide white sail with an image of a fish whose tail had been cut and formed into legs by the Krystr god.

CHAPTER SIXTY-FIVE

Mandulane stood in the middle of his ship as it cut cleanly through the sea toward the vessel carrying rebels. He loved battle because it called for his finest clothes. This morning he'd taken his time dressing and selecting his garb. Black leather shoes fastened with polished buckles, made by the finest cobbler in the Southlands. Billowy dark red pants imported from the Far East, sashed in matching material. A well-fitting linen shirt. A long, flowing black cloak fastened to his shoulders with a row of silver broaches, fashioned by the craftsmen of the Northlands and fancifully shaped like the dragons they so feared. And over the sleeves of his shirt, Mandulane wore dozens of silver bracelets on his upper arms and forearms, announcing to the world his wealth and power.

"Unscar!" he shouted, while keeping an eye on the ship ahead.

"Yes, your lordship!" the young soldier called out as he raced across the rocking deck. Moments later, he knelt as Mandulane's feet.

"Is that the one?"

"I believe so. Yes, sir!" Unscar stared at the wooden floorboards. "The clerk is dead, but he claimed to see many women with swords and axes fighting alongside the men from the Western Islands. They must be the same women I encountered. And that dragonslayer woman."

Mandulane grunted. In truth, the morning's breakfast continued to disagree with him, but he enjoyed the way his grunt made the young man at his feet squirm. "I imagine this is proof they still live."

Unscar trembled. "Those women looked dead at the time, your lordship."

"Fine," Mandulane shouted as the wind whipped around him, making his fine red pants dance around his legs. He closed his eyes briefly at the pleasure of the feel of the silky cloth against his skin. Going into battle always provided a fine excuse to parade about in eye-catching fashion.

"I guess they were just pretending to be dead. But those dragons were real, and they killed your soldiers."

Had there been no wind, Mandulane would have spat at the reminder that a ragtag band of women who believed themselves to be warriors had claimed responsibility for killing Krystr soldiers. The very idea was an affront against the Krystr god himself. "Never mind," Mandulane said. "Rise to your feet and make your weapon ready."

The two ships collided with a loud crash. Unscar jumped up and followed the other soldiers as they stormed aboard the enemy ship. Mandulane smiled with approval. Chaotic shouts rose above the waves slapping against the sides of each vessel. Mandulane strolled toward the bow of his own ship and watched the battle unfold before him, especially delighted when one of his men delivered blows at women who dared to think so high and mighty of themselves.

"Chop them down to size," he said.

Unscar's heart raced as he jumped onto the enemy ship. Buoyed by waves, its deck rose to meet his feet sooner than he expected, and the sudden impact jammed his ankles. Unscar cried out from the pain and dropped to his knees. His fellow soldiers, as always, had each found an enemy to fight one-on-one. He quickly scanned the deck and saw a nearby woman taking an ax from underneath her belt and eyeballing the back of a Krystr soldier already embattled with an islander man.

Without taking the time to rise to his feet, Unscar threw his body forward, grabbed the woman's ankles, and jerked her legs out from under her. She gasped as she fell, and the impact of her body on the deck jarred her enough to loosen her grip on the ax. Unscar yanked it from her hand and then buried its blade in her stomach. Her scream reminded him of sheep at slaughter time.

Ignoring the pain in his ankles, Unscar teetered as he rose, looking for the next place where he could be useful. Hearing the moan of a man behind him, Unscar turned to see a fellow Krystr soldier fall as a woman withdrew her sword from his chest. Before she noticed Unscar's presence, he knocked her sword aside and tackled her. She cried out as he scrambled up to pin one knee against her chest and the other against her arm holding the sword.

She struggled but couldn't move under Unscar's weight. He wrenched the sword out of her hands and into both of his. Before he could drive the blade down toward her throat, she bashed the side of his head with her free fist.

Shaken by the blow, Unscar maintained his grip on the sword with one hand while pinning her arms to the deck. It took all his strength to keep the thrashing woman under the weight of his body, but he finally managed to drive the pointed tip of her sword through the base of her throat.

The ship pitched, making Unscar take care in rising to his feet as he looked for his next target. But when he recognized Mandulane's throaty yell, Unscar looked up sharply and back at his ship in search of his master. Unscar stared in horror at the sight of a woman aboard Mandulane's ship, clinging to the rigging as she lifted her body and kicked Mandulane squarely in the chest with both feet.

"Mandulane!" Unscar shrieked.

The force of the woman's kick propelled Mandulane over the side of his ship and into the sea below.

"No!" Unscar yelled as he ran to the side of the enemy ship. Looking down, he saw Mandulane bob above the water's surface for one moment only to disappear the next. Unscar faced Mandulane's men and called out, "Fall back! Mandulane is fallen! Fall back!"

A nearby soldier who had just killed an islander man looked up and picked up Unscar's order. "Fall back!" the soldier called to his peers. "Mandulane is fallen!"

Unscar hauled himself onto the ship's side and then hurled himself into the sea below.

※※

As Mandulane slowly regained consciousness, he instinctively batted the air in front of him, filled with the terror of drowning. But when he saw the faces of his soldiers hovering above his, he pretended to reach for an imaginary hand to help him rise.

Quickly, Unscar extended his and Mandulane accepted it.

Mandulane's head swam and the world went fuzzy for a few moments. He allowed Unscar to help him sit up. "What happened?" Mandulane said.

"Unscar saved your life," an unfamiliar voice answered.

Mandulane didn't worry that he hadn't recognize the soldier's voice. He depended on their simple uniforms to identify them as his own men. He rarely recognized individual faces or voices. But he did recognize Unscar as the one man who for a while had successfully tracked the dragonslayer woman that had escaped Mandulane's camp, as well as the self-important women who helped her.

When Mandulane shivered, someone quickly placed a blanket around his shoulders. His nose wrinkled at its distasteful odor and coarse texture. Like smelling salts, the foul smell cleared his senses immediately. "Did you steal this from the back of a donkey?"

The men surrounding him paled, their eyes widening with fear. And yet Unscar had the audacity to speak with a soothing tone of voice. "You could have drowned. We simply want you to stay well and keep from catching ill."

Mandulane struggled to his feet, and the Krystr soldiers stood with him. Only Unscar dared to lend a helping hand to Mandulane's elbow when he teetered for a moment.

Mandulane took the offensive blanket off his shoulders and threw it to the ground. The sea wind made him shiver and realize his clothes were soaked. His voice sank in disappointment. "Look at these pants! They are ruined. Completely ruined. And I acquired them only a week ago." Mandulane reached down to the wet fabric, moaning in deeper disappointment when the dye left his hands red. "Perhaps they can be salvaged once they dry." He examined his chest. "What happened to my shirt? It's streaked with black! Is that from my cloak?"

But when Mandulane reached back, he felt nothing draped behind him. In fact, when the chill wind blew, it seemed to cut through his clothes to his damp skin. In a tone as icy as the breeze raising his flesh, Mandulane said, "Where is my cloak?"

After a stretch of silence, Unscar cleared his throat. "It wrapped itself around you and would have pulled you into the depths of the sea like a monster. I had to pull it off you."

At first, Mandulane assumed he'd misheard the soldier. "My cloak is gone? It cannot be gone. How is that possible?"

The other soldiers backed away from Unscar.

"Your cloak would have killed you," Unscar explained. "Your life is what matters."

Mandulane shivered just as his attendant arrived with a dry cloak in his arms. It was simple and for everyday wear, not the fine, rich cloak he'd saved for battle wear. While his attendant arranged the everyday cloak across his shoulders, Mandulane said, "It was my best cloak. A very expensive one. Pinned with my finest silver broaches. I suppose the broaches are lost as well. And look! The silver I wore on my arms is missing."

"Yes, and I'm sorry for the loss," Unscar said. "But you are more important than anything you might purchase."

Mandulane nodded. "Of course. I should count my blessings that we have defeated the enemy and taken their ship. Perhaps they have something worthwhile on board."

The other soldiers took another step back from Unscar.

Mandulane took a few steps away from them and scanned the sea surrounding his ship, only to spot the rebel ship sailing away in the distance.

"I killed two of the women," Unscar said hopefully. "And a few of the islander men were killed. Not all of them escaped with their lives."

"Not all of them," Mandulane murmured dreamily. He pointed at Unscar. "On your knees."

Unscar obeyed.

Mandulane circled him slowly. "Lie with your face on the floor."

With his face twisted and red, Unscar obeyed again.

Mandulane grabbed the hilt of a sword sheathed to the nearest Krystr soldier, ripped the sword free, and yelled as he delivered a forceful overhead blow that cut off Unscar's head.

Handing the sword back to its rightful owner, Mandulane said to his stunned soldiers, "Clean that up."

As they scrambled to follow his orders, Mandulane stood at the ship's side, watching the enemy sail out of sight.

Enjoy your freedom while you have it. Because it will not last much longer.

CHAPTER SIXTY-SIX

Komdra believed the Krystr soldiers would most likely strike the Northlands through its busiest port of Gott. To reach it, Komdra's men sailed diagonally across the sea from the Southwest to the Northeast, taking two days to cross the water. During that time, they saw no sign of Krystr vessels. Having the seas to themselves, they gave appropriate ocean burials to Jewely, Efflin, and the islander men who had been killed by Mandulane's Krystr soldiers.

Flanked by the Iron Maidens, Komdra, and his men, Astrid walked through the bustling village on a long and wide walkway of wooden boards that ran parallel to the sea. Komdra's men had tethered their ship between dozens of others that filled the docks next to the walkway. Astrid suppressed a chill at the sight of the crates and goods set up in front of each merchant ship, forming the marketplace opposite rows of wooden houses jammed against each other. Here, she had first met Margreet and Vinchi a year ago last winter, and the sudden memory of walking the boards where they'd met made Astrid's heart ache with bitterness and regret. They'd understood the danger but had failed to elude it.

Astrid scanned the faces of the merchants selling their wares to the townspeople. She caught herself looking for Vinchi's familiar face and then silently scolded herself. Vinchi had returned home to his native Southlands and now spent his days teaching his fellow countrymen and women how to protect themselves from the Krystr soldiers. Vinchi would never come to Gott again. Remembering Mandulane's map, she realized Vinchi's home had probably been overrun by Krystr soldiers by now. She wondered if he still lived.

Astrid caught sight of someone and froze, oblivious as the Iron Maidens and men walked past her.

In front of a ship with a tattered and stained sail stood a broad and tall man who had the large, meaty hands of a butcher, sorting through his pile of furs on the crates in front of him. Astrid remembered that he'd once sported an unkempt yellow beard, although his face was now as bare as his shaved head.

Gershon. Margreet's husband.

Astrid swiftly drew Starlight from its sheath as she shouted, "Murderer!"

❧❧

Although Astrid kept her gaze fixed on Gershon, she sensed the Iron Maidens and Komdra's men closing rank behind her. Taking one hand off of Starlight's grip, Astrid pointed at Gershon. "Murderer!" she shouted again, tears welling in her eyes.

Gershon's eyebrows drew together in anger as his potential customers backed away from his displayed furs. Seeing Astrid pointing at him, Gershon pointed back. "Lie!" he shouted.

Gripping Starlight with both hands again, Astrid strode toward him, keeping her sword's tip pointed at him as everyone in the marketplace backed up to form a circle around them. "Krystr!" she shouted.

Gershon recoiled as if she'd slapped him across the face. "No!" Gershon bellowed. "No Krystr!" He slammed his open palms down on the crate's surface, and the furs piled on top of it trembled. He grimaced as if disgusted by the accusation.

Astrid narrowed her eyes, staring into his as she held Starlight steady, ready to slice him into pieces. "Killer!"

Startled by the accusation, Gershon returned her stare, searching her eyes until his face hardened with suspicion. "No weapon," he said evenly, holding up his empty hands as proof. "Work. No fight. Live in peace."

His words only served to enrage Astrid deeper. "I saw you murder Margreet!" she screamed.

Gershon's suspicious expression fell away, replaced by astonishment. He studied Astrid's face, only to look confused and bewildered as he struggled to recognize her. "Trial," Gershon said, his voice softer now. "Fair fight."

Of course, Astrid realized. *He doesn't recognize me. He's never been able to see the results of shapeshifting because he doesn't drink lizard blood or eat its meat. He met me as a one-armed boy covered in scars. This is the first time he's seen me since Norah restored my arm and rid me of my scars forever. Gershon doesn't know who I am.*

Before Gershon could blink, Astrid took a few quick steps and struck the crate between them with her sword, wood cracking loudly as the blade split the crate open. Wrenching the sword free, she pressed its tip against his nose. He stood frozen in place as Astrid said, "Do you remember me now?"

Gershon stared into Astrid's eyes. His face sagged in resignation. Still bewildered, he finally seemed to recognize her. "Margreet friend," he said. "You and Vinchi."

Astrid nodded. "You were her husband. You were supposed to love her. Protect her. You were supposed to keep her from harm." Astrid paused, taking a deep breath and focusing on her hatred of Gershon instead of her love for Margreet. "But you beat her. You drove her away from you."

"You steal Margreet," Gershon said, his voice soft and quiet. "She no leave."

"To save her from you!" Astrid cried. "To keep her alive. And in the end she wanted to stay with us, not you." Taking another deep breath, she added, "She chose us to be her family, not you."

Instead of continuing in broken Northlander, Gershon spoke rapidly in his native Midlander language. Having no idea what he said but convinced he was scrambling to gain sympathy from the crowd surrounding them, Astrid stood her ground, shouting, "Liar!"

Flushing with rage, Gershon placed his meaty hands on the remains of the crate before him and ripped it apart, throwing the shards to either side. He pushed Starlight's blade away. Astrid dropped and then circled the sword above her shoulder, bringing it down to rest against his neck. Gershon stopped, breathing heavily with frustration. Staring into Astrid's eyes, he said, "Love Margreet." Tears burst from his eyes and ran down his cheeks. "Miss Margreet. Every day."

Before she could slit his throat, Astrid found herself pulled back by the Iron Maidens flanking her.

On her right, Kikita dug her fingers into Astrid's biceps, holding her back from Gershon. "He claims it was a trial by combat," Kikita said. "Word of this trial spread throughout the Midlands as well as the Southlands. Everyone knows of it. Even Vinchi says it was a true and legal battle."

Astrid struggled only to find more Iron Maidens holding her back.

"No!" Astrid cried out. "She did nothing to harm him! She was innocent!"

Kikita frowned. "It was combat. Margreet had a weapon."

Ignoring her, Astrid's chest heaved as she struggled against the hands holding her back. "He could have just left."

"In the eyes of the law," Kikita said, "he did nothing wrong. If you want to fight him, you must challenge him."

"Have you forgotten what the Krystrs did to Efflin?" Astrid cried. "To Jewely? He did the same to Margreet. He's a killer! A monster!"

A slow trickle of blood stained Gershon's shirt from where Starlight's tip had nicked his neck, but he took no notice of it. "Monster," he said, considering the word. Still weeping, he took a long look at Starlight. His face softened, as if the world suddenly made sense to him. Shifting his gaze to Astrid, he said, "Dragonslayer."

"Yes," she said as the Iron Maidens continued holding her back. "I kill lizards. But I can kill monsters, too."

Gershon nodded slowly. Sweeping his arm across another crate to clear away the displayed furs, he then knelt and put his head on the crate. He spread his arms out to either side, seemingly waiting for execution.

Astrid's heart flamed with elation.

"That is not why we are here," Kikita said as she and the Iron Maidens pulled Astrid farther away.

"The law is the law. And we all obey it." Thorda gently pried Astrid's fingers from Starlight's hilt. "Do not be like him," Thorda said.

Astrid shook with rage when she saw Komdra and Hevrick approach Gershon and speak with him.

She turned her attention to Thorda, suddenly hating the Iron Maiden. "Who are you," Astrid said slowly, "to tell me not to kill?"

Chapter Sixty-Seven

"Gershon was in league with the Krystrs," Astrid said, trying to calm herself in an effort to be heard. "You killed the Krystr clerks easily enough. Why not kill Gershon, too?"

Gershon stood from the crate where he'd knelt to offer Astrid the opportunity to cut off his head. Now flanked by Komdra and Hevrick, he listened closely as they spoke to him in the Midlander language.

"This not battle," Thorda said in a soothing voice. "This is village. We keep peace here." She placed an equally soothing hand on Astrid's shoulder.

Astrid shoved Thorda's touch off angrily. "Then you're putting all our lives in danger. Have you forgotten that Mandulane's men murdered Efflin and Jewely and some of Komdra's men? What makes you think he won't try to murder the rest of us?"

Kikita eased her way to stand between Astrid and a teary-eyed Thorda. "There is only one of him," Kikita said. "And there are still many of us."

"What if he murders us in our sleep?" Astrid shouted, pointing an accusing finger at Gershon.

"That will not happen," Kikita said. "We have safety in our own numbers and those of Komdra. Gershon cannot harm us."

"But he could betray us. What do you think will stop him from telling Mandulane?"

Astrid struggled to keep what she had left of her composure, worried as Kikita and Thorda exchanged doubting glances. Kikita then called out a question in Midlander to Hevrick, who answered with a nod.

"Gershon no longer follows the Krystrs," Kikita said. "He could face his own danger by approaching Mandulane."

Astrid learned that Gershon did not want to stay on the coast and join the ranks of Northlander men preparing to fight the inevitable Krystr invasion. Instead, he agreed to spread the word as he journeyed throughout the Northlands, selling his goods.

The morning Gershon left, Astrid stalked him, convinced he could not be trusted. Unable to sleep, she rose before the others and waited outside the home where Gershon boarded. But before he exited the house, a hand clapped Astrid's shoulder. Jumping in surprise, Astrid turned to see Komdra standing behind her.

Komdra squeezed her shoulder, his brow knotted with worry as he shook his head.

Astrid jerked herself free from his touch. She crossed her arms.

Komdra sighed in resignation and called out, "Kikita!" Moments later, the Iron Maiden appeared carrying a basket of fresh food she must have just purchased.

"Leave me alone," Astrid whispered.

Komdra pointed at the house, gave Kikita a knowing glance, and said, "Gershon."

"Gershon can't be trusted," Astrid explained.

Kikita seemed to weigh her words before offering them. "So you plan to murder him? How will you pay for that crime? By handing over your sword? Do you have any other means to pay the fine for killing a man? Or have you forgotten the consequences for murder in your homeland?"

A chill overcame Astrid. Kikita spoke the truth. Killing Gershon would be cold-blooded murder. By law, Astrid would have to confess to killing him and pay a hefty fine for her crime. And killing Gershon wouldn't bring Margreet back to life.

What is happening to me?

"Will you stay with me to make sure he leaves this morning, as he said he would?" she said.

Kikita nodded.

Although Komdra didn't understand their words, he also stayed until Gershon left that morning, and Astrid felt the islander's sharp gaze upon her the entire time.

The Iron Maidens, Komdra, and his men formed small groups to travel first to well populated sections of the Northlands then work their way to smaller regions.

Astrid agreed to travel with Kikita only, feeling disenchanted by the others after their encounter with Gershon. Afterwards, they'd looked at Astrid with no attempt to hide their horror and concern.

Hypocrites.

She hated them for choosing to kill the Krystr clerks instead of sailing away from them, and she hated herself for becoming one of them.

But most of all, she hated Mandulane, his soldiers, and everyone who had decided to force their new god down the throats of others. If not for Krystr, none of this would have happened. If not for Krystr, DiStephan would still be alive, and she'd be living the happy life of a blacksmith in Guell among the people she loved.

At least she would see them soon. With Kikita at her side, Astrid hiked the familiar mountains between the port village of Gott and the path that would lead her home.

⁂

Days later, Astrid and Kikita walked in silence on a forest path. The hot summer sun shone brightly through patches in the canopy of trees above, flanked by patches of clouds. A light rain pattered loudly against the leaves, and a few warm drops slipped beyond the leaves to land on the women's skin.

Suddenly, three young lizards bounded into sight from around a bend in the path. In a heartbeat, they neared Astrid, raised themselves on their hind legs, and leaned upon her. For the first time in many days, Astrid laughed as their weight made them all collapse to the ground. "Smoke," she said in delight as the lizards regrouped to curl around her. "Fire. Slag."

Kikita stood nearby, smiling as she crossed her arms. "You have the most unusual friends."

Astrid scratched each young lizard's nose as she rose to her feet. "I don't understand why they're here. We saw them weeks ago. It makes sense they migrated north and swam across the sea between here and the Midlands. It's what all lizards do at this time of year. But it's peculiar to find them here, unless they're returning to where they hatched." Suddenly concerned, she stared at the animals. "What have you done?"

The lizards' jaws hung open, full of sharp teeth and deadly spittle, as if smiling.

Astrid broke into a run, and the lizards and Kikita followed.

Smoke, Fire, and Slag launched themselves past the women and reached the gates of Guell first.

Astrid paused, remembering the day Trep had brought her to the new gates of the fence built by the blacksmiths to surround and protect Guell from anyone or anything that might harbor the intention of harm. Long iron pikes forged by Randim and his men stood inches away from each other in a row, shackled together to form the fence. But the sight that still chilled her to this day was the hundreds of bone fragments bound to the fence and gates by thin ribbons of iron. When the blacksmiths had created this fence, the ghosts of those murdered in Guell by Drageen and his men volunteered their bones to frighten intruders away.

Seeming to smile joyfully at Astrid, the lizards sank into a happy pile in front of the gates.

Astrid's heart leaped at the sound of a familiar voice.

"Miss Dragonslayer?"

Chapter Sixty-Eight

Donel, the seventeen-year-old butcher's boy who had become Astrid's blacksmithing apprentice, unlocked the gates and eased them open an inch or so. Although he'd grown even taller since she'd last seen him in the fall, he'd kept his berry-brown hair short and let it naturally curl like wood shavings. He kept a cautious eye on the young lizards resting outside them. "Watch out for the dragons, Ma'am. Better get your sword out."

Astrid laughed. "It's all right, Donel. I know these dragons. I saved them from being eaten by a lizard when they were hatching. They know me. They remember me."

Donel's fingers curled tightly around the bars of the gates. "They came here some days ago and won't leave."

Astrid knelt by the pile of young lizards and patted Smoke's head. "They hatched just outside of Guell. I suspect they consider this their home just as much as any of us do."

"I see," Donel said, still clinging to the gates and keeping them mostly closed. "But don't you think we're surrounded by enough dragons already? We've got Dragon's Head to the west, and there's no telling how many dragons are swarming that place right now. Do we need more dragons at our gates?"

Astrid patted Smoke until the young lizard fell asleep, breathing so heavily and rhythmically that his siblings dozed off, too. Rising to her feet, Astrid spoke softly to keep from waking them. "The only people I've seen them attack were men who tried to kill us." She gestured to Kikita. "This is my friend. She's an Iron Maiden."

Donel frowned as he gazed suspiciously from the sleeping lizards to Kikita, who stood quietly behind Astrid. "What did you say she is?"

"Let us in, Donel, and then gather everyone up. It's time for us to talk."

❧❧

Word spread quickly throughout Guell of Astrid's return and the Far Eastern woman who traveled by her side. With Kikita's assistance, Astrid built a large fire in the center of the village, and the townspeople brought root vegetables and grains and a large iron cauldron filled with fresh rainwater to cook a communal soup. As the meal simmered over the fire, Astrid spoke to the crowd of blacksmiths, their families, and the original residents of Guell who circled around the open hearth, sitting on large stones and logs yet to be split for firewood. Their familiar faces brought her comfort, and her heart soared when she saw Lenore, Randim, and Trep, who each greeted her with a long and hard embrace. But while Astrid told the story of what had happened when she traveled this year's winter route to the Midlands and Southlands, every face she saw turned grim.

"Komdra and his men and the other Iron Maidens are spreading the word throughout the Northlands," Astrid said. "Everyone needs to decide whether to stay here in Guell to protect our homes if the Krystr soldiers succeed with their invasion of the Northlands or head to the lower coasts to try to stop them before they can reach us."

"No worries," Randim said, holding Lenore's hand as they sat next to each other on a log. As always, he'd rubbed his eyes throughout the day while blacksmithing, unintentionally smudging his face with soot. "Guell is a coastal town. We stay here, we protect Guell and the coast at the same time. What is there to decide?"

"It's not so simple," Donel piped up from where he sat near Astrid's side. "Guell is different. You're forgetting about Dragon's Head. With all the dragons that come to lay their eggs there, no merchant ever comes here by sea. The few that dare make the journey come by land. If that wasn't enough, the waters between our beach and Dragon's Head churn so much that no ship can survive it."

Lenore squeezed Randim's hand. She'd left her long dark hair loose today, and the wind whipped it across her face as she spoke. "Even if the Krystr soldiers wanted to invade us by sea, between the dragons and the lack of a safe port, they'd probably die before they could reach us."

"Makes us safe on the coast," Trep said. As always, he'd dressed his long blond hair in narrow braids that now draped across his shoulders. Normally, bright and breezy in nature, worry broke his voice. "How many men need be on the coasts below us? How many need be to stop these demons?"

"I don't know." Astrid swallowed hard. She gazed at the people surrounding her and beyond them to the blend of cottages that graced the village of Guell. If the Krystr soldiers destroyed Guell, it would be gone forever. Mandulane's men would transform it into an unrecognizable and unthinkable place. And the only way that Krystr soldiers could reach as far north as Guell would be by conquering nearly all of the Northlands. Suddenly, that threat seemed impossible to avert. "No one will know until our people reach the coasts and come together. We can't predict how many soldiers Mandulane controls or where he'll send them until it happens. All we know is they plan to invade the Northlands, and most likely it will happen soon."

"I've heard tales of another world beyond the Western Islands and across the ocean," Donel said. "What if we all pick up and set sail?"

Without realizing it, Astrid looked at Kikita, who kept an even temperament no matter what anyone said. Astrid understood Donel's wish. Not long ago, she'd only wanted to be with the people of Guell and had no care for anyone who lived outside their village. But that was before she met Margreet. "We could consider that," Astrid said gently. "But what would happen to the people we'd leave behind? The Bog Landers in the Far North? Or the people in the port town of Gott in the Lower Northlands? Or Far Easterners like Kikita? Or the Midlanders or the Southlanders or the islanders?"

Donel hung his head in shame. "I was only thinking of us sticking together like we've done before."

"No shame in that kind of thinking," Trep said.

Randim sighed. "Is any man ready to leave his home for the sake of guarding the coasts beneath us?" Before anyone could answer, Randim released Lenore's hand and rose to his feet, soon followed by Trep and every other blacksmith, including Donel.

"No!" Lenore protested. "You can't leave Guell in need of a blacksmith. At the very least, we need someone to keep our plow blades and hoes in good repair."

"Donel is the youngest," Randim said. "He can stay."

Donel failed to hide the relief on his face as he sat once more. "What about Mistress Dragonslayer?"

"I stand with the Iron Maidens," Astrid said. "And if we take enough iron with us, I provide another set of hands for making dragonslayer swords."

"Dragons?" Randim said, sinking to sit next to an increasingly worried Lenore.

Astrid felt hatred burn at the back of her throat. "It's the best type of sword to kill a dragon. It's less likely to bend or break. Why not forge them for Northlanders to use against the Krystrs?"

They talked into the evening, weighing options and making plans. Astrid found herself taking long looks at each blacksmith, drinking in his face and voice and manner so she could remember him in case he didn't survive the Krystr invasion.

As the evening grew late and the sun began its slow descent to skim along the horizon for the next several hours, she realized that she no longer saw Trep among the friendly faces surrounding her.

Chapter Sixty-Nine

Although Astrid invited Kikita to spend the night at her home, Lenore quickly insisted that she and Randim already had a spare mat for the Iron Maiden. Astrid thought Lenore's behavior odd and secretive, but she felt too tired to argue. As the villagers dispersed to their homes in the pale evening light, Astrid walked through Guell toward the spit of land she called her own. She enjoyed the quiet stretch of land between the edge of Guell and her cottage and smithery, surrounded by a row of poplars and separated from the sea by Dragon's Teeth Field. Here, she felt safe.

She entered the smithery first, smiling to see all her blacksmithing tools lined up as neat and clean as she'd left them. She unhooked the sheath from her belt and hung Starlight up on the hooks Donel had forged and nailed to one wall, certain that no one would steal the sword from her again. She lingered as she ran her hand across the cool surface of her anvil, the same one her master Temple had used the day he'd bought her from the child seller. That night, she'd slept in the smithery, finding comfort by embracing this same anvil.

For a moment, Astrid wished she could go back in time. If she'd never argued with DiStephan, he wouldn't have left Guell and would still be alive today. Maybe his disappearance had caused the first bloodstone to emerge from her foot, which had set in motion a chain of events. If the stone had never come out of her foot, Drageen would have left her alone. Everyone in Guell would be oblivious to the impending Krystr invasion, and Drageen would most likely be gathering forces to protect the Northlands.

But if the stone had never come out of her foot, she never would have met Randim or Trep or the other blacksmiths. Lenore wouldn't have met Randim or found such happiness with him. Astrid never would have met Vinchi or Margreet or Kikita, because Vinchi would have had no cause to train women to use weapons. The Iron Maidens wouldn't exist. Thorda and Kikita and all the other women who knew how to defend themselves with weapons might already be dead.

Or worse than dead, Astrid thought with a chill, remembering the women with the blue skin who serviced Mandulane.

Astrid froze at the sound of a faint shuffle in the distance. Breathing quietly, she cocked an ear toward the direction of the sound. Silence. She thought about the sound she'd just heard. It hadn't been the casual sound of a foraging animal or the skittering of an inquisitive bird or squirrel. It might have been a footstep. It might have come from inside her cottage.

Slowly, she removed Starlight from its place on her smithery wall, reminding herself that an attack on Guell from the sea couldn't happen. There were no Krystr soldiers in Guell.

Not yet.

Keeping a solid grip on Starlight's hilt, she eased on quiet feet from the smithery to the door to her cottage, which stood slightly open. Hesitating, she kept listening but heard nothing. Placing Starlight's tip on the door, she used the sword to push it open with care.

She sensed someone's presence inside her home. She smelled the scent of potatoes and herbs on someone else's breath, wafting through the air. She felt someone else's chest rising and falling with every breath. She detected a slight heat from another body.

"Show yourself," Astrid said, keeping a firm grip on her sword.

As she took a few cautious steps inside, she saw a dim figure move out of the twilight that seeped into her cottage from the open door. Pointing Starlight's sharp tip at the figure, she said, "Stop."

"He's dead," a familiar voice said.

Astrid froze, suddenly worried. She lowered her weapon. "Who's dead?"

A familiar hand took Starlight out of her hands, closed the cottage door, and used the sword to lock the door shut. "DiStephan. Your dragonslayer. He's long dead."

He placed his hands around her waist, letting them linger as if waiting for an answer. "I'm alive, Woman. And I'm here."

Astrid waited until her eyes adjusted enough for her to recognize Trep's long braids of hair to make sure it was him. "I don't understand," she said, lying to herself as well as him.

"Ain't nothing wrong with grief so long as it don't keep you from loving another."

Astrid shuddered for a moment. Why hadn't DiStephan's ghost made himself known to her for such a long time? Had someone released DiStephan's spirit in the same way she had released Margreet?

"Let me stay or let me go." His hands rested against her waist like ships ready to set sail.

He'd welcomed her into Randim's blacksmithing camp with delight when she'd first been sold to them. While some of the other blacksmiths had questioned her ability or Randim's judgment in buying her, Trep had always treated her the same as any blacksmith. Trep had believed she'd escape Tower Island and find her way back to the blacksmiths.

And when she'd come back to Guell after Margreet's death, Trep had been the one to sit with her through the night, watching the moon change from pale yellow to blood red, telling her about his sister and the man who might have killed her had she not escaped.

Astrid realized she felt as safe in his arms as she did in her own home. With a start, she also realized he'd likely leave with the rest of blacksmiths for the lower coasts of the Northlands. "Don't go," she said, raising her hands to cup his face.

He kissed her. Astrid happily sank into his arms and let the rest of the world melt away, forgetting about Starlight, the sword that kept her cottage door shut and gave them safe harbor for the rest of the night.

CHAPTER SEVENTY

Astrid dreamed of a bright, clear day where the blazing sun hung high over a stretch of beach. She walked barefoot in the white, fine sand, as soft as a lamb's wool against her skin. The briny scent of cod stank so much that she almost gagged. The ocean waves rolled strong in whitecaps for as far as she could see, crashing loudly when they finally reached shore.

A patch of sand rose between Astrid and the incoming waves in the dream. When it stood up to her height, the sand took the shape of a man and pointed at her. Ignoring the strange sight, she walked past it quickly but more men of sand bubbled up from the beach and surrounded her, their eye sockets empty and mouths filled with pebbles.

Astrid reached for Starlight, but she found only an empty sheath strapped to her belt. Without her sword, she instinctively held her hands up, palms open wide, to ward off the sand specters even though it appeared that they couldn't move, like animals caught in a mud pit.

"Stay away," Astrid said. "I mean no harm."

The sand specters screamed, and the sun plummeted from high above and landed on the horizon. A wayward beam of sunlight caught the center of Astrid's hand, illuminating the stone of darkness embedded at the center of her palm. At first, the stone caught the sunlight and magnified it, sending sunlight beams radiating from her hand in all directions.

Bloodstones rained from the sky, seemingly out of nowhere. Each gem thudded softly on the sand in front of Astrid and formed a path leading her toward a stone mansion nestled in the center of a nearby field. As she followed the path created by the bloodstones, they glowed from where they'd fallen among the grass and weeds. The sand men moaned as Astrid turned her back on them and walked away. She thought she could hear the heaviness of slow, thudding footsteps behind her and quickened her own pace.

Running through the field, Astrid slowed to a walk as she saw the path of bloodstones continue on a cobbled walkway and up the stone steps to the mansion. For a moment she felt anxious because it looked deserted. In the distance, she heard the scraping sound of sandy footsteps against grass and hurried inside the mansion.

Astrid found herself inside a huge circular room. A pit had been built at its center, and she caught her breath as she recognized Mandulane standing inside it with only his shoulders and head showing. A crowd of brown-robed clerks huddled about fifteen feet from the edge of the pit, conversing as loudly as geese.

Light emerged from the stone of darkness and flooded the room, forcing the clerks to shield their eyes from its brightness. Astrid squinted and turned her head, pushing her lighted hand away. She saw Norah and Taddeo standing in an arched doorway made of yellow bricks. Norah held out a hand to Astrid, gesturing for her to join the dragons.

But a sudden hunger rumbled in Astrid's belly. She didn't have time for dragons. She longed for blood.

Taddeo's voice carried on the wind. "If you don't keep an eye on who you are, you can turn into someone you don't recognize."

I know who I am, Astrid told herself. *I decide who I am every day.*

As if some invisible hand moved them, the bloodstones that had led her inside the mansion picked themselves up and piled into a black leather pouch resting by the pit's edge.

The light emitting from the stone of darkness narrowed into a beam and fell upon the black leather pouch full of bloodstones. Astrid had the ability to produce bloodstones because her grandfather and father were dragonslayers. Her brother Drageen had set in motion a series of events acting as a catalyst for Astrid's body to create bloodstones, but he'd been absorbed into the stony surface of Dragon's Head before he could harvest them. When dozens emerged later, Astrid had hidden them in a box and buried it near her cottage, keeping them safe in case she should need them in the future.

Astrid stared at Mandulane, who leaned against one wall inside the pit. Smiling with utter confidence, he balanced a dagger on one fingertip.

She removed the empty sheath from her belt. What good would it do her now? Letting it clatter on the smooth stone floor beneath her feet, Astrid walked toward the edge of the pit and swept the leather pouch into her hands. It weighed heavier than she imagined, and the weight felt good in her hands. A cold, hard feeling coursed through her veins as she kept a close watch on Mandulane, who now wrapped his fingers around the grip of his dagger.

Astrid circled the edge of the pit, holding the leather pouch by its long drawstring and letting the pouch's weight swing back and forth like a pendulum.

Mandulane eased into the center of the pit, turning slowly in place as he tracked Astrid's every step. He held the dagger below his waist and rested his thumb on the blade, keeping it pointed at Astrid's heart.

She took a swing at Mandulane's head with the weighted pouch, but he ducked and missed the blow. Off balance, Astrid stumbled but regained her footing.

Mandulane lunged and stabbed at her ankle, but she stepped away before he could touch her. His face dark with anger, Mandulane hurled himself toward the pit's edge and slashed at Astrid's leg, but she pivoted back on one foot before the blade could touch her.

"DiStephan taught me how to kill lizards. I can just as easily kill men." Astrid pivoted forward and smacked Mandulane in the head with the pouch filled with bloodstones. She pivoted away from the pit before Mandulane could respond.

He clutched his head, gazing at Astrid in horror. "You struck me!"

"You challenged me to this fight!" Astrid looked for an opening to deliver the next blow. "You could have walked past me when you saw me. You could have left the Northlands alone."

Furious, Mandulane tried to climb out of the pit, but Astrid placed one foot on his chest and kicked him back down inside it the same way she had kicked him off the ship and into the sea. Springing forward, she dealt a sudden blow to the side of his head. Surprised, he hesitated, failed to block it, and his head rattled when the pouch struck him. Mandulane dropped to his knees, and then fell to the bottom of the pit.

Astrid kept a good distance and watched his face closely. For a moment, his eyelids fluttered.

Mandulane sprang to his feet and reached for Astrid's ankles, but she stepped away from his reach and hit him in the head with her pouch of bloodstones.

Dazed, Mandulane relaxed his grip on the dagger, and it slipped on to the floor by Astrid's feet. She swept the dagger up with one hand and plunged it into Mandulane's back. He cried out once before collapsing back into the pit.

The on looking clerks shrieked and ran away from Astrid and toward the mansion's entrance. Their sandals clattered like rain against the stone floor as they ran, and their brown robes billowed like sails.

Comforted by the heft of the pouch still in her hands, she watched the pit while walking away from it. By the time she reached the mansion's entrance, she discovered herself alone.

But when Astrid walked outside, she stopped abruptly, stunned by what she saw.

Slaughtered bodies covered the land surrounding the mansion for as far as she could see. At first, Astrid recognized hundreds of Krystr followers by their brown robes. Beyond them lay the bodies of Komdra and his men.

A wave of fear rushed through her. Astrid wished she had the comfort of Starlight's grip in her hands. Missing it, she tightened her grip on the pouch of bloodstones. She couldn't stay here. She felt an urgency to walk through the field of bodies she faced and leave them all behind.

Astrid picked her steps carefully as she walked among the dead. She caught her breath and stopped when she recognized Thorda lying on the ground a few paces ahead. Like the others, her skin had paled to a bluish-white, and her empty eyes seemingly stared into nothing.

"No," Astrid said as she knelt by Thorda. Picking up the Iron Maiden's cold hand, Astrid shook it. "Wake up, Thorda. It's time to go. Wake up."

Thorda's arm flopped. A rotting stench filled Astrid's nose. Dropping Thorda's hand in horror, Astrid rose quickly to her feet as she covered her nose and mouth with her hands. Letting her gaze wander, Astrid saw the bodies of other Iron Maidens scattered across the field, those who now lived and those who had already died. Jewely. Efflin. Even Banshi.

How can this be? Didn't Mandulane's men kill Jewely and Efflin? Didn't Banshi die weeks ago? Didn't a lizard's bite already kill her?

As if in response to Astrid's questions, Banshi's body deteriorated until all her flesh vanished and her bright white skeleton basked in the sun.

Astrid shuddered and kept picking her way through the field of bodies. For a moment, she brightened with hope at the realization that she hadn't found Kikita's body.

"She must be alive," Astrid said out loud, gaining confidence at the sound of her own voice. Thunder rumbled, and when she looked up, lightning flashed across the sky. The ground trembled beneath her feet, and a stormy wind whipped around her body.

When Astrid walked past the last dead body and toward the shore, she noticed large heaps of sand dotting the beach. The sand specters rose out of those heaps, struggling to move their wet legs toward her.

No. You won't kill me like you killed them.

She shifted the heavy pouch of bloodstones from one hand to the other.

I'm a dragonslayer.

The sand specters dragged themselves toward her. Astrid whipped the pouch at the closest one. The pouch connected cleanly with its grainy head, which burst apart. The headless specter stumbled over its own feet and fell to its knees, exploding on impact.

That's right, Astrid thought, relishing the sweet sting of power that shook her to the core. *Try to hurt me, and I will kill you.*

The other specters kept pressing forward, and Astrid charged toward them, swinging the pouch of bloodstones with fury. One by one, the specters fell or collapsed into piles, leaving Astrid standing alone.

Astrid smiled, congratulating herself silently.

The piles of defeated sand moved and shifted until they formed dead bodies.

Astrid's harsh joy vanished when she began to recognize the bodies. Randim. Lenore. Donel. Beamon. Kamella. The blacksmiths of Guell.

DiStephan.

The air chilled with silence.

I killed them. I murdered the people I love!

The ocean no longer crashed against the shore. Instead, the sea had become as still as a mirror.

With an inexplicable urge, Astrid hurried toward it. Kneeling, she stared into the still water at her feet.

Her eyes had turned lavender. Unwittingly, her shape had shifted so that she now looked like her brother Drageen.

Chilled, she stared at her reflection, thinking, *I am no better than any other murderer who walks in this world.*

CHAPTER SEVENTY-ONE

Astrid woke up screaming and punching the air with her fists. It took a few moments for her to become aware of strong arms embracing her from behind and the heat and soft hair on a muscular chest pressing against her back.

"Ain't nothing but a dream," Trep said. "I got you."

Astrid breathed hard and fast, gasping for air. "A dream," she said. "I had a dream."

Trep kissed the back of her neck, his lips soft and tender, and then held her close.

She gave herself the luxury of relaxing into his arms and listening to his quiet breath with every rise and fall of his chest. A faint scent of smoke from the blacksmithing forge lingered in his hair from yesterday's work. Astrid took one of his hands in hers, cherishing the familiar sooty smudges around and under his fingernails. When she was a blacksmith, her hands had looked like his.

The sudden sound of distant shouting filled the air.

Without another word, Trep sprang out of bed, tossed Astrid's clothes to her, and then reached for his own.

Astrid dug her heels into the soft grass beneath her feet as she raced to keep up with Trep. They sprinted to the outskirts of Guell and then into the village center, where they found everyone crowded around Donel. The young blacksmith kneeled in the middle of the road, pinning a blue-skinned woman face down on the dirt.

"Let her go!" Lenore pleaded as Randim held her close, surrounded by the other blacksmiths, their families, and the other villagers. "Donel, you're hurting her!"

Astrid pushed her way through the crowd until she faced Donel and the strange woman. "What happened?"

Donel's face darkened in a way she'd never seen before, and

his eyes filled with hate. "Your young dragons found her at the gate. They toyed with her but didn't bite." He blew away a strand of hair that drifted across his eyes. "Don't know why they didn't. They should have."

"Donel!" Lenore cried out in horror.

Donel recoiled for a moment as if she'd struck him. The blue-skinned woman beneath him tried to wriggle free, but he pressed his knee harder against her back, keeping her pinned to the ground. "How'd you like it if she'd killed you or your man in your sleep?"

Beamon and Kamella, two of Astrid's first neighbors from the old days in Guell, held hands as they stood across the crowd from Lenore. Now married, Kamella's belly bulged with the presence of their first child. "She wouldn't do it," Kamella said. "She couldn't." She looked at Beamon. "I wouldn't, so how could she?"

"Stop," Astrid said, holding up her hands to the crowd for emphasis. "This woman belongs to Mandulane. Remember, he colors their skin against their will to mark them as his own. She's probably a Midlander or Southlander. She might even be from the Northlands." She placed a gentle hand on Donel's shoulder. "Let her stand."

"You don't understand," Donel said, looking up to meet Astrid's gaze. "The dragons don't like her. They had her cornered against the gate. They banged their tails against the fence to give us alarm. When I opened the gate, the dragons hissed at her. They never do that with any of us."

Astrid squeezed his shoulder. "Everyone in Guell surrounds us. We have her cornered now. What could she possibly do with all of us standing guard?"

Reluctantly, Donel released his knee and stood, hands balled into fists and ready to fight.

The blue-skinned woman rose. Astrid took note of the long robe she wore. Hadn't the women in the port city of Gott worn clothes like this?

The woman hunched over as if in pain and brushed the dirt from her clothes.

"Who are you?" Astrid said. "Why have you come here?"

The woman threw the back of her elbow into Donel's face, knocking him to the ground. She then sprang and wrapped her hands around Astrid's throat.

At first, Astrid felt paralyzed, stunned by the pain of the woman's sharp fingernails digging into her neck and the crushing pressure against her throat. Then she panicked, feeling the same desperation as if discovering she needed to breathe while swimming deep under water and not knowing if she could reach the surface in time.

Gagging, Astrid clawed at the woman's steadfast hands.

The hands loosened and fell away.

Gasping, Astrid collapsed to the ground. She looked up to see the blue-skinned woman clawing helplessly at an elbow smothering her nose and mouth from behind. The woman thrashed, but whoever stood behind her stayed as still as a rock. Her muffled cries pierced the silence surrounding her. No one crowded around her seemed to move or even breathe.

Finally, the blue-skinned woman's struggle slowed and her body went limp. The arm pressed against her face waited for another several moments as if to be certain and then released her, letting the stranger's body slip to the ground. Only then did Astrid recognize Kikita as the one who'd just now saved her life.

Gradually, Astrid noticed the men circled around them with weapons drawn or fists clenched, ready to step in. Randim and several others held daggers they'd withdrawn from their belts. Trep had picked up a stone as big as his hand. It took several minutes for them to let their hands soften and put their weapons away. Relief washed across their faces.

Kikita stepped forward, extended her hand, and pulled Astrid to her feet. Speaking so soft that only Astrid could hear, Kikita said, "It's best to keep a man from having to live with the memory of killing a woman."

Astrid nodded, and then turned her attention to Donel, who struggled to keep his balance as he stood. "I'm sorry, Donel. You were right. I should have listened to you."

He wiped away a thin stream of blood trickling from his nose and nodded.

Staring at the dead body of the blue-skinned woman, Astrid knew what she had to do for the sake of Guell, everyone she loved, and all of the Northlands.

CHAPTER SEVENTY-TWO

DiStephan's ghost stood on the final step of the stairway that wound from the ground floor of the tower on Tower Island to its very top, where the iron cage that had once held Astrid and Norah captive now stood as a sculpture of a woman bearing a sword, her hair flying free in the wind. But because Fiera had worked her magic beginning at the top of the tower, DiStephan now stood at the bottom, and from here he could gaze through the open door leading to the courtyard outside.

I'm almost free. Then they'll let me return to Astrid. He no longer cared that she would never be able to see him again. He only cared about being by her side, ready to guide her if she needed him.

Taddeo paced near the open door, casting a nervous glance at Fiera as she focused on releasing the last bit of darkness from the stairway.

Fiera eased her head back while a look of ecstasy lit up her face. Her cheeks glowed pink as her arms drifted parallel to her shoulders and sparks danced across her fingertips.

A whooshing sound plummeted throughout the tower, spiraling around the staircase. A column of black smoke seeped out of the last step, carried up and out of the top of the tower by a powerful wind.

Taddeo rushed to Fiera's side and placed his hands on her waist. He turned her slowly until she faced the wall opposite the step where DiStephan stood, then guided her into it.

The wall shimmered and dissolved, opening up like a door to a passageway leading deep underground.

Taddeo glanced back and smiled at DiStephan. "Fare well, dragonslayer."

If DiStephan had been alive, he would have felt his heart race. A pressure seemed to lift from his essence, and he felt free once more.

Fiera's arms fluttered back by her side. She seemed to wake up and notice Taddeo and the passageway before them. Puffing up like a peacock, she preened, running her fingertips through her own hair. But when Taddeo took a step forward, an invisible force stopped him. "No," Taddeo said in disbelief, touching the empty but solid space before him. "The passageway is still blocked! It's impossible for us to leave!"

As DiStephan focused on his memory of Guell and felt himself dissipate, he saw Taddeo spin to face him, shouting, "Find the last dragon and tell her we need her!"

CHAPTER SEVENTY-THREE

"I have something for you."

Inside Donel's small cottage, Astrid placed the box she'd dug up from her yard at his feet.

His eye had already blackened from where the blue-skinned woman had elbowed him before attacking Astrid, but he seemed to have cheered up after carrying the woman's body back to the gates and tossing the fresh meat to Smoke, Fire, and Slag. Donel looked down at the box, covered in sandy earth. "What is it?"

She knelt by the box, and he followed suit. Opening the lid, she said, "Bloodstones."

"What are bloodstones?"

Astrid sank her fingers into the dozens of gems inside the box, remembering the first time one had broken through the bottom of her foot. "Protection. But you need to find an alchemist who knows how to release the power from each stone. Once that happens, anyone can use it to protect their skin. We can fight against the Krystr soldiers and kill them, but they won't be able to hurt us."

Donel's face brightened with hope. "Then we can keep the Northlands safe." He hesitated. "But why bring them to me?"

Astrid grinned. "Because right now I need a good blacksmith."

❧❧

After leaving Donel's cottage, Astrid stayed mindful as she took one last walk through Guell. *Lenore will be angry. And Trep. But if they knew what I'm about to do, they'd stop me. They haven't seen Mandulane. They don't understand how deadly he can be.*

Astrid gave herself the luxury of sauntering, taking in every glorious face and sight of the village. They'd decided to spend a few days making sure everyone who remained in Guell had what they needed, especially in terms of farming tools. Several of the black-smiths worked at the large forge in the center of the village, making extra nails and hoe blades and everything else they thought necessary. Astrid breathed in the wonderful smoky scent and smiled at the sound of the bellows pumping. *Will I have a memory?* she wondered. *Or will everything simply end?* She decided it didn't matter.

She worried when Lenore ran out of her cottage to catch up and walked the road a few paces with her. Lenore gave Astrid a knowing smile and said, "Did you sleep well last night?"

Astrid remembered Lenore's insistence that Kikita stay with Lenore and Randim instead of Astrid. *She knew Trep waited for me at home*, Astrid realized. Smiling wistfully, Astrid said, "I slept quite well, thank you."

Lenore kissed Astrid's cheek and whispered, "I'm so pleased for you. It's time for you to be happy again."

Astrid took a long look in Lenore's eyes, wishing to remember them forever. "I'm grateful we became friends."

Lenore gave Astrid a quick hug. "As am I. But I must hurry back to the bread I have baking before it burns."

After Lenore bustled back inside her home, Astrid picked up her pace, still careful not to walk too fast for fear of attracting attention. As she passed through the outskirts of Guell, she heard the sound of ringing iron from her own smithery. Trep must be working there. Good. When he worked, he focused on nothing but iron. She walked past her smithery and cottage without looking back.

Astrid continued onto the wooden walkway and crossed Dragon's Teeth Field. Once she reached the shore, she waded into the ocean and then swam toward Dragon's Head.

Chapter Seventy-Four

The dream convinced Astrid she could make Taddeo hear her from this place that connected dragons and Scaldings. Once she completed her swim to Dragon's Head, she climbed the rocky outcrop to its peak. For most of her life, this peak had taken the shape of a dragon, but now it bore the outline of her brother and his alchemist. Trees with twisted limbs dotted Dragon's Head, and their plump green leaves rustled as young dragons scurried to hide among them. The sun baked Astrid's skin, a welcome relief from the chilly seawater.

She faced the statue-like figures, not sure how this would work. "Taddeo!" Astrid shouted into the wind that whipped mercilessly across Dragon's Head. "You were right!"

The wind died suddenly, making the leaves on all the surrounding trees fall still. Was Taddeo listening?

A chill swept through Astrid like a sharp winter wind. *How could I have been so stupid to trust that woman? After all I've seen of Mandulane and the followers of Krystr, why did I think one of them would come here for any reason other than to spy on us? How can I have been so reckless to think I could help one of Mandulane's women? Why can't I learn better judgment?*

What is wrong with me?

"You were right!" Astrid shouted again. "You warned me. I failed to keep an eye on who I am. I turned into someone I don't recognize." She paused and gathered the strength she needed to speak the truth about herself. "I've become someone thirsty for blood. A murderer." Her voice dropped to a whisper, but she still found the courage to speak out loud. "A monster."

Astrid looked down at her hand knowing it contained the stone of darkness, convinced that if she tried to help Guell she would only cause its destruction. The gothi Spathar had warned of the things that can break people. Greed and envy and arrogance. Astrid had become greedy for revenge. Envious of power. And arrogant in believing herself above anyone who wasn't a dragonslayer like herself.

Astrid braced herself, sickened at the feelings rumbling inside her. She spoke to the empty, quiet air, hoping that Taddeo could hear. "I don't know what happened. I don't know when or how I stopped thinking about who I want to be. I failed when I let my anger get the better of me and killed the clerks on Slaughter Island. I wanted to murder Gershon, and my friends kept me from doing it. I assumed too much and failed to protect everyone in Guell from Mandulane's woman. I can't find my balance." Taking a deep breath, the deepest truth struck her. "I have lost myself."

Astrid choked back tears, determined not to let one fall. *Blacksmiths don't cry.*

She waited, not knowing what to expect. The leaves rustled again on trees all around her. Otherwise, Dragon's Head stood in silence.

A speck of bright white light glowed in the center of her palm. Astrid stared, baffled by the light. The stone of darkness bore a black color as deep as a starless night. But the pinprick of white light glowed from where she'd seen and felt the stone vanish inside her skin.

Astrid looked up with the hope of seeing Taddeo or Wendill or maybe even Norah, but she found herself still alone. She raised her voice. "Krystr soldiers and Mandulane are coming for the Northlands. We need someone ruthless. Someone who is willing to do whatever is necessary to drive away these soulless, hateful men."

The ground rumbled beneath Astrid's feet, and she took it as a good sign. Now, she chose to speak to Dragon's Head itself. For all she knew, it might be a living, breathing thing. "I know there is some pact between dragons and the Scaldings. You've kept one or the other of us in your embrace for many years."

Seized with inspiration, Astrid stood again and walked to place her hands upon the stony figure of her brother Drageen. As soon as she touched it, the white speck of light on her hand spread across her entire body, sizzling and popping, although she felt no pain.

"I am the daughter of a Scalding dragonslayer. I am the granddaughter of Benzel Scalding, known as Benzel of the Wolf. If you need a Scalding, take me and set Drageen free."

The ground cracked beneath her feet, revealing a molten fire beneath. Shallow chasms opened up all around her, and she stood still as the molten fire crawled up toward her. Astrid caught her breath at the shock of the fire's touch when it grabbed her ankles and snaked up around her, too surprised to register the depth of pain.

Astrid barely noticed the wind picking up again, but this time she saw something shimmer in the wind, like waves of heat off flat stones on a summer's day. The invisible waves took a familiar shape, and her last act was to smile wistfully when she recognized the faint outline of DiStephan's ghost.

❧❧

Drageen felt groggy, as if he were waking from a long dream. Eyes closed, he thought he felt layers of rock fall from his skin, exposing him to the sharpness of an ocean wind.

At once, his eyes opened and he drew in his first breath in years, wheezing and hacking. He tried to speak, but his voice had been too long out of practice. He managed nothing more than a faint gasping sound. And the sun nearly blinded him.

Using his arm to shield his long-closed eyes from the sun, he realized the bright light didn't come from overhead. Instead, it came from the stony figure forming beside him.

Drageen took a step, only to fall to his knees. Although his body still worked, it had been out of commission too long like a rusted tool in need of polishing. Focusing on the task at hand, Drageen thought, *And so he arose out of the depths of anguish to stand like the majestic warrior of legend.* Steadying himself, Drageen stood again and croaked, "Bashing, thrashing, crashing like waves against the rocks of Dragon's Head, I come forth, back into the world I so richly deserve to rule!"

He stared at the statue-like figure of Astrid raising her arms to the sky as if to embrace it. Blinding white light surrounded the figure until the stone of darkness finally fell from its hand and onto the ground.

"Alchemist!" Drageen shouted when he saw a different figure emerge out of the stone. Elated, Drageen looked across the ocean and spotted Guell, the meaningless village he'd decimated however long ago, and the sight of it gave him hope.

He walked toward the stone-like figure of Astrid and picked up the stone that had fallen from her hand. Larger than a bloodstone, its faceted surfaces looked smooth and polished. "Alchemist!" he yelled again.

The white-haired woman groaned as she shook off the last bits of rock from her shoulders and held herself stiffly while she minced her way toward him. "Hello, Drageen. It is nice to see you, too."

Ignoring her comment, Drageen showed the stone to her by holding it up between his fingers and letting the sunlight strike its heart.

Drageen's jaw slackened and the alchemist paled as the dark color of the stone evaporated into wisps of curling smoke carried away by the wind. The vanishing color left the stone as clear and flawless as a diamond. Willing his hand not to tremble, Drageen said, "What is this?"

Squinting as she peered closer, the alchemist said, "I believe it is a stone of light."

Drageen swallowed hard, taking a moment to make sure he'd heard her correctly. "Then when I picked it up, I held the stone of darkness."

"I believe so."

"Then everything my father told me is true." Drageen smiled as he held the stone up higher and watched it cast prisms of rainbow color around him. "I have what I need to reclaim my rightful place in the Northlands."

About the Author

Resa Nelson's first novel, The Dragonslayer's Sword (Book 1 in the 4-book Dragonslayer series), was nominated for Nebula Award. It was also a finalist for the EPPIE Award. She attended the Clarion Science Fiction Writers Workshop and is a longtime member of Science Fiction and Fantasy Writers of America (SFWA). Her short fiction has been published in Science Fiction Age, Fantasy Magazine, Aboriginal SF, Tomorrow SF, Brutarian Quarterly, Paradox, Oceans of the Mind, and several anthologies, including Marion Zimmer Bradley's Sword & Sorceress 23. The Dragonslayer series is based on two short stories originally published in Science Fiction Age magazine: "The Dragonslayer's Sword" and "The Silver Shoes," both of which were nominated for the Nebula Award. About her standalone novel, Midwest Book Review said, "Our Lady of the Absolute is a riveting fantasy, very highly recommended."

Nelson was the TV/movie columnist of Realms of Fantasy magazine from 1999 until its demise in 2011. She was also a regular contributor to SCI FI magazine and has written nonfiction articles for a wide range of publications.

While researching her Dragonslayer series, Nelson took a course in blacksmithing, where she learned how to build a fire and forge iron and steel. She also took a course to learn how to use a medieval sword at the Higgins Armory Museum in Worcester, Massachusetts. She soon joined the Higgins Armory Sword Guild and took more courses in German long sword and Italian rapier and dagger. She also studied foil fencing for a year. Nelson participated in the guild's study of fight manuals from the Middle Ages and the Renaissance and participated in demonstrations of historically accurate sword techniques at the Higgins Armory Museum, science fiction and fantasy conventions, and other venues in New England. The sword work in this novel and other books in the Dragonslayer series is based on her study of these techniques.

Nelson has also studied screenplay writing and participated in the making of three short independent films, two of which are based on her short stories. She has been a quarter-finalist in the Nicholl Fellowships in Screenwriting and a semi-finalist in the Chesterfield screenwriting contest. She lives in Massachusetts.